ASHES TO ASHES,
CRUST TO CRUST

St. Martin's Paperbacks titles
by Mindy Quigley

SIX FEET DEEP DISH
ASHES TO ASHES, CRUST TO CRUST

ASHES TO ASHES, CRUST TO CRUST

MINDY QUIGLEY

St. Martin's Paperbacks

This is a work of fiction. All of the characters, organizations, and events portrayed in this novel are either products of the author's imagination or are used fictitiously.

First published in the United States by St. Martin's Paperbacks, an imprint of St. Martin's Publishing Group.

ASHES TO ASHES, CRUST TO CRUST

For information, address St. Martin's Publishing Group, 120 Broadway, New York, NY 10271.

www.stmartins.com

ISBN: 978-1-250-79245-7

Our books may be purchased in bulk for promotional, educational, or business use. Please contact your local bookseller or the Macmillan Corporate and Premium Sales Department at 1-800-221-7945, ext. 5442, or by email at MacmillanSpecialMarkets@macmillan.com.

Printed in the United States of America

St. Martin's Paperbacks edition / May 2023

10 9 8 7 6 5 4 3 2 1

To Lori Hohenstein, coolest of moms

ACKNOWLEDGMENTS

This story owes a lot to my sister Jaime Gagamov, who fought hard for happy endings for the characters she likes and provided helpful insights about financial crimes and quirky Eastern Europeans. Our plot talks feel like an extension of the hours-long Barbie melodramas we acted out as kids.

I appreciate Molly McClintock, Laura Rettberg, Marti Larson, Sonya Steckler, and the Heyer family, especially J5, for being game to lend their names to my characters. Apologies to Caitlin Frates for putting your last name on the wrong side of the law.

Thanks to Danna Agmon, Tanya Boughtflower, Tracee de Hahn, Charlotte Morgan, and Jessica Taylor for reading drafts and providing valuable insights. I am so blessed to have you all in my life. Megan and Jesse Bongartz, my dear sister and bro-in-law, helped me poison some folks (on the page, not IRL) during a snowy MLK weekend. Thank you. Special shout-out as always to Paul, Alice, Patrick, and the rest of my family for supporting me.

To the members of the New River Writers Group, especially Tom McGohey, Charlie Katz, Elisabeth Chaves, and H. Scott Butler—I feel so fortunate to know you all and benefit from your talent. Thanks, also to early readers, Jane Goette and Christina Polge. The members of the Unitarian Universalist Congregation of the New River Valley have been so supportive over the years. Ditto Akiko Nakata and Lori Tolliver Jones, my yoga buddies, who give me a confidence boost with a side of asanas. Thanks to Joe Hoyt for sharing his experience in the restaurant industry and for always being highly entertaining.

My "day job" colleagues at the Virginia-Maryland College of Veterinary Medicine have been so accommodating as I've transitioned to becoming a professional novelist. Special thanks to Terry Swecker, cow doctor extraordinaire, who got roped into advising me on bovine ailments, despite his better judgment.

Thanks to Danielle Christopher and Mary Ann Lasher for the pretty covers. I love your rendering of Butterball!

I'm grateful for the savviness of my agent John Talbot of Talbot-Fortune. Hannah O'Grady at St. Martin's is a fabulous editor, and I am blessed to have her as my guiding light. Hannah, your encouragement means so much to me. The whole Minotaur-St. Martin's team— including Steve Erickson, Kayla Janas, John Rounds, and Kelley Ragland—is truly the bomb, with Sarah Haeckel and Sara Beth Haring providing especially bombastic marketing and PR help. Many thanks to John Simko for his careful copy edits. I feel like John and I are good friends, even though our entire relationship takes place in the Track Changes function of Microsoft Word.

CHAPTER 1

"Son, come and taste this," I called, holding up a fork and summoning Sonya Perlman-Dokter, my best friend, sous chef, and the namesake "Son" of my pizza restaurant, Delilah & Son. She stood at the counter near me, prepping for the dinner service.

Sonya pivoted toward me with her eight-inch gyuto chef's knife leveled at my chest. As always, she wore a full face of flawless retro-style makeup, with matte red lips, heavy powder, and a fluttering expanse of false eyelashes. A blunt-cut midnight black bob framed her gray eyes, which held a glint almost as steely as the razor-sharp edge of her knife.

"If that's another bratwurst sample, I can't be held responsible for my actions," she said, putting a menacing arch in her perfectly plucked eyebrow.

Sonya threated to kill me at least once a week, which showed great restraint considering how often my uncompromising culinary standards put the bonds of our friendship to the test. "Just one more?" I waggled the fork in front of her nose. "This bite could be worth ten thousand dollars."

With our first summer season drawing to a close, I'd hatched a plan to see the business through the leaner

winter months, and finding the perfect bratwurst was
a crucial first step. Our Geneva Bay, Wisconsin, location is a paradise in the high season, the Midwest's answer to the Hamptons. A massive, glittering blue lake
is ringed by mega-mansions built for mega-wealthy
families whose names are synonymous with turn-of-the-
century industrial success—Wrigley, Sears, Schwinn,
Vick. In the winter, though, the wealthy Chicagoans and
other assorted tourists flee back to the city or to vacation
spots in warmer climes. The seasonal pattern meant that
businesses like mine had to count on stockpiling at least
three-quarters of our annual revenue during the fleeting
summer months.

Luckily, I'd hit on the ideal opportunity for a last-
minute revenue boost—Geneva Bay's Taste of Wisconsin
Cook-Off, the marquee event of the town's yearly Labor
Day weekend festivities. All of Geneva Bay's top restauranteurs would be vying to take home the grand prize
for the dish that best showed off our region's local flavors. The winning restaurant would receive a three-page
write-up in *On the Water*, the Chamber of Commerce's
popular magazine, top billing on the Visitors Bureau
website, and a ten-thousand-dollar cash prize.

"I don't care if it's ten thousand dollars or ten million."
Sonya gestured toward her knife and toward me. "The
killing of Delilah O'Leary would be self-defense and not
a jury in the land would convict me."

I gently disarmed her, placing the knife on the worktop. "This one's different. I asked them to grind in more
back fat and use less cardamom."

Sujeet and Big Dave, the restaurant's meat suppliers,
had spent the last few weeks creating variations on a
custom sausage mixture for my planned entry in the contest: a new deep-dish recipe with locally sourced pork

bratwurst, pickled onions, a beer-infused cheese sauce, and a soft pretzel crust. I'd hit on the basic idea early on, but I still hadn't found exactly the right balance of flavors. I knew every element had to be perfect, or the concept could risk coming off as, for lack of a better word, *cheesy*.

Sonya huffed, crossed her arms, and reluctantly opened her mouth to allow me to feed her. I watched as she slowly chewed the morsel.

"Well?" I prompted.

"It tastes very much like samples twelve through fourteen," she replied.

"Do you think it needs a finer grind?"

She took my hands in hers and peered into my face. "I can allow you to abuse our friendship, but remember I'm also your employee. There has to be some kind of workplace safety regulation against forcing me to eat this much bratwurst."

"No doubt. Please submit your formal complaint to the HR department," I teased, gesturing to the large ceramic bin of food scraps we kept for garden compost.

She gave me a good-natured punch in the arm and turned back to her work. I popped another piece of bratwurst into my mouth, and shook my head as I chewed. Definitely needed a finer grind. And maybe this last version had overdone the salt by a smidgeon.

Sonya, with her uncanny ability to read my mind, called out, "Dee, it's fine. The last five iterations have all been excellent."

I walked back toward my prep area, while Sonya opened a large can of whole peeled San Marzano tomatoes. She grooved her hips as she turned the crank on the opener, humming along with the B-52s song on our "Chop and Bop" playlist.

"You know," she said, "I've been thinking of getting back on the dating scene."

"Really?" I replied, almost choking on the meat I was chewing.

Much as I wanted Sonya to find her soulmate, her romantic track record was akin to the Detroit Lions'—that is to say, one long, ugly losing streak. Always one to lead with her heart instead of her head, Sonya's most recent relationship had been among her all-time greatest disasters. She'd somehow gotten herself tangled up in an affair with her previous boss's wife. That ended with said boss humiliating her in front of the entire staff by firing her on the spot and dumping a full pan of jellied veal demi-glace over her head during service. Even all these months later, she was still recovering from the loss of that job and the damage to her reputation.

"Yeah, life's short, right?" Sonya said. "No sense in crying over spilled milk."

Or spilled demi-glace, I thought. Out loud, I said, "That's great, Son. I hope you find someone who really makes you happy."

I took another bite of bratwurst, then another, stuffing my mouth, lest I utter aloud my silent prayer—*Please let her find someone nice this time. Someone employed. Someone single. Someone who doesn't empty their joint bank account and skip town in the middle of the night with Sonya's car and half her record collection.*

Sonya must've caught me staring because she apparently mistook my concern for her as fixation on the quality of the bratwurst. She called out, "It's time to stop testing, Dee. How many pigs have lost their lives in service of your nitpicking? More importantly, my body can't take it anymore. My blood is now fifty percent gristle."

I sighed and swallowed. She had a point. I could feel

myself going down the rabbit hole of perfectionist obses-
sion, and it was messing with my palate as well as my
head. Usually I could just look at ingredients and see a
dish, the way a sculptor can look at a block of marble and
see a finished statue. But this recipe had been a struggle
from the start. Maybe the bratwurst wasn't the problem.
Maybe the problem was me.

My mind summoned a vivid memory of one of my culinary school instructors warning me and my classmates
about the dangers of compulsive self-criticism, a common
occupational hazard among chefs. "Being a chef," she'd
said, "isn't a job so much as a personality type." Demanding, detail-oriented, hard-charging. We'd all been late in
plating our veal blanquettes, having wasted our allotted
time futzing with the sauces and seasonings. Fixing her
firm gaze on us, she cautioned us not to become our own
worst critics, not to let ourselves be controlled by "that
tiny voice that sits inside your head, quietly judging your
every action against some unreachable standard."

Ha! Good one, lady. There was nothing quiet or tiny
about my inner perfectionist voice. My perfectionism
came with a built-in megaphone and a surround-sound
speaker system.

I'd hoped that when I opened my dream restaurant,
Delilah & Son, a lakeside spot specializing in hand-
crafted cocktails and unique deep-dish pizzas, I'd be
able to hush my ever-screaming inner voice. For the first
time in my career, I'd have complete control over every
aspect of the food—choosing every supplier, inspecting
every ingredient, tasting every dish before deeming it a
worthy addition to the menu. Surely, with total author-
ity, I'd finally be content. But in the three months since
Delilah & Son opened its doors, I'd found that the opposite was true, and that perfection remained tantalizingly,

maddeningly, just beyond my reach. Of course, it didn't help matters that the restaurant's stuttering launch had been ever so slightly overshadowed by a murder and subsequent police investigation.

"You should get your love train back on the track, too," Sonya said. "Maybe it would help you focus a little less on meat." She turned her head toward me with a seductive tilt. "Or focus a little more . . . on meat."

I threw a kitchen towel at her, and she caught it with a laugh.

The restaurant's financial problems had definitely been worsened by my ill-timed breakup with my former fiancé and business partner, Sam Van Meter, aka the guy who'd been bankrolling the whole shebang. I'd been confident that the restaurant could stand on its own following our split, so I'd refused Sam's offer of financial assistance. To tell the truth, that decision might've been driven by pride as much as confidence. Whatever my motivation for going it alone in the financial wilderness, southern Wisconsin's rainiest summer on record put the restaurant's spacious lakeside dining patio out of commission for much of the tourist season, which put a literal damper on the restaurant's profit forecast.

While I knew my problems remained blessedly smaller than the life-or-death stakes that greeted the restaurant's opening, I still couldn't get over the feeling that my dream scenario of complete control and contentment was continually tiptoeing along the edge of an abyss.

A high-pitched voice interrupted my ruminations, calling out, "Knock, knock."

Harold Heyer, president of the Geneva Bay Convention and Visitors Bureau, scuttled into the kitchen cradling a stack of papers. My first reaction when he pushed through the door was to bum-rush him out of my kitchen.

Civilians were not allowed to casually stroll in. However, Harold was in the process of assigning locations for the upcoming festival. Each participating business's tent would be placed in a more or less prominent spot in the town's large waterfront park, and those placements could be crucial to getting good foot traffic and the revenue and exposure that came with it. In an economy as tourist dominated as Geneva Bay's, Harold's position carried outsized influence and power. The Visitors Bureau, in addition to housing the local Chamber of Commerce and publishing *On the Water* magazine, was in charge of organizing big public events—all of which gave Harold the ability to provide a huge marketing boost to businesses he featured.

Although his job gave him the potential to play favorites or even wield Mafia don–level dominance over Geneva Bay's small business community, Harold was more Muppet than Mussolini, radiating a level of positivity that fell somewhere between a Disney princess and a high school cheerleader on amphetamines.

Harold sported Bermuda shorts and a lime green plaid sweater vest, despite the August heat, and the sheen of sweat on his steeply domed bald head glistened under the kitchen's bright lights. Harold's uncanny resemblance to Humpty Dumpty—with his rail-thin appendages, short stature, egg-shaped body, and bald sphere of a head—was something of a running joke between me and Sonya, a small act of mischief that allowed me to tolerate his high-octane personality.

"Harold, what can I do for you?" I asked, coaxing my mouth into a smile.

"I just wanted to pay a call on my two favorite deep-dish divas to pass along some good news," Harold said.

"Oh?" I said.

"Yes indeedy. But first, tell me how is your delightful aunt doing these days? Such a gem of a woman."

My no-nonsense octogenarian great-aunt, Elizabeth "Biz" O'Leary was known to most locals from her decades as an accounting and personal finance teacher at the high school. Over the course of her long career, she'd taught everyone from Harold Heyer to the mayor to the chief of police, a man who apparently still had anxiety dreams about being late for her class. Auntie Biz could be . . . vocal. And . . . decisive. And any number of other euphemisms for being a stubborn old battle-ax. But a "delightful gem of a woman"? Harold's rose-colored glasses needed a good cleaning.

"She's the same as ever. Kicking ass and taking names. Have you decided on our placement for the festival?" I asked, encouraging him to cut to the chase.

"Still ironing out a few teensy details." He stopped to examine a stack of glossy-skinned eggplants. "My, these are lovely. Of all your wonderful creations, your Eggplant Nduja pizza is my absolute favorite. A scrumptious blend of umami and spice."

He patted each eggplant in turn, pinching the top one to test the firmness. I'd have to rewash them now. I dug my nails into my palms, trying to stem the steady trickle of irritation rising in my body. *Smile, Delilah. Be pleasant.*

"Oh," Sonya said, eyes twinkling with mischief, "you like the *egg*-plant pizza?"

Harold nodded. "It really is exceptional."

"Did you hear that, Dee? Harold thinks our *egg*-plant pizza is *egg*-ceptional."

I envied Sonya's gift for parrying life's annoyances with humor. I shut my eyes and counted to ten. When I opened them, though, Harold was still there—an unauthorized civilian, in my kitchen, fondling my eggplants, shoveling out inflated compliments, and making pointless small talk in the midst of dinner prep.

Over many years working in restaurants and hotels, I'd developed a certain level of immunity to pranks, come-ons, bullying, hijinks, diva tantrums, ego trips, and foul language the likes of which a seasoned trucker would be ashamed to utter. Harold's over-the-top flattery and ham-handed schmoozing shouldn't have even registered on my Richter scale of kitchen-related annoyances. However, nothing triggered my temper quite like an intrusion into my inner sanctum. Especially by a guy so seemingly clueless about how much power he held over my future. And that went double for someone who was basically a walking smiley-face emoji.

"Everything you make here is exceptional. Just as exceptional as those who prepare it," Harold said, pausing as he passed Sonya. "Sonya Perlman-Dokter, have I mentioned that you're looking radiant as ever? How are you this fine Tuesday?"

She flashed a tolerant smile. "In *egg*-zellent health. And how *egg*-zactly are you?" The occasional sly Humpty Dumpty joke clearly helped her maintain cordial relations with Harold—maybe I should try it.

"I'm about ten shades of wonderful, thanks for asking," Harold replied. He spun on his heel and approached my work area. "And Delilah O'Leary, the pizza prodigy of Geneva Bay, is all well with you? Can you believe all the rain we've had?"

"Yes. Rain. Lots," I said. "Now, you said you had some news for us?"

"Whatever you're cooking in here smells divine. Are

those bratwurst pizzas? Two of my absolute favorite foods combined." He took a long pull of air through his bulbous nose. Given that he stood all of five-foot-four, he had to rise up on his toes to peer inside the pizza oven. "What's on the menu for today?"

My patience with him hung by a microscopic thread. Harold was such a human cannonball of peppiness that sometimes having a corrupt Mafioso in his place sounded preferable. As he reached for the oven handle, I instinctively took a step toward him with balled fists. No one touches my oven.

Sonya, well accustomed to putting out my internal fires, rocketed over and placed herself between me and my intended victim.

"We're so grateful you stopped by, Harold," she said. "Did you want to talk to us about something? Let's get to it. We really have to get back to dinner prep. Like, now."

"Yes," I agreed, drawing in a calming breath. *Must not pummel the guy who controls your destiny.* "You said that you had good news? Is it about the celebrity judge for the cook-off?"

Last time I'd seen him, Harold had hinted that he was in talks with a big-name chef who would bring major publicity and star power to the competition.

"You must be as clever as you are charming, because that's just what I came to talk to you about," he said. Behind Harold's back, Sonya picked up an egg and danced it on the edge of the worktop.

My boiling blood cooled ever so slightly as I struggled to suppress a grin. Harold, oblivious to our childishness, plopped the stack of flyers he'd been carrying down on my workspace and pointed to the top one. "You won't believe what we have in store this year."

I barely registered the bright banner headline announcing "Geneva Bay's 25th Annual Taste of Wisconsin Cook-Off" or the list of names of the competing restaurants. Instead, my attention snagged on a full-color photo of this year's celebrity chef judge. The person who would decide the winner of the contest. Harold was right to say I wouldn't believe it. My heart thudded and blood rushed to my ears.

"We've managed to secure Graham Ulrich, head chef of Quotidien," Harold gushed, giving voice to the news my brain was struggling to accept. "He has his own Food Network show now, as I'm sure you know, so this is going to be a huge draw. Huuuuuge," he sang, smiling broadly. "Definitely the most memorable in Geneva Bay history."

I heard the sound of an egg cracking on the floor, and looked over to find Sonya, mouth agape, staring straight ahead with horrified eyes.

She mouthed the name *Graham Ulrich*, but no sound came from her lips.

"Oh, dear, you've dropped your egg," Harold said, rushing over to help clean up the mess. Sonya didn't shift positions or so much as blink. "I can understand why you're a bit overwhelmed," he soothed, patting Sonya's hand, which seemed to be frozen in midair. "Graham Ulrich is by far the biggest celebrity judge we've ever hosted. But don't let it intimidate you. You and Delilah are top-notch chefs and you'll do just fine in the contest." He turned to me. "Frankly, I was amazed he agreed to come. We've been trying to get him for years, but he always said no. Then suddenly out of the blue, *he* called *me* and said he wanted to take part if the offer was still open. Quite a boon for our humble festival."

While Harold blathered on, Sonya's eyes were locked

on mine. Graham Ulrich. Her former boss. The one who'd practically run her out of town on a rail after discovering her fling with his wife. I was sure Sonya was thinking the same thing I was—our hope of winning the cook-off was shattered. All the king's horses and all the king's men wouldn't be able to put *that* together again.

CHAPTER 2

After Harold's revelation about this year's celebrity judge, I shuffled him out the door as fast as politeness would allow. My next order of business was to get Sonya perched on a stool at the restaurant's bar with a tall glass of white wine in her hand. I didn't have the magical mixology skills of our talented bartender, Daniel Castillo, but I knew how to use a corkscrew. Sonya sat at the empty bar now, glassy-eyed and stunned, looking like a taxidermy version of her usually vibrant self.

"It's going to be fine, Son," I consoled. "You don't have to go to the festival. Ulrich will never even need to know you're in Geneva Bay."

She glared at me. "As if he doesn't already know I'm here." She picked up her glass and drained half of it in one long gulp. "You know how small the culinary scene is. He probably knew I'd moved here before my bags were even unpacked."

I couldn't dispute that. The world of high-end kitchens is more inbred than a kennel full of French bulldogs. With Graham Ulrich's power and connections, there was no way he hadn't clocked where Sonya was working. I'd hired Sonya because she was my best friend and a phenomenal cook. What I hadn't known until later was that this position had been her only option. Ulrich had used his influence to blackball her from most respectable jobs on the Chicago culinary scene. If Delilah & Son failed, she had just as much at stake as I did. Maybe more.

Much as I wished it wasn't true, the more I thought about it, the clearer it seemed that Ulrich agreed to judge Geneva Bay's competition because of Sonya. Even among top chefs, he had a reputation for being temperamental and vindictive. He would almost certainly use his "celebrity judge" platform as an opportunity to further humiliate Sonya, which in turn would damage the restaurant. I reached for another wineglass and poured myself a generous serving.

We roosted there for a few minutes, drinking in silence. I took in the restaurant's ambiance with a sense of impending doom. This place was my baby, and I loved it with a mother's unreserved adoration. Metallic-gray wallpaper shimmered gently along one wall, while the honey-colored wood floors created a homey feel. The funky, mismatched pink and red dining chairs added an element of whimsy. Over our heads, huge, vivid portraits of famous Chicagoans—both notorious gangsters like John Dillinger and notable celebrities like Michael Jordan—hung suspended from the high ceiling, adding a sense of artsy drama that evoked the city where deep-dish pizza originated. Stylish as the interior was, the restaurant's best feature doubtlessly came in the form of the huge wall of windows that looked onto the outdoor patio and beyond to the shimmering blue expanse of the lake. I had to think of a way to save this place.

Usually, I loved enjoying a few moments of peace before dinner service began. The restaurant stayed open six days a week. Wednesday through Sunday, our hours ran from eleven a.m. to ten p.m., the typical brutal restaurant schedule that meant a string of fifteen-hour days. On Tuesdays, we gave ourselves a little break, opening at five p.m. for dinner service only. Not that I was ever "off." Mondays were for ordering, shopping, and accounting. On Tuesdays I devoted myself to getting a jump on prep for the coming week. If you value downtime, don't open a restaurant.

"I'll quit," Sonya suddenly blurted out. "Then Graham will judge you fairly."

"Don't even think about it. There's no way I could have gotten through the past three months without you. Heck, there's no way I could've gotten through the last fifteen years without you," I said, scooting closer to her and resting my head on her shoulder. "Plus, your name's above the door, and I can't afford a new sign."

She let out a hoarse laugh.

"Are you going to be okay here?" I asked. "I need to make some headway in the kitchen."

"Don't worry. I just need a minute to wallow in regret. Besides, I won't be alone." Sonya gestured to the bottles that lined the back shelves of the bar.

"It's not your fault, okay? We'll figure it out," I said.

I squeezed her shoulder and headed back to the kitchen. I would've loved to stay and comfort her, but the distraction of Harold's visit had already thrown our prep schedule off-kilter. Luckily, I'd finished mixing several batches of our signature pizza doughs earlier that morning. While chopping and sautéing could be fast-forwarded to some degree, the natural process of yeast breaking sugars into carbon dioxide bubbles took between one and two hours, depending on the air temperature, the kitchen's humidity, and the recipe's ingredients. Fast-forward that process, and I might as well close down the restaurant.

Close down the restaurant.

Without the cash prize and the publicity that would come with a good showing in the contest, that could be just where I was heading. I brooded my way through a mound of onion chopping and cheese grating.

Piercing the dark thoughts that swirled around my head, Melody Schacht, Delilah & Son's perpetually perky front-of-house staffer, burst in the kitchen door, arm in arm with my great-aunt Biz.

I unknit the crease of worry on my forehead and faced them. If there was one thing I didn't doubt, it was my ability to project the outward appearance that all was well. My family rarely "did emotion," preferring to conceal personal problems and vulnerabilities behind a thick curtain of overachievement. This way of being translated perfectly to life as a chef. No matter what kind of chaos brewed in the kitchen, I always saw to it that the plate that reached the diner would be flawless.

"What are you two conspiring about?" I asked, launching a forced smile toward Biz and Melody.

"I'm telling her what a live wire her grandmother was back in my day," Biz said. "Shirley McClintock used to ride up and down Broad Street on the back of that old crook Rocco Guanciale's Harley like she was the Queen of Geneva Bay."

"I can't picture Grandma Shirl on a gangster's motorcycle," Melody laughed. "She crochets blankets for all the newborn babies at church, for heaven's sake."

"They were an odd couple even back then. It lasted maybe a summer. Everyone knew Rocco was trouble and your grandma was a goodie-two-shoes. This was all when Rocco was just a little punk kid, mind you, before he became a crime boss." Biz shrugged. "You never know what makes two people connect."

Looking at the pair before me, I couldn't have agreed more. I'd been a little uncertain when I suggested that Melody move into the spare room of my aunt's house. Melody, with her blond curls and girl-next-door lovability, was the ultimate odd couple match for my curmudgeonly aunt.

But Melody had desperately needed cheap accommodation in town so she could save money for college, and Auntie Biz couldn't stay alone in her ramshackle lake-front cottage unless she had some live-in help. For a hot second, I'd thought about moving in with her myself, but immediately realized that the combination of close living quarters and our two inflexible personalities would've caused a combustion of epic proportions. Better for me to stay in my own small apartment above the restaurant. The sweet and sour pairing of Melody and Auntie Biz had worked out far better than I'd expected.

"That's not the half of it," Biz continued. "She and Rocco wore matching black leather jackets."

Melody let out a peal of laughter as she escorted Auntie Biz to a sturdy high-backed stool we called "the perch." Auntie Biz was a grade-A home cook, and she'd taken to lending a hand in the kitchen most days. Although her mind was as sharp as my Wüsthof carbon-steel paring knife, her petite frame—all ninety-five pounds of it—was fragile, and she was prone to the occasional bout of dizziness. "The perch" allowed her to stay firmly planted while she chopped and mixed.

"I can't wait to tell Mac about Grandma Shirl's walk on the wild side," Melody said.

"Who's Mac?" I asked, sweeping a pile of sliced mushrooms into a sauté pan.

"My cousin, Molly McClintock," Melody replied. "The one who grew up on the farm with me."

I shrugged.

"I've talked about her a million times. She's been my best friend since forever." When I continued to stare blankly, she clarified. "You know, Molly? Looks like me only tall? The family all calls her Mac? Or Mickey Mac? Or Molly Olly Macintolly? I've definitely mentioned her."

"Oh, yeah," I said, nodding as if a lightbulb of recognition had gone off. It hadn't. Could anyone blame me for not keeping track of the extended Schacht clan? Melody was forever mentioning this niece or that uncle. Her family tree covered half of southern Wisconsin, and every one of them seemed to have about twelve different nicknames.

Melody hauled a bin of clean silverware off a shelf, getting ready to head out front and set up for service. Biz pulled an apron off the hook next to her.

"Hey, before you get started, I want you to taste the latest bratwurst," I said.

"Don't tell me we walked into another bratwurst taste test," Biz complained.

I thought I heard a little retching noise escape from Melody's lips.

"As a matter of fact, you have. I've got two variations of the cheese and brat deep-dish pizza recipe in the oven. I thought we could have them for family meal with a spinach salad. I made up some score cards for your tasting notes," I replied. "But first I want you to try the sausage on its own."

I walked toward the counter where I left the remaining brats I'd browned earlier. The cutting board was empty. I stood there for a moment, blinking.

"You look like you've seen a ghost," Auntie Biz said, coming over to where I stood.

"There was a sausage on this cutting board and another

one on this plate. I'd only cut off a couple of small pieces for Sonya and me to taste." I looked around the counter and even on the floor, but the only hint of the sausages' existence was a crescent-shaped sheen of meat grease on the empty plate. "If we were upstairs," I said, "I'd blame Butterball, but unless he's figured out how to unlock doors, there's no way for him to get down here."

Butterball, my loveable oversized kitty companion, was under house arrest in my apartment after his most recent string of cat fights had left him with an injured paw and severely wounded pride. Much as I would have loved to be able to bring him to work with me, the obvious health code violations and his tendency to gobble up every remotely edible substance within his reach made such an arrangement impossible.

"Maybe Sonya took them?" Melody offered. "Where is she anyway?"

"Probably in hiding, if she knew this was coming," Biz muttered.

I shot a dark look at Biz. "She'll be back to help in a few minutes." My continuing sausage search came up empty. Maybe Sonya really had hit her limit and chucked them. "She's out front . . . taste-testing some new wines," I said. True enough. "Oh, and Melody, that new server is starting today. Can she shadow you for the first few tables?"

"Sure thing," Melody said.

We'd been through four different servers since opening, a regular rogue's gallery of incompetence, laziness, and, in one case, downright criminality. I didn't have high confidence in the latest hire—Jarka, a gangly, Bulgarian thirtysomething whose previous restaurant experience was limited to serving as a "tavern wench" for a local medieval-themed dinner theater. Serving jobs were plentiful in Geneva Bay during the high season, meaning employers sometimes had to take what they could get.

"Where's Daniel?" Melody asked. A slight blush rose in her cheeks as she spoke his name. "Not that I need to know. I mean, it's just that he's usually in by now." It was a secret from exactly no one that Melody had a massive crush on our handsome bartender.

"He's stopping by that new organic smoothie place on the corner of Cook and Main, Juice Revolution," I said. "He heard they have a supplier for some rare tropical fruits he'd like to use in summer cocktails, so he's going to try to get the details."

"Mac can help him! She's got a job there!" Melody squealed, fluttering her hands with excitement. "She just started a few weeks ago. Have you tried it yet? Biz and I went there last week. It was *uh-mazing*."

I looked at Biz. "Since when do you drink *uh-mazing* organic smoothies?"

"I drink what I want," she snapped. "Speaking of which, when's Daniel going to be back? I'm ready for my gin fizz."

Ever since the restaurant opened, it had been a tradition to have "family meal," our pre-service staff meal, just before the doors opened. Auntie Biz always accompanied her food with her signature drink, prepared to her exact specifications by Daniel.

"It's not even three o'clock," Melody replied, playfully nudging Biz. "What would your doctor say?"

Looking at the clock, I slapped my palm to my forehead. "Shoot. I was supposed to drop Butterball off with Sam at two."

"How's Butterball's diet going?" Melody asked.

"It started off great, but lately he's plateaued. Last time

I had him for the week, he actually gained weight. Sam thinks I'm sneaking him extra food," I said.

When my fiancé Sam and I split up, we'd agreed to share custody of Butterball. Sam was gung-ho about putting the poor thing on a diet and exercise regimen to try to get his ballooning weight under control. I wasn't totally sold on the undertaking, but I didn't want to risk looking like a bad co-parent. Butterball had originally been Sam's cat, so allowing me to have fifty-fifty custody was already something of a favor.

"*Are* you sneaking him food?" Biz asked.

"No," I said, putting my hands on my hips. "I've followed his fitness plan to the letter. He hasn't had a single bite that isn't detailed on Sam's spreadsheet."

Biz put up her palms and pointed her chin downward. "Excuse me for doubting, but you also said that you were going to do a makeover on your own diet, and I've seen you eat about forty bratwursts this week."

"Sampling doesn't count," I grumbled.

"Have you eaten a proper meal today?" she pressed.

"I haven't had time," I snapped. "Some of us have a restaurant to run."

"You're surrounded by healthy food, but you eat junk."

We faced each other, jaws clenched, neither of us backing down.

My eating habits *had* nosedived as the stress of the restaurant had risen, and I was experiencing a knock-on effect on my energy, stamina, and waistline. Powering through marathon workdays on my feet in a roasting hot kitchen fueled only by caffeine, cheese, and sugar had taken its toll. Sure, I wanted to fit into my size-fourteen jeans without needing Spanx and an industrial-strength shoehorn, but it was more than that. My thirty-sixth

birthday loomed on the horizon. Chefs tend to peak by
forty. The grueling hours and constant adrenaline often
led to stop-gap solutions like smoking and alcohol. I
wanted Delilah & Son to become a mainstay of the Geneva Bay restaurant scene, and that simply wasn't going
to happen if I dropped dead of a bratwurst-induced coro-
nary next week.

On some level, Biz was right. I knew that. Much as I
knew her criticism was her way of caring. After all, nothing says "I love you" like pointing out a person's flaws
with painful accuracy. Sometimes it felt like Biz said "I
love you" too damn much.

Melody slowly backed away from our standoff. She
cradled the silverware bin in one arm and chewed on her
opposite thumbnail.

"Is it okay if I start setting up out front?" she asked.
The poor girl's demeanor reminded me of Butterball's
when Sam and I used to argue—all saucer eyes and for-
lorn mewing. I nodded, and she ran past Biz and me like
she was dodging through the line of fire in a war zone.
Which, I supposed, she was. I thought again how glad I
was that Biz and I didn't live together.

I sighed. I wasn't in the mood for traumatizing my staff
or having a blowup with Biz. In the O'Leary family, dis-
cussing our personal lives was like tap-dancing in a mine
field. Food talk was our neutral zone. "There's still a mountain of prep to do," I said. "I'm going to be so late for Sam."

"I'll handle it," Biz said, pulling the strings of her
apron tight as she reviewed the outstanding tasks on the
day's prep list.

"It's a lot of work," I said.

"Do you think I'm helpless?" came her sharp reply.

"Of course not, but I need to double-check the seasoning on the salad dressings, and I wanted to process those

fresh herbs from your garden," I said. "Sonya will be back any minute, and Rabbit can jump in once he arrives," I said, walking over to the huge commercial fridge.

Our other member of staff, Robert "Rabbit" Blakemore, a recently paroled single dad, had been hired as a dishwasher, but had proven himself adept at all manner of kitchen work. I'd quickly promoted him to "assistant kitchen supervisor," a sort-of back-of-house Swiss-army-knife position I'd invented. His hard work deserved recognition, but the accompanying pay raise was yet another item that cost money I didn't have.

I started pulling ingredients from the fridge. "I'm going to try incorporating chervil into the asparagus and goat cheese pie, and I still have to—"

Biz cut me off by rapping her knuckles on the worktop and putting her finger to her lips. Like every experienced classroom teacher, she didn't even need to make a shushing sound. The mere motion of the index finger rising toward her lips was enough to stop a charging rhino dead in its tracks. "I said I can handle it. Don't treat me like a child."

Her tone had a sharpness that went beyond our usual give-and-take bickering. There was some kernel of pain there, some trip wire of feeling, that took me aback.

"I'm sorry, I didn't mean—"

"You're not the only person on the planet who knows how to cook," she said. She dismounted her perch, her facial expression deescalating from the mask of ire that I'd unwittingly provoked into its usual cantankerous frown. "Family meal will be on the table when you get back. The prep list will be done." She shoved me toward the door, showing surprising strength for a woman who stood five-foot-nothing and weighed a hundred pounds soaking wet. "Get going."

CHAPTER 3

I hustled up the outside stairs that led from the restaurant to my apartment, instantly breaking a sweat as my skin hit the sultry air. I was already almost an hour late to drop Butterball off at Sam's lakeside mansion. I took my phone from my back pocket as I opened the door. Dang. Three missed calls from him. The din of the kitchen often masked the buzz of incoming calls, and other distractions had abounded that day.

I dialed his number. "I'm so sorry I'm late. Crazy day at the restaurant." I spoke quickly, trying to cram my apology in before Sam could open his mouth. "I'll be over in ten minutes."

"It's always a crazy day at the restaurant," Sam replied. Although his tone was mild, the whiff of reproach in his voice was unmistakable. For the three years we were a couple, Sam had reluctantly tolerated the way I often prioritized my job over our relationship. Now that we were broken up, though, his patience tended to wear a little thinner. I kept having to remind myself that my Get Out of Jail Free card had expired.

"Well, this was *unusually* crazy," I said.

I looked around the small open-plan kitchen/living/dining area. No sign of my sweet kitty. Typically, he came charging toward me like a Pamplona bull at the sound of the deadbolt turning. He was always more like a dog than a cat in that way. I dashed into the bedroom and pulled the cat carrier off the shelf, as I scanned the bedroom for Butterball. Since he was over sixteen pounds and sported several inches of lemony-orange fluff, hide-and-seek wasn't his strong suit.

I covered the phone's microphone with my palm. "Where's my little Butterbuns?" I called. No reply.

"What did you say?" Sam asked.

"Oh, I was talking to B-man. I just need to herd him into his carrier, and we'll be at your house before you can blink."

I flipped up the duvet cover and peered under the bed. There was at most four inches of clearance between the bottom of the platform bed and the floor, but Butterball was known to squeeze his ample form under there when he was angry at me or guilt-stricken about something he'd done. As I crouched down, I found myself face-to-face with a pair of accusatory jade green eyes. Bingo.

"I'm already on my way into town to meet a friend," Sam said. The sound of rushing traffic in the background proved the statement.

"I can come by your house later," I offered.

"Don't you have a dinner service to run tonight?" Sam replied.

"After that, I mean."

"I'm not going to wait up until one a.m." Sam sighed. "Dee, when we agreed to joint custody, I expected you to hold up your side of the bargain. First you won't cooperate with his diet and now this."

My heart beat a little faster. Surely Sam wasn't implying that he was rethinking our arrangement? Could he even do that?

"I am. I mean, I will. And I'm not giving him extra food." Even as I said the words, I hurried back to the kitchen and took a jar of forbidden homemade cat treats from a shelf. Desperate times.

"Come on, Butterbutt. Help me out," I whispered. Crouching next to the bed, and putting my hand over the microphone again, I gave the jar a shake. Butterball let out a cranky screech, refusing to budge.

I reached under the bed to extract him, but he shrank away from me, his eyes focused on a spot over my shoulder. I glanced backward and saw that I'd left the cat carrier right in his line of vision. Shoot. He hated car rides with the fiery passion of a thousand burning suns. Previously the carrier had mostly been reserved for rides to the vet necessitated by his frequent brawls. Now that Sam and I split custody, though, Butterball was back and forth every week. I'd been making good progress on acclimating him to the trips using the crunchy homemade treats I'd concocted from bacon grease, smoked mackerel, and brewer's yeast. His new diet, however, left those strictly off the menu, and left me trying to entice him with "treats" like shredded zucchini.

"Uh, how about I meet you in town?" I suggested, giving the jar another shake. "I'll buy you a smoothie at that new place and then you can meet your friend. I know how much you love organic juices."

"As a matter of fact," Sam said, "I'm meeting my friend at Juice Revolution. I've been spending a lot of time there lately."

"I'm not surprised. That place sounds like it was made for you," I replied. Although Sam and I shared a passion for good food, his taste tended to veer further into kale extract and hydroponic microgreens territory than mine did. For me, old-fashioned good flavors always trumped new-fangled wellness trends. "Butterball and I will be there in ten minutes."

Ten minutes turned out to be an ambitious target. Butterball wasn't merely hiding or cowering under the bed; his excess bulk had gotten him stuck between the wooden slats. I finally enlisted Sonya and Melody to help me lift the bed and wrangle him into his carrier, aka his torture dungeon. He fought us literally tooth and nail, and we succeeded only after bribing him with the illicit goodies. *I've created a monster. A giant, ravenous monster*, I thought, as I pulled into a parallel parking spot in front of the painted brick building that housed Juice Revolution. I sighed, hoping Sam wouldn't be able to smell the cat treats on Butterball's breath.

As I eased my Jeep Wrangler to a stop, Butterball let out an almighty yowl of fury. I could see him in the rearview mirror, plastered to the back of his cat carrier, looking like he'd endured a ride on a runaway roller coaster rather than a one-mile journey through a treelined 20-mph zone. Butterball yowled his protest again as I hefted the carrier out of the back of my Jeep. I hoped that Sam would forgive me for being late twice over and that Juice Revolution's owner wouldn't object to me bringing Butterball inside. It was too hot for him to stay in the car, even for a short time.

Although I grew up in Chicago, I'd been coming to Geneva Bay for as long as I could remember, spending at least a month at Auntie Biz's tiny cottage every summer of my childhood. The basic architecture of the downtown's two-story brick-and-glass storefronts hadn't changed, but the businesses that filled them—yoga studios, art galleries, purveyors of high-end kitchen gadgets and artisanal chocolates—now overtly catered to well-heeled tourists and weekend homeowners, rather than workaday locals. Across the street from Juice Revolution stood the large building that had once housed Heyers, the town's long-defunct department store. When my sister and I were little, Biz bought all of our presents from Heyers. I still associated Christmas with their signature dark green boxes embossed with gold lettering. The store had been out of business for the better part of twenty years, and its former space had long ago been subdivided into an arcade-style shopping plaza.

While I held as much nostalgia as anyone for the locally owned hardware stores and five-and-dimes that dotted the downtown when I was a kid, I had to admit that the ongoing fancification made the environment more welcoming for businesses like Juice Revolution and my own upscale pizzeria. There weren't many other towns in southeast Wisconsin where you could get away with selling Eggplant Nduja pizzas or expensive organic juice concoctions.

I used my hip to push open the glass door to . . . what to call it? The juice café? The smoothie bar?

"Welcome to Juice Revolution, your local lifestyle juicery," a cheery voice chirped from behind the counter.

I looked up to see a statuesque woman with an avalanche of golden curls flash a smile from behind a sleek Formica counter. She wore a tight-fitting plum minidress with a mandarin collar and offset black buttons, the kind of outfit a Star Fleet cadet might wear; all that was missing was a ray gun. On the other side of the counter from the blond goddess stood Daniel, Delilah & Son's bartender, looking equally attractive with his sun-kissed complexion and spiky pop-star haircut. Side by side, they could have been mistaken for models on a break from shooting an advertisement for expensive fragrances or Swiss watches.

Stepping away from his close conversation with the "juicery" employee, Daniel moved to help me with Butterball's unwieldy carrier. "Chef, we were just talking about you," he said, easing the carrier onto the floor next to one of the few empty tables. "Hey, buddy," he cooed. He wiggled his fingers through the bars of the carrier.

I took hold of his arm and pulled it away. "Maybe give him a minute to relax," I cautioned. Butterball's usual disposition was gentle and tolerant, but when he had a strong opinion about something, he wasn't averse to throwing a couple open-clawed punches. A sharp hiss emanated from his carrier, followed by a series of thumps as Butterball flung himself against its sides. Clearly, I'd judged my cat's mood accurately.

Daniel held up his hands and backed away as if Butterball had drawn a gun on him. "Okay, man, take it easy. I thought we were friends."

"Don't take it personally," I consoled. "He's been a little touchy since Sam and I separated. And this godawful diet Sam has him on . . ." I shook my head. "I'm pretty sure he'd rake us all to shreds if I let him out right now."

Although there were several people waiting to be served, the blond woman dashed from behind the counter and dropped gracefully to her knees in front of the cat carrier. "Oh my gosh! Is this *the* Butterball? Melody talks about him all the time!" She peered through the bars. "Wow, Melody wasn't kidding, you've got curves for days. They look amazing on you, honey." She spoke as if she were giving a pep talk to a girlfriend who was self-consciously trying on bathing suits. "It's all about body confidence, and embracing your floof. Love yourself inside and out and good things will follow, am I right?"

I was surprised to hear a small mew of agreement emerge from the carrier and even more shocked to see Butterball smoosh his face against the bars for her to stroke.

The woman petted him for a moment and then sprang up with balletic elegance, somehow managing not to flash the entire shop, despite her microscopic skirt. Pivoting toward me, she stuck out her hand, "Molly McClintock. You must be Delilah. I'm super pumped to meet you. You can call me Mac. Everybody does. We were just talking about you."

"So Daniel told me," I replied.

Before she could reply, a low, thickly accented voice called from the other side of the counter.

"Mac, why you are talking to this people? Other customer are waiting."

"Jarka? What are you doing here?" I asked, approaching Mac's fellow employee, a woman I recognized as the server I recently hired. I was bewildered. She was scheduled to report to the restaurant in less than two hours, and yet here she was, wearing a plum dress similar to Mac's and apparently working. She had accessorized her outfit with leopard-print leggings and a cardigan made of teal faux fur. Her hair, dyed the color of a maraschino cherry, was slicked back into a flaccid ponytail. Her overall style was high in volume and low in good taste.

"Oh, hello, chef." Jarka's voice betrayed no emotion, and her pale lips barely moved when she spoke. "I work here as well as your restaurant. And also I am morning delivery newspaper person." She turned back to Mac and gestured to the growing line of customers. "You want to help customers like you are paid for or you want to play with cat and have flirting?" She tipped her head toward

Daniel. "Jordan said you go down to cellar and get more lemons and kales."

"On my way, Jark-ster." Mac flashed her coworker a smile that held no discernable hint of annoyance, and then turned back to me. "Lemme just pop down to the storage room for a hot sec and then I'm totes going to make you the most *uh*-mazing smoothie."

I stared after Mac, not sure how to categorize my impression of her. Butterball was a pretty solid judge of character, and he seemed to be buying whatever she was selling. Like her cousin, she spoke at a speed typically reserved for commercial actors reciting the potential side effects of prescription drugs. She also bore a strong physical resemblance to Melody, although she had the advantage of tamer curls and a good six inches in height on her younger cousin, not to mention a strongly expressed charisma gene in place of Melody's jumpy timidity. While on the surface she was as relentlessly upbeat as Harold Heyer, her obvious zest for life was hard to dislike.

Daniel pulled out a chair for me at the table where he'd placed Butterball's carrier and took the seat opposite. "What brings you here, chef?" he asked. "Dropping off B-ball with Sam?"

"Yes," I looked around the place, taking in the hip pharmacy-meets-botanic-garden ambiance. Real plants—succulents, ferns, and tiny flowering shrubs—grew from pots that stretched the full height of one of the forest green walls. Rows of see-through containers of all sizes and shapes lined the sleek shelves on the wall behind the counter and filled the glass-doored fridges. Some held recognizable ingredients like bananas; others held exotic-looking powders and tinctures.

The customers were mostly the usual Geneva Bay

assortment of younger, bearded hipster types mixed with
the Boomer-aged tennis and Pilates set. The one outlier
was a ruddy-complexioned brute of a man with a white-
blond goatee who roosted at a corner table, looking about
as jolly as a Soviet tank. All told, there were a dozen customers in the small space, and none of them was Sam.

"I take it you saw Sam, unless you've been moonlight-
ing as a mind-reader. Did he already leave?" I checked
my watch, anxious about being away from the restaurant
for too long.

"He went into the back office a couple minutes ago
with the owner, Jordan. She's going to print off the supplier details for those fruits I want to order."

"Sam went into the back office?" My forehead creased
in confusion. "He said he was meeting a friend."

Daniel shrugged. "Maybe she was the friend. It seemed
like they know each other."

Interesting. Sam had never mentioned this "friend" to
me before.

Jarka called out an order, saying a name that sounded
like *Missile*—maybe *Michelle*? *Melissa*?

"Do you think her iffy English skills will be a problem for our diners? Delilah & Son can get pretty loud
when it's busy," I said to Daniel.

He clicked his tongue. "Accents are sexy. Good for getting tips."

"Yours is different," I countered. "Everyone loves
Puerto Rican accents. They remind people of piña cola-
das and beaches. Her accent makes me think of bread
rationing and Borat."

"Honestly, *jefa*, when you speak Spanish, your accent
sounds worse than hers. It's like you're talking with broken glass in your mouth, but I can still understand you.
Mostly."

He barely dodged the wadded napkin I threw at his head.

A peal of laughter drifted into the room, ringing out over the noise of whirring blenders and the earnest harmonies of the indie pop duo that played from hidden speakers. Sam emerged from the hallway to the left of the counter, smiling widely, in the midst of an (apparently) hilarious conversation with a petite, athletic-looking woman. Choppy layers of ebony hair framed her strong chin and wide black eyes. While her looks weren't quite as traffic-stopping as Mac's, she was no slouch in the beauty department. Sam, of course, looked as effortlessly handsome as ever, his knife-blade cheekbones covered by a layer of rugged stubble.

When Sam saw me, his smile tightened. He greeted me with a cheek kiss, and I caught a whiff of the familiar toothpaste and lemon-zest scent of him, a smell that always made me want to nibble my way along his warm skin. *Stop it. You're broken up.* He cleared his throat and ran his hand through his shoulder-length brown hair. "Delilah O'Leary, meet Jordan Watts, owner of Juice Revolution."

As I shook Jordan's hand, I caught a glimpse of myself in the large-framed mirror affixed to the wall behind her. Standing almost five-foot-ten and taking up a non-negligible amount of curvy width, I dwarfed the petite woman in front of me, which allowed me to get a good eyeful of the perspiration-stained Smashing Pumpkins T-shirt and torn jeans I was wearing. My coppery chestnut hair was prematurely graying at the temples, a fact even more evident with my long waves swept up into a sweaty scrunchie bun. I made an urgent mental note to spend some quality time with the Clairol box that night after service.

"So nice to meet you," Jordan said. "Sam's told me so much about you."

So, today was National Talk about Delilah O'Leary Day. "Really?" I said, eyeing Sam.

She nodded. "And I see you brought Butterball," she observed, tapping the cat carrier with the side of her shoe.

This woman knows my cat? It was going to take some getting used to the idea that Sam and Butterball now had a life independent of mine.

"I hope that's okay," I said. "I couldn't leave him in the car in this heat."

"No prob." She dismissed my concern with a wave. "Here's that supplier info you wanted, Daniel honey." Jordan waved a sheet of paper in the bartender's direction.

"Finally, a way to get fresh guavas and carambolas." Daniel brought the paper to his lips and kissed it. "Now, if you don't mind, I have to head to work. I have so many ideas for the cocktail list and I want to start planning."

"Biz's gin fizz better be your first priority if you know what's good for you," I called after his departing form.

Sam chuckled. "Some things never change."

An uneasy thought drifted across my mind, recalling Biz's sharp response to me earlier. In all our years together, through our countless arguments, I never remembered her using that tone. I'd touched a nerve, and I wanted to understand it.

With a name like O'Leary, people expected me to come from a big, boisterous Irish American family, chockablock with cousins and convivial family gatherings. In fact, my dad was an only child whose alcoholic parents had died before I was born. Auntie Biz was his only close relative. My mom died when I was twelve, and she'd been estranged from her family since her teenage years. Other than my older sister, Shea, and her kids, Biz and I were the only branches on our sad little family tree. Although our love was deep, my aunt and I had always had a fraught relationship.

The bell over the door dinged and Mac welcomed a new customer to the "local lifestyle juicery."

I turned to see Harold Heyer strolling in, still carrying his now slightly diminished stack of flyers. He made his way over to us. "How wonderful to see two of Geneva Bay's finest new business owners together," he gushed. "I'd seat the two of you next to each other at the next Chamber of Commerce breakfast, but I don't know if Geneva Bay could cope with such beauty and talent concentrated in one place for too long." He turned to Jordan. "Can we talk?"

"Shush," Jordan cut in before Harold could continue. Her body went taut, her dark eyes locking on to my face and widening with a sudden realization. She held up her hands, palms out, and used her index fingers and thumbs to frame my face. "Wow."

"Wow . . . what?" I prompted, my forehead crinkling in puzzlement.

The air seemed to still as we all waited for Jordan's reply. She nodded slowly, as if settling on the answer to some internal conundrum. "Your body is screaming for the One in a Melon Cold Brew Juice Fusion. It's packed with cumin to release the excess bile in your liver."

"Excess bile?" I asked.

"When I say your body is screaming, I mean that literally," Jordan said.

"My bile is screaming?" I struggled to keep the skepticism from my voice.

"It is. Loudly. That's why I got into this business. To

heal people." She tapped her fingers on her chest and then on mine. She lowered her voice to a ministerial whisper. "Now, let's get you that juice."

I threw Sam an "is this chick for real" look, but he was too busy nodding in earnest admiration to notice. Really, I shouldn't have been surprised. Ever since Sam sold his software company for a (not) small fortune while he was still in his twenties, he'd devoted himself to seeking enlightenment. If ascribing to a nutty mishmash of mystical fads was an actual job, he'd have been promoted to regional manager of Nutty Fad, Inc. long ago. Sam ushered me toward the counter, where Jarka was punching in an order from an older Asian man in a pink polo shirt and his perky, twinset-wearing wife.

"Jordan trained with some of the world's top herbalists and Ayurvedic healers," Sam said, his expression sincere. "She's tuned into karmic frequencies. Sometimes the messages are very palpable to her."

Harold followed us to the counter and tapped on the stack of flyers. "Jordan, I have something exciting to talk to you about." My stomach flip-flopped as I caught a glimpse of Graham Ulrich's picture again.

"Sure thing, but first"—she gave him a hard stare and then snapped her fingers—"Maximum-Wattage Anti-Tox Mocktail. That's what you need."

I, personally, wasn't so sure Harold's wattage needed to be cranked any higher than it already was, but then again, I was blessedly deaf to screaming bile.

Harold turned to me. "She's great at this, isn't she? We've known each other since we were kids. She can always sense what I need to balance my chi."

Mac had reemerged from the storage cellar at some point while we were talking, and Jordan summoned her and Jarka with a snap. "Can you make a One in a Melon for Delilah, please? And a Maximum-Wattage Anti-Tox Mocktail for Harold," she added. "On the house, of course." She tossed a smile in our direction. "I'll have an Anti-Tox Mocktail, too. Sam, do you want something for the road? You look balanced, but a Jackfruit Blast with Citrus Power Boost never hurt anyone."

He shook his head. "Nope, I'm good."

Mac began pulling ingredients from the fridge. Jarka shrugged with the resignation of a life-term convict who'd just had another year added to her sentence.

Jordan spun to face Harold. "Let's be quick. My boyfriend and I are heading out on his new sailboat. Don't want to miss any more of this glorious day after all the rain we've had."

As she spoke, my eyes locked onto her hand, which came to rest on the small of Sam's back. I had a brief, nonsensical thought about what a strange coincidence it was that Jordan's boyfriend and Sam had both recently gotten new boats. But reason quickly returned. Part of me had known it from the first moment I saw them together. Sam and Jordan were way more than friends.

Sam must've seen the realization dawn on my face—only three months after we'd ended our engagement, he'd moved on. He had a new girlfriend. A girlfriend with a well-balanced aura, who was on a first-name basis with my cat.

CHAPTER 4

With his usual deft ability to dodge potential conflict, Sam hustled over to Butterball's carrier and hoisted it off the ground. "Better get this guy home. Don't want to waste any more daylight," he said. Then, calling to Jordan, he added, "Meet you in the car."

I stood rooted to the floor, feeling like I was suddenly in the back row of the nosebleed section, watching a recast version of a play I used to star in.

The blender whirred to life again as Mac mixed another smoothie. Jordan, who stood at the counter looking at the festival poster with Harold, blew Sam a kiss. Her expression morphed into a tight smile as she turned back to Harold. She nodded mechanically at regular intervals, clearly only half listening to whatever he was saying. Harold, by contrast, seemed fully engaged, and I again doubted the need for the additional "wattage" in his promised smoothie. Jordan stole a glance at her watch. Apparently, I wasn't the only one whose patience Harold strained. Yet another thing Jordan Watts and I had in common.

Mac slid a plastic cup containing a concoction that glowed a radioactive green down the counter to the collection area. Jarka plunked down the drink she was making and yelled out something incomprehensible. She spun back around to fill her next order as the pink-shirted man brushed past me to collect his drink. The clockwork timing of their movements added to the strange disconnect I felt.

As the sound of the blender finally died down, Jordan made her escape, clutching her own cup of super juice. She stopped briefly as she passed me. "So nice to meet you, Delilah. I'm sure we'll be seeing a lot more of each other. Never thought I'd be step-parenting a cat," she added with a laugh.

I was still too shell-shocked to do more than nod. *What was I still doing here again?* Jarka barked out a series of sounds that I slowly registered as my name. *Oh, yeah. My bile-cleansing super juice.*

The queue of customers had abated, and Mac zipped around the counter as I picked up my cup. The beverage had two layers—one a subtle pink foam, the other a pale peach juice. I took a tentative sip.

"What do you think?" Mac asked. "Be honest."

"Honestly? It's not bad. A bit overcomplicated, though. It tastes like a cantaloupe that got a PhD and wants to tell you all about his research at every party."

Mac pointed at me and grinned. "You're totally right. I've never been able to put it into words, but it *is* like a really stuck-up melon."

I glanced up at the colorful wall-mounted chalkboards that held Juice Revolution's menu. "Mine costs *nine dollars*?"

"Actually fourteen dollars. The basic One in a Melon is nine dollars, but by the time you add in the Fusion Power Booster and the cold-brew upcharge, it's fourteen," she explained.

She gestured to Harold, who was chatting with Jarka

at the other end of the counter and sipping his smoothie. "Harold's is even more. The Maximum-Wattage Anti-Tox Mocktail isn't even officially on the menu. Jordan has one every day, and with all the add-ins, it's about twenty-five dollars. The Anti-Tox add-in blend has some kind of special, like, extinct seaweed in it or something," she explained.

"How can you serve something if it's extinct?"

She waved her hand, unbothered by facts. "Whatever, it's rare and costs, like, fifty bucks an ounce. Jordan gives them to us sometimes if our chi is super jacked up."

I looked again at Harold, who seemed to be downing his drink with gusto. "Is it any good?"

"Hard no. It's like dragging your tongue across the bottom of the ocean."

"How can you sell drinks that don't taste good and cost a fortune?" I asked.

Mac flipped a stray curl of hair out of her face. "Knock it all you want, but since I started working here my poops are like clockwork and my skin looks incredible. Plus my chi is, like, phenomenal."

"Where did Jordan get her start-up capital for the business?" I asked, hoping to sound casual. I wondered if Sam had fronted her the money, like he had with my restaurant. He'd told me he'd done it because he believed in my talent, that he would've wanted to invest in my career even if we weren't together. Did he believe in Jordan's talent, too? "A bank loan, or . . . ?"

"Nope, it's her own money," Mac said. "She's self-made."

I wasn't sure if that made me feel better or worse.

Mac's voice lowered as something caught her attention. "OMG, don't look now, but I think Harold has a thing for Jarka."

I cast a subtle glance toward the opposite end of the counter. Indeed, Harold seemed spellbound, leaning across the counter and gazing with doe eyes at Jarka. He was no doubt laying on his usual ten-inch-thick snow job, but instead of being nauseated by it, Jarka seemed flattered. Her mouth, while not exactly smiling, seemed perhaps a smidgeon less scowly.

Behind me, the sound of a chair clattering to the floor put an end to our spying. I turned to see the pink-shirted man standing next to the fallen chair, his back hunched and his fingers clawing the air in an unnatural, silent-film-villain posture. His smoothie was a Jackson Pollock splatter of neon green across the floor.

"Are you okay, sir?" Mac called.

He seemed not to hear her, instead staring at his clothes and beginning to clumsily pick at his shirt and shorts. "Where did all of these come from?" he asked, his voice full of bewilderment.

Turning back to me, Mac whispered, "I wonder if he's drunk or something."

The man's wife rose. "Ronnie? What are you doing?" She looked around the room apologetically, her cheeks flushing as pink as her husband's shirt.

Instead of answering, he continued to peer hard at something invisible to the rest of us. He bent farther down, using his fingers to pluck at the air. "Do little stars grow here?" He gazed warily around. "Who's that singing carols?" Fear crept into his voice and his words tapered into disjointed mumbling. His complexion turned an unhealthy shade of violet as he took a stumbling step forward.

"Ronald Wong, stand up straight. What's come over you?" his wife snapped.

Jarka hurried from behind the counter. "Call ambulance," she commanded.

The hulking man I'd noticed earlier at the corner table rose and walked briskly out the door. Seeing no other movement from the shocked customers, Jarka barked directly at me. "Delilah, call ambulance *now*."

Before I could even take my phone from my pocket, Ronnie Wong sank to his knees, his hands clutching his neck. A wrenching gasp rose from his throat, like a drowning victim breaching the water's surface. His face had taken on a wild, raving-eyed violence. Just minutes earlier, he'd looked like he might play a round of golf or fire up a backyard grill.

"Ronnie? Sweetheart?" His wife rushed to his side, panic overtaking her embarrassment. Her hands shook as she helped Jarka ease him to the floor.

The 9-1-1 operator picked up on the first ring. I did my best to describe the situation unfolding before my eyes. I considered myself cool in a crisis, and this situation wasn't totally foreign to me. A few times over the years, I'd seen diners collapse during service—heart attacks, strokes, choking. I'd stood right next to line cooks who'd been careless with their knives, leading to some pretty gruesome scenes. But this was something far more disturbing. This man seemed to be losing his mind before my eyes.

"Say to them he is tachycardic with increased respiratory rate," Jarka spoke with precision, enunciating to compensate for her thick accent and dubious grammar. She gently eased the man's closed eyelids open. "Pupils bilaterally dilated." She turned to his wife. "What medications your husband is taking?"

"Um, just Benadryl for allergies," she replied, beginning to snivel.

"He has food allergy? Anaphylaxis?" Jarka asked.

"No, no. Sneezing because of the pollen. That sort of thing."

As I relayed the information, Wong convulsed violently, until all at once, his body went rigid, his back arching unnaturally high off the ground. Tiny twitches continued to course through his arms and legs and his eyes rolled back in his head. His gasps became more ragged. The twitches slowed, his body relaxed, until gradually, the riotous movements stopped. I felt a moment of relief, until I noticed that his breathing, too, had ceased. The whine of the ambulance siren drew closer. A ball of ice settled into my solar plexus, alongside the dawning knowledge that help would arrive too late. Ronnie Wong was already gone.

CHAPTER 5

Four of us—me, Mac, Harold, and Jarka—stood around an otherwise-empty Juice Revolution like survivors of a natural disaster.

"Can you call Sam again?" Mac gnawed on her thumbnail, a posture that highlighted her resemblance to her cousin. "I've already left six messages for Jordan."

"I can try," I said, "but depending on where they are on the lake, they're probably out of range. Either that or they can't hear their phones because they're working the sails."

"Do you think it was a heart attack? He looked so healthy." Mac stared at the spot where the man had fallen, hugging herself and rubbing her arms as if to ward off a chill. "And he was, what? Sixty? Seventy at most."

"Was not heart attack." Jarka nodded her head. "No, this was not so natural, I think." She picked up a wet rag and started to wipe at the table where the afflicted man had been sitting.

I looked at her closely. "How did you know all those things? The medical stuff you had me tell the operator."

"In Bulgaria, I am doctor. When I come to here two years ago, they say my English is not good enough for pass exams." She rolled her eyes, as if dismissing this absurd possibility. "So I study and work and I take test again maybe next year."

"Are you saying you don't think that man's death was due to natural causes?" I asked.

Jarka shrugged and righted a chair that had toppled onto the floor. "Did this look like normal heart attack to you? You don't have to be doctor to have such opinion."

A tingle ran up my spine. Indeed, although my medical knowledge was limited to Dr. Oz and a comprehensive understanding of the anatomy of various edible animals, I, too, was profoundly unsettled by the death I'd witnessed. I'd seen diners choke and have allergic reactions. This had been altogether different.

Jarka looked at her watch. "Is almost time for beginning dinner service at your restaurant." She gestured to the space before her, which looked like it had played host to a riot. A table was overturned. Trash littered the floor. Every surface seemed to be sticky with spilled juice. "I may be late for first day."

"Of course," I said. "Please take the night off with pay. I'm sure you don't feel up to working. That was traumatic."

"I will be there, but late." Jarka tilted her head, seeming not to comprehend. "I don't stop working only because a man is dead," she muttered.

I shivered as the word "dead" brought back the scene that had played out only moments before. The ambulance crew had rushed in and spent a few fruitless minutes performing CPR before whisking the unfortunate Ronnie Wong and his wife away. The shell-shocked customers filed out one by one in the aftermath. The last one left only a few minutes earlier.

"Dead." Harold repeated slowly. He'd been rooted to the same spot since the paramedics came, saying nothing.

When the rest of the customers drifted away, he seemed barely aware. I suspected we were witnessing what could well be the longest period of silence Harold had ever managed. "That poor man died right in front of us," he whispered. Already pale as a panna cotta, his coloring had taken on a worryingly greenish hue. He looked to be inhabiting a precarious territory between barfing and passing out.

Jarka, noticing Harold's complexion and demeanor, took off her fluffy cardigan and gently draped it over his shoulders. "Harold Heyer is having shock."

I was anxious to exit the dreadful scene and get back to my restaurant. I'd never missed service before. Even when I'd had the flu and was spiking a 102-degree fever, I always worked the whole shift. It wasn't pretty, but that was the chef's code: you work unless your arms have actually fallen off your body or you have an illness that could be foodborne. Most kitchens don't have a deep reserve of back-up cooks, and canceling an entire night's worth of bookings isn't an option. Much as I wanted to get back, though, I felt guilty leaving Jarka in charge of two traumatized people, plus a massive clean-up operation.

I walked behind the counter, my chef instincts taking over. I'd get Harold settled and then go. Usually, Tuesdays were quiet, especially this early in the evening, and that had been even more true during the sodden summer we'd had. I fired off a text to Sonya, letting her know I'd been held up. I had to hope she could hold down the fort for a few minutes until I got back.

"I'll make Harold some strong, black tea." I examined the labeled containers that lined the shelves. Licorice root extract, Chinese cinnamon powder, Omega-3 tocopherols. This place was more like a chemistry lab than a café. "Where do you keep the sugar?"

"I don't think we have regular sugar or black tea," Mac replied, her customary pep infused with a manic tinge. She continued to hug herself, her large blue eyes bulging.

I pressed the button to fire up the electric kettle. "Hot water with honey and lemon, then. You've got honey, right?" I continued my search, looking on shelves, rifling through cabinets and drawers. I noticed for the first time a folded sheet of paper nestled next to the register. It had been ripped from a notebook, the ragged edge clinging to the paper like torn lace. As I unfolded the sheet, a hard lump formed in my stomach. A dollar bill had been tucked inside, and as I opened the folded page, the money fluttered to the counter. A simple inscription was scrawled across the face of the bill in blocky red Sharpie.

ITS TIME TO PAY FOR WHAT YOU DID

I grew up on the South Side of Chicago with a rowdy set of friends, so the idea of intentionally involving the cops in a situation was foreign to me. The working-class community where I'd lived had plenty of resident cops, but on my side of the tracks, you didn't borrow trouble. The threatening note, though, coupled with Jarka's description of Ronnie Wong's death as something "not so natural"—there was no way I could've gone on without at least making the authorities aware of what I'd seen.

I stepped outside and made a call. Although both Mac and Harold were looking decidedly shaken, my secrecy wasn't due to sensitivity about anyone's fragile emotions. The truth was, I barely knew these people. And I didn't know if I could trust any of them.

Having worked in restaurants long enough, I was well aware that investigations into food-related illnesses, if they happened at all, almost never involved the police. If food poisoning or allergen contamination were suspected, the local health department might get involved. If it was a safety issue, the state occupational health and safety board might step in. Maybe an autopsy would be conducted on Mr. Wong, but it seemed equally likely that the death of an older man would be chalked up to natural causes. On the face of it, the medical examiner would have little reason to run extensive testing to determine how the man died.

I stepped back inside and busied myself making Harold's lemon-and-honey water. Less than five minutes after my call, the bell over the door to Juice Revolution clanged.

"We're closed, sir," Jarka called.

"I know." The newcomer replied. Dark jeans and a fitted khaki green T-shirt highlighted his powerful physique while also complementing his sepia-tone skin and close-cropped black curly hair.

My heart skipped a beat as I recognized Calvin Capone. The handsome police detective and I had met a few months before, as a result of the chaotic events that surrounded my restaurant's launch. I thought I'd sensed a romantic spark between us, but I'd gradually come to believe the whole thing was a case of temporary insanity or a figment of my imagination. Even if there was some glimmer of romance between us, a mountain of obstacles—everything from our cats being sworn enemies to his great-grandfather being the legendary gangster Al Capone to the fact that he, at age forty-two, was already the bona fide *grand*father of a toddler—stood in the way of anything ever happening. Damn him for looking so sexy in that T-shirt.

"Delilah," he said, stopping mid-stride. "What are you doing here?"

"Making tea," I replied, too surprised to state anything other than the obvious.

I thought some uniformed newbie would show up, take a statement, bag up the threatening note, and let me ease my conscience. I hadn't expected the dispatcher to send a detective, and I certainly hadn't expected Capone.

"How are you?" I asked, walking toward him.

"This is a"—Jarka cast a slow, appraising look up and down Capone's handsome figure—"friend of yours, Delilah?"

"We, uh . . ." Capone began.

Jarka turned to me for clarification, but I was equally hard-pressed to describe our relationship. *This is a cop I flirted with during a murder investigation?* It didn't help that Capone and I stood so close that I could feel the sultry heat of the summer afternoon still clinging to his skin. "We're kind of . . ." My hands moved in circles, as if I were trying to juggle some invisible answer.

Capone cleared his throat and turned to Jarka. "Are you the owner?"

She moved her chin up and down. "I am Jarka Gagamova."

"How long have you owned this place?" Capone asked, understandably interpreting her nodding head as assent.

"No, I only work." She stilled her nodding head. "I am sorry. Bulgarians, we nod our head for no. For yes, we do this." She demonstrated a vigorous shake of her head. "Is difficult to change this."

"I can imagine," Capone said, with a slight sparkle of amusement in his eye. "I'm responding to a call. I'm an officer with the Geneva Bay Police." He flashed his badge. "I was around the corner, doing some research for another case, when the call came in. I didn't realize you were involved," he added, to me.

"I'm the one who called," I replied.

"You called the cops?" Mac asked, still looking like she was skating on the rim of hysteria. "What for?"

"I found . . ." I paused, remembering that I hadn't mentioned the call, the note, or my suspicions to any of them. "I just wanted to be sure everything gets handled correctly. The, uh, paperwork."

The inner corners of Capone's eyebrows shot up, but he didn't challenge my thin excuse.

"Should I try calling Jordan again?" Mac asked. "She still doesn't even know what happened."

"Is Jordan the owner?" Capone asked.

"Yes, Jordan Watts. We've only been open for, like, five weeks," Mac said, her auctioneer-speed speaking pace making a comeback. Since Capone arrived, she'd sprung into action, fetching Harold more hot water and honey and pitching in to help Jarka clean. "Jarka and I work here. I'm Molly McClintock by the way. You apparently know Delilah, and you probably know Harold Heyer from the Chamber."

At the mention of his name, Harold slumped further in his chair.

"Mr. Heyer, are you all right?" Capone asked.

"That man died," he said, staring with wide eyes at the spot on the floor where Wong had fallen.

Jarka patted him on the shoulder with surprising gentleness. "Yes, he is dead." She looked at us. "I should take Harold Heyer to his home. Is not good for him to be here. Mac, you can finish the cleaning and try again to call Jordan?"

"Jordan was here right before the guy died," Mac

explained to Capone, "but now she's out on the lake with her boyfriend, Sam Van Meter, and we can't reach them."

"Your ex, Sam?" Capone turned to me.

"Uh, yeah," I replied.

Realizing it was going to be difficult to have a private conversation with Capone in the small café, I said, "I'm late for dinner service." That much was true at least. I'd sent a few quick text updates to Sonya, but I was sure my crew would be wondering if I'd fallen into a black hole. "Any chance you could give me a lift back to the restaurant?"

Capone looked around Juice Revolution and then at me. "Sure. I can always come back later if there's any . . . paperwork that needs to be cleared up."

CHAPTER 6

As I climbed into the passenger seat of Capone's black, police-issue Dodge Charger, I was already beginning to regret my impulsive decision to report my suspicions.

I had enough sense to realize that a creepy note and a tingly Spidey-sense wouldn't suffice to get a search warrant, much less to open any kind of investigation. For all I knew, Ronnie Wong had a preexisting condition of some kind. The note could've been a prank, unrelated to his death. Even if there was something devious behind Wong's death, what business was it of mine? I feared I was becoming one of those pathetic small-town types who calls the cops every time their neighbors leave their trash cans out an extra day.

"If you wanted a lift to your restaurant, you could've ordered an Uber," Capone said, pulling his car on to Main Street.

"Actually my car's right there." I pointed to my Jeep Wrangler as we drove past it. I covered my face with my hands and shook my head. "Let's just forget this, okay? I don't know what I was thinking. I have a restaurant to run. I don't have time to get mixed up in . . ." I trailed off, not quite knowing how to finish.

"A murder?" Capone put words to the thought that had

been roosting in the back of my brain. A thought I hadn't even allowed myself to fully acknowledge.

"Some middle-aged guy keeled over," I said. "I let my imagination run away with me."

"Really?" Capone pursed his full lips. "Delilah O'Leary, level-headed, uncompromising bad-ass chef, accidentally butt-dialed nine-one-one?" He took his eyes off the road to throw a brief, penetrating look in my direction. "Why don't you tell me what happened at Juice Revolution and we'll go from there?"

The drive was only a little over a mile, and I barely had time to relay a broad outline of the events of the previous hour before we pulled into the restaurant parking lot. I wasn't at my most eloquent either, distracted as I was by Capone's proximity and the cedar wood and vanilla scent of him. Maybe I did need to join Sonya in getting back on the dating scene.

"That's when I found the note," I finished, a little breathlessly.

The parking lot was unusually full, and Capone pulled into one of the few open spaces near the lakeside patio. Seeing the tables filled with diners, my blood pressure spiked. I'd almost forgotten that I left a distraught Sonya and my frail octogenarian aunt to finish all the prep and get service underway. Melody and Daniel would be scrambling to handle the front of house without Jarka's help, and Rabbit would probably be shuttling back and forth to fill the gaps. Of all the Tuesday evenings to have picture-perfect weather and a packed patio.

"This note," Capone said, bringing me back to the matter at hand. "You've got it with you?"

I plucked the paper-enfolded dollar bill out of my purse, holding it by the corner with a tissue. I carefully removed the bill with another tissue. Capone looked it over, without touching it. He tilted his head to one side as he read it, but he made no comment on its contents. He reached across my body, pulling an evidence bag from the glove compartment and gesturing for me to deposit the note inside.

"So that's what I've got. I witnessed a freak death and moments later, I found a threatening note, so I called."

Capone looked at the bagged note and then at me. "Just to be clear, you're insinuating that your ex-boyfriend's new girlfriend's juice bar just played host to a suspicious death, and you want the police to shut the place down and investigate?"

When he said it like that, my motives didn't sound as altruistic as they had inside my head. "I knew I shouldn't have gotten the police involved," I muttered.

"Yes, you should have. I only wish you hadn't been the one to find this evidence," he added. "You, who knows better than almost anyone that opening a criminal investigation will likely result in a serious disruption to her brand-new business." He pressed his fingers to the bridge of his nose briefly and then looked at me. "I'm glad you called. But you do have a special way of making my job difficult."

"We could just pretend I never said anything," I said, reaching for the door handle.

"Unfortunately, I know from bitter experience that you've got a good eye for evidence, and your instincts are often correct. I think you know it, too. If this guy's death gave you a reason for suspicion, at the very least, I'm going to get this note fingerprinted and make sure Ronald Wong doesn't go into the ground without an autopsy and full tox screen. At least I know from the outset that this case, if it turns into a case, will be a hot mess." He leaned on the center console, his arm brushing mine.

Startled by the contact, we turned to face each other, my dusky blue eyes locking with Capone's gold-flecked ones at close range. Although the lively patio was only a few yards away, the interior of the car was pin-drop quiet. The background chatter on the police radio had fallen silent, and only the whirr of the car's air-conditioning and the whisper of our mingled breathing disrupted the stillness.

Capone cleared his throat, breaking the tension. "How's Butterball been?"

"He's . . ." I began to say "fine," but stopped. Something about the intimacy of the space made me drop the pretense. "Not good," I answered. "He's been really stressed. Lots of hiding, more fighting than before, constant drama. He's mad at me all the time. It's like having a teenager. And don't even get me started about the diet Sam has him on."

Capone chuckled. "Brujo was a bit like that when we moved up here," he said.

I'd met his cat, a huge, pointy-eared Maine Coon, a few months earlier, when he and Butterball had declared war on each other. The cat was originally owned by Capone's mother, a jazz singer who still performed a few nights a week at a club in the city. She'd moved to Geneva Bay to help care for Capone's granddaughter while the little girl's single dad finished up his medical studies at Northwestern. Magellan himself would struggle to navigate his way around the who's who of the Capone family. As I contemplated Capone's chiseled jawline and inviting lips from close proximity, it was important to remind myself that his tangled family arrangement was just one reason why I needed to give my raging crush a cold shower.

"Brujo was used to living in my mom's townhouse in the city," he continued. "He didn't know what to do with himself when they first got here. We tried moving him back and forth for a while, when she was in the city on the weekend, but he was tearing his hair out—literally. Chewing bald spots into his fur. His vet said it was best to leave him in one place. My mom hates to be apart from him, but she realized she had to put his needs above hers."

I swallowed hard. I'd never had a pet before Butterball, but it didn't take a kitty whisperer to realize that my cat was trying to tell me something. I'd been chalking his rebellious behavior up to the diet, but I hadn't wanted to see the truth. The shared custody arrangement was a bust. I'd known it deep down, but facing that meant accepting the reality that Butterball had originally been Sam's cat. If only one of us could have him, it probably wasn't going to be me. The story of King Solomon threatening to divide the baby floated up from the murky depths of my childhood catechism classes.

Capone must've noticed the pained expression on my face. He covered my hand with his. "I didn't mean to imply anything. I'm sure Butterball will adjust. He's a resilient cat."

A sharp rap on my window startled me, and I turned to find Melody standing outside the car, holding a bus tub. Capone rolled down the passenger window using the control on his side.

"It *is* you," Melody said, pressing her hand to her chest. "Thank goodness you're back, chef. It's mayhem. We're so deep in the weeds. Jarka didn't show up, but then Graham Ulrich *did*. He didn't have a reservation and there weren't any tables and I didn't know what to do, so I seated him at the bar, but I didn't tell Sonya and now we have to keep Sonya in the kitchen so she doesn't see him." Her lip quivered and I feared that she might have a nervous breakdown right on the spot.

"Did you say Graham Ulrich is here?" I was out of the car like a Derby horse from the starting gate. As a card-carrying control freak, a part of me always suspected that the world would fall off its axis if I didn't personally keep it spinning. This was case in point.

Capone got out of the car, too, and came around to the side Melody and I were on. "The TV food guy?" he asked.

"Yeah," Melody said. "The one from *Restaurant 9-1-1* who goes into a failing kitchen and rips the chef a new . . ."

I interrupted Melody before she could finish that anatomical Mad Lib. "He seems to be haunting me today. Why on earth would he come here?"

"For an Eggplant Nduja pizza, he said, but it's not on the menu tonight," Melody explained. "I tried to convince him that the Deep Dutch is just as good, but he seemed pretty annoyed. He said he wanted to speak to the chef, but I couldn't let Sonya see him, so I told him the chef was busy, but I wasn't sure how long I could keep stalling, and . . ." Her face crumpled. "Cripes, I'm just so glad you're here!"

I cursed under my breath. "I've gotta go," I told Capone. "Sounds like tonight is shaping up to be an epic goat rodeo."

"Yes, it does." Capone clicked his car's remote lock. "Why don't I pitch in until Jarka turns up? I waited tables all the way through high school."

"Really?" I asked.

"You don't believe me?" he teased. "Mr. Walker, who managed Ja'Grill back then, has been dead for twenty years, so getting ahold of my references won't be easy."

"Very funny. I meant are you really willing to help?"

"I'm off the clock, and I've got nothing better to do with my Tuesday night," he replied. "Everyone at the station knows your menu backward and forward from all the take-out we've ordered."

"You're hired. Welcome to the goat rodeo," I said.

Melody rushed back to her expectant diners on the patio, while Capone and I went in through the back door. As we entered the kitchen, I was relieved to see that nothing was actually on fire. At least nothing that wasn't supposed to be on fire. However, it didn't take a professional cook to see that chaos reigned. I've always run a clean, methodical kitchen, and usually Biz, Sonya, and I ascribe to the same prep-cook-clean-repeat rhythm that keeps service running without a snag. Messy stations, a dish-stacked sink, a ticket printer firing out orders like a trigger-happy squaddie—these were hallmarks of impending doom.

At the sound of our entrance, Auntie Biz turned on me like a guided missile. "Where in the bloody blue blazes have you been?" She gestured to the stack of order tickets next to her, which hadn't been touched, much less filled. "I should be home watching my *Matlock* by now."

Sonya rushed over and clutched my arm. "I was worried. Your texts where so cryptic, I thought you'd been kidnapped." She looked at Capone and paused, a frown line creasing her forehead. "Wait, were you kidnapped?"

"Long story. Too long for right now. Jarka is going to be late," I explained. "Capone's going to lend a hand." I ignored Biz's and Sonya's astonished looks as I handed him a black apron and notepad. "Take over the window side of the dining room from Melody. Tables one through six."

"Rabbit's covering the window side," Sonya said. "He just seated a twelve-top."

"He what?!" This wasn't impending doom. This was the End Times.

Serving a group of twelve could be a nightmare juggling act for even a seasoned pro. Rabbit had only been "on the outside" for a few months, after a string of lengthy jail sentences. He still had the close-cropped hair, wary eyes, and jumpy demeanor characteristic of many long-incarcerated men. Although he was a pro at dishwashing, shelf stocking, and expediting, the subtleties of face-to-face customer service still eluded him. I'd used him as a back waiter occasionally—helping to bring out finished dishes from the kitchen and refilling water glasses—but his social graces were still heavily oriented toward life behind cinder-block walls. He'd worked in the prison kitchen, but five years of experience ladling mystery meat onto shatterproof trays wasn't entirely translatable to an upmarket dining context.

I peeked through the door into the dining room. Rabbit stood at the head of a large table of raucous women, pencil in hand, looking like he was facing down a mounted regiment. "You've got to be kidding. The twelve-top is a bachelorette party. That woman has one of those little white veil headbands." I spun to face Capone. "Can you take over from Rabbit?"

"Don't worry. If I can coordinate a multi-agency racketeering investigation, I can handle a table of rowdy women." He peered over my shoulder in time to see the bride-to-be stuff a dollar bill into Rabbit's waistband. The other women whooped and cheered. "But to be on the safe side, let's ask Daniel to water down their drinks."

CHAPTER 7

Once Capone headed out to get control of the unruly bride-to-be's table, Rabbit returned to the kitchen, safe but shaken.

"I've never been so happy to see a cop in my life," Rabbit said. He set down his order notepad alongside a handful of dollar bills he'd plucked from his waistband. He gripped the edge of the worktop for a moment to steady himself. His face, already careworn, seemed to have aged ten years in the space of an evening. "You know I'd do almost anything for you, chef, but not"—he pointed emphatically in the direction of the bridal party—"that."

"I'm sorry, Rabbit. You really took one for the team," I consoled, handing him his dishwashing apron. He clutched it briefly to his chest, closing his eyes with gratitude. "I need you to rally, though. We're in deep. Can you organize and restock the stations?"

"I got you, chef," he answered, his round, green eyes taking on a determined gleam.

I spent the next few moments in army medic mode. My first order of business was to relocate Auntie Biz upstairs to my apartment and get her set up in an armchair with an episode of *Matlock* from the DVR. She'd shown surprising stamina, but I knew by her lack of argument that she'd reached her limit. Either that, or she was still mad at me after our argument earlier and giving me the cold shoulder. No time to get to the bottom of that now.

Back in the kitchen, I twisted my hair into a bun and quickly threw my chef's coat—essential protection from steam, spills, and heat—over my grubby T-shirt. With the breathing room afforded by Rabbit's return to the back of house, Sonya and I began to triage orders and expedite the dishes that could still be completed somewhere close to on time.

Deep-dish pizzas take no less than thirty minutes to cook, so our diners knew better than to expect instant service. But leave people waiting for too long without a crumb to eat, and hanger would start to get the better of them. An onslaught of one-star "my food was late" Yelp reviews was the last thing we needed right now. Based on the behavior of the bachelorette party, another danger was that my patrons would keep ordering cocktails on empty stomachs. Of all the nights for the dining room to turn into a live reenactment of *Lord of the Flies*. Not what I wanted Graham Ulrich to see.

Ugh. Graham Ulrich. I dreaded facing him, but ignoring him wouldn't make him go away. If it was confrontation he wanted, I had a cup full of piping-hot whup-ass brewing especially for him. How dare he come to Geneva Bay to ruin our contest chances and then walk into my restaurant to rub it in Sonya's face? Tempted as I was to have Rabbit and Daniel toss him into the street, I wasn't going to let him leave until he tasted my food. If he was going to try to sabotage Delilah & Son, I wanted him to know deep down in that little coal black heart of his that I was the rightful winner of the Taste of Wisconsin.

I surveyed the stack of "no way in hell those people are getting their food in under an hour" orders and came up with a plan. Drawing upon my mental recipe file, I threw together lightning-quick appetizer plates of pancetta-wrapped dates and crostini topped with goat cheese, local honey, and strawberry slices.

Melody burst through the swing door, her blond curls flying like she'd ridden to the kitchen in an open-top convertible. "How are we doing on those Red Hot Mama pies for table eleven?"

"Fifteen minutes," Sonya said.

"You said that fifteen minutes ago," Melody moaned.

I shoved one of the app trays at her. "Take these to eleven, on the house, and thank them for their patience. If the pizza still isn't out in twenty, tell them that's on the house, too." I pointed to the other trays. "These are for three, nine, and fourteen. Same deal." I peeked into the pizza oven. "Tell two, seven, eight, and twelve their food will be out ASAP."

"What about the small Deep Dutch for the bar?" Melody asked, widening her eyes meaningfully behind Sonya's back.

Sonya scanned the orders on the ticket rail in front of her. "Dang, they've been waiting awhile, but it should be out in five."

"That one is to-go," I said. "Melody, when it comes out of the oven, can you box it up and bring it out? I'll let them know it's on the way."

Sonya pointed to the ticket. "It doesn't say carryout."

"Trust me, the customer has to go," I said.

Melody shot me a worried look before she headed off on her appetizer-bribery mission.

As I entered the dining room, I paused for a moment, gauging the mood. One or two sets of expectant eyes glanced up when I came through the door, but not as many as I'd feared. Once the entire room started eyeing the waitstaff like lions roaming the savannah, you knew desperation was setting in. We weren't there just yet. Near the windows, Capone stood poised to take down an order. Seeing me, he threw a subtle nod in my direction, indicating that he had the situation in control. I breathed a little easier. Capone's help plus the gambit with the free apps would probably be enough to pull us back from the brink. There was, however, still one problem that remained to be tackled.

I made my way toward the bar, where the sleek, silvery mane of Graham Ulrich stood out like a beacon. Ulrich and I had crossed paths more than once in our professional lives, even briefly overlapping in the kitchen at the Kimpton Hotel in the Chicago Loop a decade earlier. Even back then, he was an egotistical jackass. As if that amazing head of hair and the plummy British accent meant he could treat the rest of us like peons. Unlike almost anyone else who ever worked in a big-city restaurant kitchen, he never bothered to learn a word of Spanish, so his only communication with the large contingent of Mexican and Central American workers was in the form of shouting and angry gestures. We'd called him "Cabeza," literally "head." He took it as a recognition of his superior position, not knowing we used it to mean "arrogant chump." Since he'd opened his splashy haute-cuisine restaurant and landed his TV gig, his ego had ballooned to the size of a parade float.

I slid onto the barstool next to Ulrich and signaled for Daniel to pour me a drink. Although rosé was my usual tipple of choice, Daniel reached for the liquor bottles on the top shelf. He had a keen intuition for situations when wine wasn't going to cut it.

Ulrich turned toward me, his thin lips twisting into a smile.

I spoke before he could. "Why don't you tell me what you're really doing here?"

As far as I was concerned, Ulrich had become my enemy the day he humiliated Sonya. On some level I could concede that his anger toward her was justified. After all, she'd had an affair with his wife. I couldn't help thinking he had it coming, though. Besides, when it came to Son, there was no right or wrong—my loyalty to her was absolute.

"Delilah O'Leary." He narrowed his deep-set eyes and drawled out the vowels in my name in his sonorous BBC accent, an accent he was rumored to have adopted to re- place the slangy Cockney of his upbringing. He cast a disdainful glance at his Rolex. "I'd hoped you'd be bring- ing me my food."

"Kitchen's a little backed up, so we had to prioritize the orders of everyone who isn't a jumped-up little hosebag." I'd already kissed my chances in the contest goodbye, so why pretend this was a catch-up between old friends? I could just about muster enough politeness for harmless pests like Harold Heyer, but I wasn't going to let a snake like Graham Ulrich think for a millisecond he could come on to my turf and mess with me or Sonya.

Daniel pressed my drink into my waiting hand, and I took a long sip, letting the bittersweet tang of the Old Fash- ioned steel my nerves. Daniel had clearly overheard what I said to Ulrich, and his lips rounded into an O as he turned back to fill his next orders.

"Such hostility. I really am quite appalled that this is how you treat a former colleague." Ulrich's lip turned up in a smirk that seemed equal parts sinister and amused. "I thought you'd be excited for the opportunity to show off your—what is it you make here? Oh, yes. Pizzas." He spat the word as if he were trying to expel something unpleasant. "I'm so looking forward to handing out the little blue ribbons or what have you at this charming little contest. I presume Geneva Bay's other entries will be just as elevated as your offerings. Perchance cheese curds, or even a cheeky hot dog. With such displays of culinary prowess"—he fanned himself with his hand—"my taste buds won't know what to do with themselves."

"I can think of a thing or two." Daniel's murmuring was audible even over the din of the dining room. He'd stayed nearby during our conversation, wearing an expression that was more "Army Daniel" than "Bartender Daniel." I got the sense that he was ready to leap over the bar and throw this guy off the end of marina pier if I gave the signal.

"One more chance," I said. "Why are you here?"

"I need to speak with Sonya," he said. As he leaned toward me, his face fell into shadow, and for a moment, his polished veneer melted away. "She's trying to take something that isn't hers."

I paused, unsure what he was referring to. Did he think Sonya and his wife were still an item? I was positive they hadn't spoken in months. No matter. The only thing he needed to know was that I wasn't going to stand for his bullying.

"Fat chance," I replied.

"You're making a mistake, Delilah. If you do as I say, it could turn out quite well for you. But if you make things difficult . . ." He let out a mirthless laugh. "Well, I'm afraid to say it may end very badly indeed." A cold menace filled his flinty blue eyes.

I drained the last of my cocktail and stood up, using my body to shield the still-seated Ulrich from the rest of the dining room. I rested my index and middle fingers on the soft hollow of his throat, allowing just enough pressure to maintain his attention. "If you so much as breathe in her direction while you're in Geneva Bay . . ."

I felt a tap on my shoulder. "Sorry to interrupt. One Deep Dutch, to go." Capone loomed into view, holding a small pizza box. Although he'd addressed me, his eyes were focused squarely on Ulrich, his thick brows drawn low. In tone and expression, he retained his usual calm self-possession, but the corded muscles in his neck and jaw told a different story.

I took the still-warm box from him and placed it into Ulrich's hands. He eyed it as if it might contain plastic explosives. "So sorry for the wait, sir," I said, flashing an acid smile. "This one's on the house." I crossed my arms, daring Ulrich to try anything.

Me. Ulrich. Capone. Daniel. No one moved, our gazes flitting from one person to the other. Daniel leaned in, pressing his forearms hard into the smooth wood of the bar, showing off the solid definition of his biceps. "Your order was to go," he said.

Graham Ulrich might have a flashy lifestyle and his own TV show, but none of that was a match for the wall of testosterone on my side. He straightened his spine, gathering his pizza and what was left of his pride as he marched out the door.

CHAPTER 8

Another hour passed before Jarka arrived for her shift. By then, the dining room crowd had thinned out, the kitchen was almost caught up, and the bridal party had blessedly decamped to a bar in town to continue their debauchery. The immediate danger of me spontaneously combusting from stress had passed.

"Hello, chef and Sonya." Jarka greeted us in her usual monotone as she walked through the kitchen to the sink and began to wash her hands. She'd changed out of her Juice Revolution tunic and into a black velour tracksuit with a gold zipper and wide satin collar. Bedazzled onto the seat of her pants in black rhinestones were the words "Cutie Pie." It was a deeply inharmonious combination of fabrics and styles—not quite what I had in mind when I created the simple "wear all black" dress code for Delilah & Son's front-of-house staff.

"I am here, but late because of dead man and Harold Heyer having shock," Jarka continued. "Poor, poor Harold Heyer. Such a tender and beautiful man. This death has affect him deeply." She clutched her fists briefly to her heart. "After I leave sweet Harold Heyer, I went back to the Juice Revolution because Jordan returned from the lake and wonders what has happen and why is Mac upset and why is the Juice Revolution very messy. And then Jordan and Sam also have very much shock because of dead man." She dried her hands on a paper towel and tossed it into the trash. "Now everyone is finished with their shocks, and I am here, but late."

I'd given Sonya a broad overview of the earlier events at Juice Revolution, but her mouth nonetheless hung agape at Jarka's blunt recounting.

"I appreciate you coming in," I said. "You really didn't have to."

Jarka shrugged. "Is no problem." As she donned her apron, she inclined her head toward the dining room. "Why that policeman is waiting tables? Does he also work second job for extra money?"

"He's only lending a hand," I explained. "I better go release him now that you're here."

I found Capone on the patio, his handsome face illuminated by the globe lights that hung crisscrossed overhead. A welcome breeze lifted the sweat-damp hair on my neck as I watched him slicing into a pan of deep-dish with a deft movement of a serrated spatula. He seemed impressively undaunted by the thick umbilical cord of mozzarella that coupled the slice he was serving to the main pizza, using a quick flick of his wrist to sever the connection. Behind him, the lake had deepened into the indigos and purples of twilight. A thin golden rind of sunset hovered just above the horizon. He finished serving out slices and then came over to join me.

"Jarka's here to take over. I can't thank you enough for helping out tonight," I said. "You've earned my eternal gratitude, and from what I hear, you also picked up some pretty decent tips. Melody said that bachelorette party left you twenty-five percent plus three different phone numbers, including the bride's. And that thing with Graham

Ulrich . . ." I shook my head. "If you hadn't been here, I really don't know how that would've ended."

He smiled. "I took an oath to serve and protect. Tonight, I ended up taking that more literally than I'm used to."

"Delilah, is that you down there?" Auntie Biz's voice cut through the tranquil chatter of the patio diners.

I looked up to see her tiny figure backlit by the illumination coming through the sliding glass doors of my apartment. Auntie Biz was leaning on the railing of the small balcony that jutted off my living room and overhung the restaurant's patio.

"Auntie Biz?" I called.

Capone and the other diners on the patio looked up as if they were expecting Auntie Biz to break into an aria. The fact of me living directly over the restaurant had never been particularly significant in my mind. Either I was working, which meant the apartment was empty, or I was home, which meant the restaurant was closed. I hadn't given much thought to the proximity of my domestic life to my work life.

"Is someone going to drive me home, or what? I ran out of *Matlock*s on the TV thing," she said.

I grimaced. "Melody usually takes her home before service starts," I whispered to Capone. "I had to stash her up there because everything was so crazy when we got here, and then I kind of forgot about her."

"Let me grab my keys," I called to her. I took a step toward the restaurant, but stopped in my tracks. "Oh, shoot, I left my car downtown."

The faces of the restaurant diners pivoted back and forth between me and Biz like Wimbledon spectators.

Capone put his hand on my arm. "I'm leaving anyway. I can take her home."

"I can't let you do that," I said. "I already owe you big-time."

"Well, one of these days, maybe I'll need a favor from you."

Was there an innuendo in his raised eyebrow, or had I been single too long? I hoped the flush of my cheeks was hidden by the growing darkness. It had been years since I'd flexed my flirting muscles, and I'd forgotten how uncomfortable the whole dating game made me. I hated the uncertainty of it, the lack of control over the outcome.

"If you really don't mind, that would be a huge help," I said.

"I'll be right up, Miss O'Leary," Capone called. "I'll drive you home."

Before I could properly thank him, he was out of sight.

The remaining few hours of service passed in a whirl of cheese and dough, but without further drama. Jarka proved adept at serving, and seemed to get along fine despite her total lack of warm fuzzies. After the day my staff had all had, we flew through our cleaning and next-day prep, and by ten-thirty, I was locking the doors and heading up the stairs, ready to collapse into bed. As I mounted the last of the steps, though, the sound of familiar voices—Capone's and Auntie Biz's—drifted from inside my apartment. Much as I'd been looking forward to faceplanting onto my duvet, I felt a small sense of relief at the prospect of company. Since Sam and I had begun our custody-sharing arrangement, I'd struggled with coming home to an empty apartment on the nights when Butterball was away. Even now, as I thought of sleeping without my kitty's large, warm body snuggled next to mine, my throat tightened with a pang of loneliness.

I opened the door to find Capone and Biz planted on my couch, feet on the coffee table, with sheaves of paper scattered around them. They held matching bottles of New Glarus Fat Squirrel Nut Brown Ale, one of the local beers Daniel wanted to introduce to the bar menu. I'd taken a six-pack upstairs, meaning to taste-test it, but judging by the empty bottles that littered the table, they'd already taste-tested it very thoroughly. I noted that most of the empties were on Biz's side of the table. Tiny as she was, the woman had the alcohol tolerance of a lumberjack.

The two of them barely registered my entry. Biz was busy stabbing at one of the pages in front of her with her index finger. "It's a registered subsidiary of the consulting company that managed the corporate charitable foundation, but it's also a transactional vehicle for the real estate division of Rock Co. Enterprises," she explained.

Capone nodded in a way that made me think he had slightly more of a clue about what that meant than I did.

"Well, what do we have here?" I asked, taking a seat in the armchair next to them. "A little late-night financial tutorial?"

Capone rubbed the back of his neck and took a long pull of his beer. "Tutorial would imply that I'm smart enough to be tutored."

"I won't hear you putting yourself down," Auntie Biz scolded. "I've taught three generations of Geneva Bay's high schoolers. I can tell when I have a bright student." She reached across and gave him an encouraging pat on the knee.

Auntie Biz's devotion to her students' education was the stuff of legend. Extra study sessions, individualized curricula, breaking difficult concepts down into bite-sized pieces, and stretching students' expectations of what they were capable of. When she and I were out and about in town, people still came up to thank her and tell her how much she'd influenced their lives. For her students, it seemed, her tough veneer was softened with inspiration. She'd taught me to cook, yes, but I'd never experienced that kind of encouragement from her. Far from it. Auntie Biz's lessons came in the form of directives and criticism, meted out like blocks of ice.

I'd once come to her bursting with the confidence of the determined ten-year-old I was, full of fantasies of recreating a complicated cheese soufflé recipe I'd seen the great French chef Michel Richard make on an episode of *Baking with Julia*. As I grated parmesan and gruyere, whisked the roux, and whipped egg whites until they looked pristine and pointy as the Matterhorn, Auntie Biz hovered in the background, criticizing, inspecting, and pointing out mistakes in my technique. When I presented the finished dish, she'd simply taken two bites and given me a soldierly nod of acceptance.

I asked her about it once—why she was always so hard on me. "You have the skills and the passion," she'd said, "but that's not enough. I knew it would be hard for you—a young woman with no industry connections and no money to fall back on. To get where you wanted to go, you'd have to be a fighter, too. Would you be where you are if I'd given out gold stars and participation trophies?"

Maybe not, but ten-year-old me wouldn't have minded the occasional "atta girl."

"What's tonight's lesson?" I asked, pushing my memories aside.

Capone reached down to the floor next to the couch and hooked his finger through the cardboard holder containing the last two beers from the six-pack. He popped the top of one and handed it to me. "The financial wizardry of one Rocco Guanciale, or rather, of his accountant, a guy called Jimmy Krimins."

I took a sip of the beer. A strong scaffolding of hops holding up notes of hazelnut and barley. I could see why Daniel had suggested it.

"Rocco the gangster, who used to own this building?" I asked.

"The one and only," Capone said.

I picked up a paper from the table. A spreadsheet—row after row of debits and credits, a jumble of numbers. "What's all this?"

"It's a side project of mine. A hobby I acquired thanks to you both, in fact," Capone replied.

I raised an eyebrow. "I'm sure I'd never encourage anyone to take up masochism."

He smiled. "Your involvement was indirect. When I was working on the murder case here a few months back, I started to wonder about this property. Idle curiosity, or maybe a bit of a hunch. Lakefront parcels in this town don't tend to linger on the market, and yet this place sat for years. Empty."

"The realtor told Sam and me it was because it needed so much work," I said. "Honestly, I was so distracted at the time by my dad's cancer that I didn't give it a second thought."

"The condition of the building was part of it, maybe. I haven't lived in Geneva Bay very long, but I've seen developers buy multi-million-dollar mansions and tear them down to build bigger mansions. The idea that people would be put off by a renovation project struck me as odd."

"This place is full of people with more money than sense," Biz sniffed.

"I started looking into it. When you called earlier from Juice Revolution, I was able to show up so quickly because I was already downtown, at the county assessor's office, requesting old property records," he said. "Turns out, despite what everyone thinks, Rocco wasn't the actual owner of this building."

Auntie Biz held up a piece of paper. "It was held by a shell company. Rock Co. Enterprises."

"Rock Co.—that's a pretty thin disguise," I observed. "Our realtor didn't mention any of that. She thought it sat empty for so long because of the combination of it being practically derelict and having an association with crime."

Capone inclined his head. "Sometimes an association with crime is the attraction."

"I guess you'd know, being Scarface Junior and all," Biz said.

I cringed, but Capone didn't seem flustered. I guessed he must have come to terms with his relation to his famous great-grandfather long ago.

"That's my point," he said. "The criminal association of this building might've scared people off for a year or two, but eventually people forget the harm. Chicago has gangster bus tours. There's a mob museum in Vegas. People talk about Al Capone like he's just another famous person from the old days, like Babe Ruth. Hardly anyone thinks about the brutality. How he ordered hits on dozens of people. Probably killed more than a couple himself, too, although he was never convicted of that."

We were all quiet for a moment, drinking our beers. I toyed with replying with something consoling, but what? There's a reason they don't make Hallmark cards that say *Sorry your grandpa was one of history's most notorious murderers.*

Capone cleared his throat. "Anyway, the Feds were the ones who prosecuted Rocco Guanciale, a RICO indictment, way too big a case for the Geneva Bay force to take on. They were very motivated to get a handle on all his assets. Everything they could prove he owned, according to the statute, the government could seize." Capone drained the last of his beer and set down the empty bottle.

"I've seen that in movies," I said. "Mob wives with a duffle bag full of cash hidden in the back of a closet to evade the Feds?"

"Exactly. That statute is designed to keep criminals from profiting off their illegal activities. The Feds managed to get Rocco's house in Geneva Bay, his place in Florida, cars, and every penny in his bank accounts. But they couldn't get their hands on the Rock Co. Enterprises holdings. Three commercial buildings in Geneva Bay. It seemed obvious that Rocco was the money man behind those purchases, but it wasn't provable. His accountant had placed the buildings into a complicated charitable trust to shield them from being confiscated. But it also meant they couldn't be sold easily. Must've driven the Feds crazy. The accountant ended up getting locked up on a state tax evasion charge."

"Just like Scarface," Biz observed. "If the fuzz can't get you, the IRS will."

"They threw the book at him," Capone said. "Probably trying to get him to flip, but he never did. He got six years at Oakhill, which is a lot on a relatively minor charge." Capone paged though a binder of documents. "I've been slowly gathering the pieces—real estate titles, financial filings, tax records—but I couldn't put it all together. I needed a specialist." He winked at Biz.

Biz leaned back in her seat. "I asked him what he was working on these days, just to be polite. He mentioned it was a financial case, and I offered to take a gander."

"She put it together in less than an hour. Our forensic accountant has been looking at it for a month."

"Don't try to butter me up," Biz replied. "Your accountant did all the hard work. I just came along and opened the jar lid he'd already jiggled loose. A fresh set of eyes. Nothing more."

"She can do tax stuff in her sleep," I said. "She's a whiz with numbers."

I turned to Biz, but my smile was met with a scowl.

"I knew you taught accounting, but how do you know so much about real estate laws and property taxes?" Capone asked her.

"I'm self-taught," Biz replied, her voice flat and bitter. She crossed her arms over her thin chest and sank deeper into the couch. Geez, what had either of us said to deserve that dark look?

Capone, still paging through the documents, didn't notice Biz casting the evil eye. "Apparently, investors made offers on this building over the years, but were always put off by the complexity of the finances," he explained. "I talked to a realtor who tried to put in an offer on behalf of a client a couple years ago. She said she struggled to even find out who to contact to put in the bid, and her client eventually got frustrated and bought a different property."

"So how was Sam able to buy it so easily?" I asked.

"The accountant died of cancer in prison two years ago, with no heirs. The estate was unwound in probate, including the charitable trust. The court-appointed executor sold the assets off over the past year or so."

"I don't have to worry about this building getting seized, do I?"

Capone shook his head. "No, they missed their chance to prove the connection to Rocco. The criminal proceeds were well and truly laundered."

"You said there were three buildings?" I prompted.

"The first one that sold is an old warehouse that's now being renovated as a craft brewery. Part of a national chain," he said. "As for the other two, there's this one, and then the building on Main that houses Juice Revolution. All the legal murkiness was cleared up just around the time Sam bought this place and Jordan bought the building where Juice Revolution is," he said.

"That's quite the coincidence," I said. "That Sam has dated the owners of two out of the three buildings that were held in that trust."

"It would be," Capone said quietly, his eyes on the papers laid out in front of him. "If I believed in coincidences."

CHAPTER 9

If Capone had a theory about the nature of the "coincidence" that tied together the holdings of Rock Co. Enterprises, he chose not to elaborate. After dropping that bomb, he skedaddled pretty quickly, gathering his papers and heading out to take Auntie Biz home. Was he implying that Sam was somehow connected to Rocco Guanciale's criminal enterprise? Or just that there had to be *some* connection within that complicated mess? Whatever the truth was, I suspected Capone, who normally played his cards close to the vest, had already said more than he'd meant to. I went to bed shortly after he and Biz left, but ended up tossing and turning for hours before finally succumbing to my exhaustion.

My dreams were punctuated with strange images—Wong's writhing body, Capone's hand on my arm, Sam's earnest face gazing at Jordan, the note written in blood-red ink, an empty plate where a bratwurst should have been. When I awakened to the buzz of my cell phone, it seemed like only moments had passed. With the blackout curtain shut, my bedroom was cave dark. A thin sliver of light from the upside-down screen revealed the source of the noise.

"Sam?" I croaked, having seen his name flash up. I

held the phone away from my face for a moment to check the time. 6:10 a.m. "What's going on?

"I'm at the hospital," Sam said.

I sat up and flung my legs over the side of the bed. "Did something happen to Butterball?" It wouldn't have been the first time one of Butterball's brawls had landed him in the pet ER.

"No, he's fine. I'm at Mercy Memorial," he said.

Recognizing the name of the nearby human hospital, I struggled to process what was happening. My head seemed to be filled with sticky cotton candy fluff. "Oh my god, are you okay?"

"I'm fine. But Jordan . . ." His voice broke. "I had to call an ambulance. She collapsed."

"That's awful. Do you know what's wrong with her? Is she going to be okay?"

"She's conscious now, but they don't know what caused her episode. She got up early to go for a run, like she always does. I heard a commotion in the kitchen and I ran down. She was on the floor, unconscious. She thinks she had some kind of dizzy spell, but can't really remember. I guess she grabbed at the pot rack to steady herself and pulled on it when she fell . . . I can't believe this is happening."

"Do you need anything? I can be there in fifteen minutes," I said. My brain had gradually cleared, but now it was my heart's turn to feel like it was mired in sticky gunk. My instinct was to rush to Sam's side, pull him close, and shield him from the pain he was in. But I was his ex, and he was distraught about his new girlfriend's health. Where was the playbook for this situation?

"No, no," he said. "There's nothing you can do here. I wondered if you could pick up Butterball, though. They're running tests on Jordan—bloodwork and checking her heart—and they said something about keeping her for observation. I don't want to leave him alone if we end up here for a long time. Julio is supposed to come over around seven. He can let you in."

"Oh, okay. Why is Julio coming?" I asked.

We'd hired Julio Jiménez, a top-notch local contractor, to oversee a complete overhaul of Sam's Queen Anne–style lakefront mansion, a house that had been purchased when Sam and I were still together. I'd made nearly all of the design decisions, from tile patterns to paint colors. The pain of losing that house—the exact kind of house I'd dreamed of owning since I was a kid—ran a close second to the pain of ending my engagement to Sam.

"He's doing an estimate for us," Sam explained. "We're renovating the kitchen."

We're renovating the kitchen? The kitchen that I had meticulously designed back when I was supposed to be the one occupying that house alongside Sam? The same kitchen that had been completed mere months earlier at considerable expense, creating a veritable chef's paradise of premium appliances and high-end finishes? Had Jordan already moved in and started gutting my dream house?

I opened my mouth, but managed to bite my tongue before any of those thoughts could be verbalized. A second ago, I'd been brimming with sympathy and ready to rush to Sam's side. Now, I had to tamp down the cruel hope that Jordan had perhaps knocked out a front tooth in her fall. This conversation felt like the emotional equivalent of riding a mechanical bull.

I took a deep breath, trying to summon my better angels. Auntie Biz was right, some people have more money than sense. Sam's spending habits were none of my business, and despite the less-than-charitable opinions I harbored about the speed of Sam and Jordan's relationship, the reality was that I still cared about Sam. If Jordan made him happy, by extension, I had to care about her well-being. At least I had to try to care.

"Of course," I said. "I'll hop in the shower and head over to your place. Please let me know if there's anything else I can do."

I hung up the phone and pulled back the curtain. Instead of a window, my bedroom had a sliding glass door that opened onto the small balcony. I stepped outside, instantly enveloped by a blanket of humidity. The thin, gray dawn light struggled to break through a heavy cloud of lake fog. I sighed. It was going to be another oppressive day.

I'd made the short walk into town to collect my Jeep, and just after seven a.m. I punched in the combination to the gate that shielded Sam's house from the road. The sun barely topped the tree line, but its roasting rays had already burned off the morning's fog. As I rounded the curving driveway and passed a small stand of trees, the house's asymmetrical façade, with its cupcake-like turret and ornately carved porch railings, rose into view. I'd chosen the exterior's authentic period color scheme— mossy green, accented by khaki and ivory details—after extensive research into the house's history. How long would that last, I wondered, now that the place was under new management?

Julio stood at his pickup, pulling his laptop case from the passenger's side door. He hailed me with a wave of his stubby fingers as I got out of my car.

"Ms. O'Leary, it's been too long. What brings ya' by?" he called in his Jalisco-meets-Sheboygan accent.

"Picking up Butterball. Sam's at the hospital with Jordan," I explained.

He raised his fingers to his stubbly chin, concern creasing his already abundantly wrinkled forehead. "She sick or something?"

"I guess so. She had some kind of fainting spell, Sam said. Hopefully nothing too serious." It occurred to me for the first time that, although Jordan didn't witness yesterday's happenings firsthand, the shock might have contributed to whatever had happened. I was made of stern stuff, but it had rattled even me.

Julio hefted the strap of his laptop bag onto his shoulder and we began to walk toward the house. "I only met her a couple, two, three times," he said. "Seemed fit as a fiddle, though, real sporty." He patted his paunchy midsection. "Exercise'll kill 'ya. That's why I don't do that stuff."

Julio unlocked the front door and we stepped into the wide entrance hall. To our right, a curved staircase swept up to the second floor. Through the opening ahead of us, we had a view of the formal living area and beyond to the bank of windows that overlooked the lake. We headed through the open archway on the left, past the twelve-seat marble-topped dining table.

"So what exactly are they renovating?" I asked.

"Pretty much everything." He gave me a sympathetic look, knowing how I'd poured my culinary soul into that kitchen. "Ms. Watts wants recycled glass countertops. She says granite isn't a sustainable material. She asked for cabinets with a low VOC finish because traditional finishes give off chemicals into the air. All the appliances changed out for the most energy-efficient ones on the market."

"So, in order to be eco-friendlier, she's destroying my brand-new, perfectly functional kitchen?" No way could I conceal the bitterness in my voice. My emotional pendulum was swinging between righteous anger and downright fury.

"You know how people are," came Julio's diplomatic response. "So where's the cat, anyway? Usually he's so friendly."

As if on cue, Butterball came padding toward us from the kitchen, the slightly striped pattern of his lemon-colored fur giving the appearance of undulating prairie grass. I crouched down to greet him, but he swerved past me, instead making a beeline toward Julio.

"Hey, man," Julio called. He deposited his laptop bag on the floor and assumed a bent-kneed squat, planting his hands on the thighs of his jeans. Julio stood five-foot-five in thick-soled boots, so he didn't have to reach too far down to scratch Butterball under the chin.

Butterball cast a sidelong glance at me as he received Julio's affections, as if to flaunt the fact that he was spurning me. I didn't know how much longer I could take this. Butterball had always been my rock, the go-to sponge who soaked up all my troubles at the end of a hard shift. I'd been his favorite human. Lately, though, he barely gave me the time of day. I watched as he continued to put on a show of exaggerated purring under Julio's hands, finally deigning to greet me after several minutes. I scooped him into my arms as we walked into the kitchen, pressing my face against his head.

I flashed back to Capone's story about his cat, Brujo. Had Sam and I been so focused on what Butterball meant to us that we'd failed to give him the stable environment he needed? This cat demanded routine and consistency with such insistence he could've gotten a side gig as a military drill sergeant. But we'd thrown his schedule out of kilter and destroyed his sense of place. A hard lump

formed in my throat as I tried to imagine letting him live
with Sam permanently.

The hard lump doubled in size as we entered the
kitchen. My dream kitchen. Sam and I had split just
before it was completed. I'd never even gotten to make a
meal with all the beautiful appliances I'd chosen, and now
they were being trashed.

The kitchen was much as it had been last time I'd seen
it, except that the large rack of copper pots suspended over
the center island was partly empty. Several of the gleaming French Mauviel pots and pans I'd selected for their superior searing and sautéing quality lay scattered across
the floor.

Julio eyed the pot rack. "Ms. Watts bumped into this
when she fell?"

"Mm-hmm. That's what Sam thought, anyway. The
sound of the pans hitting the floor is what woke him up."

"Must've been quite the fall for her to knock these
down. I installed this rack myself." Julio reached up and
gave one of the heavy saucepans a tug. Neither the rack
nor the other suspended pans budged.

"Definitely not one of those Scarlett O'Hara–style
graceful swoons," I agreed.

As I set Butterball down and leaned over to pick up
the fallen cookware, a huge, almost life-sized framed portrait of Jordan and Sam that leaned against the banquette
caught my eye. I walked toward it to get a closer look.
Sam looked as handsome as ever, his long brown hair half
swept into a casual man bun. His lithe arms were wrapped
around Jordan's petite, tightly muscled physique, her baby
doll eyes sparkling. They smiled toward the camera, looking like a billboard selling boxed happiness.

Sam, it appeared, didn't have any qualms about moving on from our relationship.

Julio nudged his head toward the portrait. "Ms. Watts wants me to incorporate that into the redesign, build it into a recess with soft lighting. I'll have to take out some of the windows to make the wall space for it."

"But what about all the natural light? And the lake views?" I protested. I'd meticulously placed every window to maximize both.

He sighed and ran his hand along the silver-specked stone of the countertop. "For the record, you designed a real nice kitchen. You should be proud."

I nodded, not trusting myself to speak without my voice shaking.

Looking around, Julio continued, "It's gonna be a bear to put together the right team for this project. I might have to bump back the demo 'cuz I still don't have my frame-out guys lined up. Ms. Watts and Mr. Van Meter want it done, like, yesterday, but some of my best subs are booked up into the new year almost. Plus, I had to fire my drywall subcontractor, and he was replacing the drywall guy I canned only last month."

Grateful for the change of topic, I replied, "What happened with your drywall guy? I remember him. Skinny guy with the belt buckle collection. He worked on this place and the restaurant, too, right?"

"He seemed like a nice guy, but I come to find out he was cutting corners, trying to get away with using cheaper materials than I specked, charging me full price, and then pocketing the difference. No way do I give a guy like that a second chance."

"Tell me about it," I said. "I've only been open for three months and I'm on my fifth server. My dishwasher is a parolee and he's more trustworthy than all of them put together."

Julio laughed, a joyful, if slightly phlegmy, sound

that echoed through the empty kitchen. "Look at us. Working-class girl from the South Side of Chicago and a farmer's son from Jalisco, standing around like we're some kind of dukes and duchesses, complaining how you can't get good help these days."

A thump sounded from the other part of the kitchen, followed by a sloshing sound. Butterball had climbed onto the kitchen table and knocked over a Juice Revolution take-out cup that had apparently been resting there. Green goop oozed from the cup, covering the table and dripping on to the floor. He pawed the liquid and leaned down to sniff it. Prior to his diet, he wouldn't have touched green juice with a barge pole, but desperation had apparently expanded his palate.

"No," I scolded, rushing over to grab him before he could cover himself in the mess. The green fluid dripped off the edge of the table, splattering the floor. A memory of Ronnie Wong's demise delivered an uppercut wallop to my brain.

I stood stock-still for a moment, watching Julio pick up the paper towel roll and wet a sponge in the sink. As he moved toward me to mop up the spill, a creeping chill rose up my spine. I put my hand on his arm.

"What?" he asked.

I looked from Julio to the splattered smoothie to the pot rack to the portrait of Jordan and Sam. She was at least a few inches shorter than Julio, and he'd stretched to reach the pots on the rack. I'd specified that they be hung at a comfortable level for my five-foot-nine frame. If Jordan knocked several of them off that sturdy rack, she wouldn't have been simply fainting, she would have been flailing. Thrashing wildly, just like Ronnie Wong did in the moments before he died.

CHAPTER 10

You were right.

At around three o'clock my favorite sentence in the English language—"You were right"—pinged my cell phone screen in a text from Capone. Usually seeing those three little words would've set my heart aflutter. Capone's text, however, sent a jolt of dread up my spine. I'd been checking my phone nonstop all day, hoping for news.

After I'd made the mental connection that Jordan's smoothie might have been tainted with whatever killed Ronnie Wong, I rushed out of Sam's house with only a minimal, frantic explanation to Julio, clutching the scraped-up remnants of Jordan's smoothie in a cup and lugging Butterball's crate with my other hand. I raced toward the hospital, calling Capone along the way.

He'd met me, grim-faced, in Mercy Memorial's parking lot. When I started to hustle the remains of the smoothie inside, he stopped me. "The in-house lab is only equipped to test for basic substances, like street drugs," he explained. "I doubt they're going to find it's been laced with heroin or cocaine. The symptoms don't sound like any overdose I've ever seen. Complex toxin cases go to the state lab in Madison for more careful testing. I'll drive the sample there."

"I can take it if it'll save time," I offered.

He shook his head. "I'll go. If you're right about this, the contents of that cup may be evidence. Might as well preserve the chain of custody from here on out."

I supposed the lab folks were more likely to take the request seriously coming from Capone than from some random chef who marched in with a half-drunk smoothie. "What about Jordan, though?" I asked. "I tried to call Sam, but he hasn't picked up. Don't the doctors need to know she was poisoned?"

"I've already been inside to let them know she might've ingested something toxic," he explained. "They were one step ahead. Some abnormalities came up in her bloodwork that couldn't be explained by an ordinary fainting episode or even a mild heart attack, and her other symptoms made them suspicious that there might be something else going on. They gave her activated charcoal to empty her stomach." A grimace of disgust passed over his usually impassive face. "I've seen that used on suspects who've OD'd, and I can tell you it isn't pretty. Anyway, they've got her stable."

After Capone left me standing in the parking lot, I went back to the restaurant. I got Butterball fed and settled into my apartment, and then I started the day's prep. What else could I do?

Lunch service passed in a nervous blur, with no word from Capone or Sam. Now, finally, it looked like there was an update. Capone's *You were right* text was followed a moment later by a second message asking me to call him.

I turned to Sonya, who was kneading a fresh portion of pizza dough. In my distracted state, I'd ruined the earlier batch by channeling my agitation into my fists and overworking the mixture. Sonya had banished me from dough duty after that, and I set myself more emotionally appropriate tasks like hacking apart the butternut squash for our goat cheese and crispy sage pie.

"Son, can you cover things here? I need to make a call," I said, holding up my phone. At that time of the afternoon, lunch service had died down, and the dining room was mostly empty while the kitchen began to gear up for dinner.

"Sam called?" she asked.

"No, it's Capone. He seems to have news."

I walked out the back door and headed upstairs to my apartment. Thankfully, Butterball greeted me at the door like he used to, gently figure-eighting around my legs until I picked him up. He must've sensed that I'd had enough drama for one day, or maybe he, too, needed a little TLC. Either way, I was grateful.

When Capone picked up, I blurted, "Was it poison?"

"We won't know for a few days, or more likely, weeks," he replied.

"What? I thought that's why you were calling."

"Afraid not," he said. "Toxicity testing is slow as molasses. It can take months sometimes."

I settled onto the sofa with Butterball. "So what was I right about?"

"You were right that there was something seriously wrong with that note from Juice Revolution. Got two matches within an hour of running the prints through the database."

"Whose fingerprints were they?" I asked.

"The first match was for Molly McClintock."

"That makes sense. She was working the register, so if someone handed over the note with their payment or left it on the counter, she probably would've touched it."

"Why didn't she say anything about it?" Capone won-

dered aloud. "Threatening notes can't be an everyday oc-
currence at Juice Revolution."

"Just because she touched it doesn't mean she read it.
It was folded." I paused. "Why did the police have her
prints on file?"

"A shoplifting arrest when she was eighteen."

I frowned. I'd done some questionable stuff when I
was younger, but by eighteen I was already going to culinary school, holding down a full-time job, and renting
my own apartment. Eighteen was definitely pushing the
envelope of a "youthful" mistake. "What about the other
set of prints?"

"That's where the real intrigue comes in. They belong to a guy named Johnny 'Cinco' Frates. Just released
from Oakhill a few months ago."

I recognized the name of the correctional facility
where Rabbit had served his sentence.

Capone's already deep voice lowered to a bass rumble.
"Cinco's serious trouble. He killed five people."

I sat up suddenly, causing Butterball to emit a hiss of
protest. He sprang to the floor and took hold of his favorite
yellow banana toy, dragging it toward the kitchen area.
I sat still, watching as my cat bear-hugged and nuzzled
his toy before suddenly delivering a frenzy of wild kicks
to it. Seemed like a pretty apt metaphor for the last few
days. I'd been lulled into thinking my biggest problem
was concocting the perfect bratwurst pizza recipe. Then
came Graham Ulrich's appearance, Wong's death, Jordan's illness, whatever weirdness was going on with
Auntie Biz, and now the revelation that the note I'd found
bore a murderer's fingerprints. Life was definitely coming at me with guns blazing.

Turning my attention back to Capone, I repeated, "Five
people?"

"*Cinco* Frates," he emphasized. "Truth in advertising."

"Why was he released if he killed five people?

"One of the five was his codefendant, the main witness against him in the other murders. They were hit men, taking out other criminals. You don't get a lot of witnesses coming forward eager to testify against someone like that. We were able to put him away for a couple years on a weapons charge, but not the killings."

"Geez," I breathed. I rubbed the goose bumps on my arms. "As if the note itself wasn't disturbing enough." I walked to the wall and turned up the thermostat. Following Capone's revelation, the air-conditioning seemed way too cold. "How did a note from a guy like Cinco Frates end up in a hipster smoothie place in Geneva Bay, and who was it meant for? Did he drop it off himself, or have someone deliver it?" I mused.

"All good questions," Capone said.

"Any connection between Frates and Wong?" I asked.

"None whatsoever. From what I've found so far, Ronald Wong's background is so clean it practically squeaks. Rotary Club, church deacon, he and his wife have had a summer place in Geneva Bay for decades." He paused. "If it does turn out that a toxic substance was involved, I have to consider the possibility that Wong wasn't the intended victim. Poison is a notoriously messy method of killing someone. Hard to get ahold of, hard to administer, hard to ensure it hits its mark. Popular in the kinds of murder mysteries my mom reads, but not so much in the real world. Guns are a lot simpler."

He was quiet for a moment, seeming to weigh his words.

"What aren't you telling me?" I asked.

"Do you remember if Jordan took a smoothie with her when she left Juice Revolution yesterday?" he asked.

I cast my mind back. "Yes, I'm almost sure she did. She

had the same blah-blah whatever magic potion she made for Harold Heyer. High Wattage something or other. I remember talking to Mac about it."

"And it was made at the same time as Wong's?" he asked.

"Yes."

"So both poisoned smoothies were made at the same time," he said.

"I guess she could've gotten another one later, though. Jarka said Jordan went back to Juice Revolution yesterday evening after she and Sam got back from the lake. Or maybe she had the ingredients at Sam's house and made one for herself," I said. "She obviously knew the recipe."

"You're suggesting Jordan made the smoothie at home in a Juice Revolution to-go cup?"

"I'm just making sure we're covering all the bases. Like, could she have gone over to her shop early this morning and made one there?"

"No. I went back to the hospital after I got back from Madison and was able to talk to Sam," Capone said.

"What *didn't* you do today?" I asked.

"Time is an important factor in investigations. That whole 'first forty-eight hours' business is surprisingly accurate. You often find out more in the first two days than you do in the whole next two months combined," he explained. He was taking me much further into his confidence than he had before, but he clearly wanted to make sure I knew which one of us was the pro and which one was the amateur.

"Anyway," he continued, "Sam was sure Jordan didn't make any drinks when they got back to the shop yesterday. They were all too shocked. He believes that the smoothie Jordan drank this morning was the one she'd brought home yesterday. She'd put it into the fridge before they went on the boat because they were in a hurry to leave. He was able to call his general contractor while I was with him and have him check the fridge. The smoothie from yesterday wasn't there, and there was no empty cup in the trash."

"It sounds like you're implying Jordan Watts may have been the real target," I said. I began pacing the floor, pressing the phone hard to my ear. Butterball, meanwhile, lolled around on the rug, stoned on the catnip that filled his banana toy.

"Impossible to say. Like I said, poison is messy. Just about everyone in that shop had some kind of drink, all made on the same equipment within a few minutes of when Mr. Wong's and Jordan's smoothies were made. Everyone except Sam, as far as I can tell."

"You can't seriously suspect Sam," I scoffed. "Butterball was there, too, and honestly, based on his behavior lately, he's a more credible suspect than Sam." As if to illustrate my point, Butterball emerged from his stupor long enough to deliver a couple more roundhouse kicks to the stuffed banana.

"Hmm . . . Should I turn my attention to Sam's spurned ex-fiancée, who happened to be there when all of this went down?" Capone said. Despite the seriousness of the subject matter, I thought—or maybe hoped—I detected a hint of teasing in his voice. Like Sonya, he seemed to have a good instinct for when my nerves needed to be soothed with a little levity.

"Yes, and I cunningly phoned the cops and handed over all the incriminating evidence," I replied, matching his sarcasm. "And then went out of my way to gather even more incriminating evidence."

"You have to admit that you have a motive," Capone countered.

"And that is?"

"To get your man back," he said.

"*I* dumped *him*," I emphasized, starting to feel my old wariness toward cops creeping in. Maybe Capone had brought me into his confidence to lull me into a false sense of security.

"And that evidence you turned over," he continued. "The Zodiac Killer sent clues to his identity and his crimes in the form of elaborate cryptograms." Okay, now he was definitely messing with me.

"Well, lucky for the innocent civilians of Geneva Bay, I can't even manage a sudoku," I replied.

"In all seriousness, Delilah, I'm keeping an open mind. I can't prove this is a poisoning homicide yet. Even if there was a poisoning, it could be accidental. Maybe one of the ingredients was tainted inadvertently." He paused. "That said, I spent my morning driving a sample of green smoothie to Madison, which should tell you something."

"No more smoothies," I said.

"You got it. Juice Revolution is closed until further notice. I'm pulling up in front of it now. I've got the CSIs gathering samples."

I repeated his theories. "Could be a coincidence. Could be accidental contamination. But then there's Cinco Frates and his note," I said, bringing us back to the original reason for his call.

"But then there's that," he echoed.

"Can't you arrest him?" I asked. "'It's time to pay for what you did' seems like a pretty clear threat."

"He's still on parole, so I'd only need a thin pretext to bring him in for questioning. But I want to keep my powder dry. This guy already beat five murder charges. If I tip him off now, he could get ahead of me. Besides, his fingerprints weren't the only ones on the note, and without context, I can't be sure it *was* a threat."

"What does Frates look like?" I asked. "You know how we were wondering how the note got there? There's a detail about yesterday that I haven't been able to get out of my head. When it became clear that something was seriously wrong with Ronnie Wong, everyone who was in the shop went into deer-in-headlights mode. Well, everyone except the wife, who was freaking out; Jarka, who's trained to deal with medical emergencies; and this one customer. He walked out. Not like panicked running. He just . . . walked."

"I'm texting you a picture," Capone said.

A beat later, the image hit my phone screen. Frates glowered from his mug shot photo, looking like someone who ate needles for fun. He sported a white-blond Hulk Hogan goatee and a neck like a linebacker. "Oh my god," I whispered. "That's him."

"You're sure?"

"One hundred percent sure."

More than that, I was now one hundred percent sure that what I'd witnessed the previous afternoon had been a murder, and that I'd been within a few steps of a murderer. Capone and I both fell silent. Despite his "open mind," I doubted that Capone truly believed that Frates's presence and the note could be unrelated to Wong's death. I shivered again, thinking how close I may have come to having more than just my screaming bile eliminated at Juice Revolution.

CHAPTER 11

Eleven p.m. found me, Sonya, Rabbit, Melody, Jarka, and Butterball on the restaurant's empty patio, listening to the gentle slap of the waves against the shoreline. A stiff breeze from the west and the accumulating clouds in the night sky signaled an impending shift in the weather. Probably even more patio-closing rain. Even that late at night, the weather was still oppressively sultry. If it weren't for the financial implications of more storms, I would have welcomed the change.

Although restaurant types are notorious for after-hours booze fests, Delilah & Son's staff weren't usually a "hang out and party after service" crew. Daniel was an early riser, keeping to a military-fitness regimen that included a daily four-mile run. Melody had tried a beer once in high school, didn't like it, and decided the party girl life wasn't for her. Rabbit, besides having a young daughter, was in recovery for alcoholism and avoided temptation. Jarka, I assumed, worked too hard to have time to relax. Me and Son? We'd been there, done that, bought the T-shirt. Showing up to a brunch service still buzzed from the previous night's exploits had lost its luster sometime around my thirtieth birthday. Still, it had been a rough few days, and when we finished clean-up and next-day prep, none of us were quite ready to call it a night.

Daniel emerged from the restaurant, carrying a tray with seven squat metal Moscow-mule cups on it. He placed one cup in front of each of us and set down the tray. "My newest creation—a passion-fruit mule. I will call her"—he paused and opened his palms in a dramatic gesture—"Nectar of the Tropics." He nodded to Melody and Rabbit. "Yours are non-alcoholic, but still"—he kissed his fingertips—"a masterpiece."

Butterball was resting on my lap, and I shifted him aside to raise my cup. Daniel had lined the rim with toasted coconut, pulverized to the texture of demerara sugar. That bittersweet, slightly charred taste hit my tongue first, followed by a flood of flavors from the cocktail. I wasn't a fruity drinks kind of gal, preferring the straightforward pungent alcohol punch of a bourbon Old Fashioned. For this cocktail, however, I could make an exception. It was some sort of intergalactic raft that transported the drinker to a Caribbean island. The sharp, citrusy passion fruit melded with the sweet spice of ginger beer and a mellow base note of pineapple vodka.

"Wow," Melody breathed.

Rabbit let out a long whistle. "Beats the hell out of a Shirley Temple, I'll say that."

Jarka rose from the table and said, "I will go now to get *banitsa* from the oven. Should be finish cooking." We were hungry after a long day, and she'd offered to whip up a batch of the traditional Bulgarian savory pastry for us to try.

"Will it go with a Caribbean drink?" Rabbit asked dubiously.

"*Banitsa* is for any time, with any drink," Jarka replied, her face full of reproach.

Once she was safely out of earshot, Rabbit whispered, "She scares the bejesus outta me."

Strong words, considering that assessment came from someone who'd showered next to lifers every day for years. I was longing to ask Rabbit if he knew Cinco Frates, but I didn't want to kill the laidback vibe.

Sonya pointed toward the drink tray. "Who's that one for, or were you counting on me going in for seconds?"

"For you, *hermana*, the bar is always open," Daniel said with a smile. "But this one is for Mac." He nodded toward the extra cup. "She texted to say she was out in town with some friends and wanted to know if we were still here."

Melody's wide-eyed look revealed that she hadn't been aware of these plans. "You and Mac text each other?"

I dove in, curious to know more. "I didn't realize you and Mac were friends." While there was no law to prevent two attractive twentysomethings from flirting, I couldn't help but worry about poor Melody's heartbreak if Daniel fell for her cousin.

"We have common interests," Daniel said, with a casual shrug. "We both make drinks to help people feel better." He winked and took a sip of his mule. "Although mine work much faster."

Before any of us could get further details, two headlight beams sliced through the relative darkness of the parking lot.

Mac pulled into the spot closest to the patio entrance. With a burst of vivacious energy, she hopped out of a gleaming white Ford Mustang convertible that still sported dealer plates. It wasn't an over-the-top glitzy car, but definitely brand new and flashier than I'd expected her to drive. She and Melody had grown up on their family's dairy and soybean farm, and I always had the impression that money was extremely tight. Melody drove a ten-year-old Honda and had to use her hostessing money to pay her way through school, a few credit hours at a time. She'd been desperately grateful for the bargain rent she was getting by living with Biz. I couldn't imagine Juice Revolution paid that much better than Delilah & Son.

"Hey, cuz," Mac called, stopping to kiss the top of Melody's head. "You're looking *très* adorbs tonight." Pivoting to Daniel she added, "Dan the Man!" She bounced into a seat next to him, lifted her drink from the tray, and took a long pull. "Yum. Nothing makes me swoon like a well-mixed beverage." She laid her hand against her forehead in a mock fainting pose, before popping up and extending the same hand to Rabbit, flashing her irresistible smile. "Molly McClintock, but everyone calls me Mac."

"Robert Blakemore, but everybody calls me Rabbit," he replied.

"Melody told me your daughter is, like, the cutest thing ever," Mac said. "I need to see a picture *stat*." She slapped her palms on the table. "Come on. Don't keep me hanging."

As Mac oohed and aahed over the pics on Rabbit's phone, I couldn't help but notice how he, usually wary around new people, warmed to her.

Mac next pivoted her attention to Sonya, introducing herself with a smile.

"Sonya Perlman-Dokter," Sonya replied, giving Mac a once-over. I hadn't shared my suspicions about a potential flirtation between Mac and Daniel, but the guardedness in Sonya's tone indicated that she caught a whiff of the looming potential for emotional disaster. If only her radar were so adept at spotting her own romantic dangers.

Undeterred, Mac amped up the charm offensive. "I am loving your makeup. Like, *loving* it. Rockabilly, but with an avant-garde edge."

Butterball, who had been alternating between napping in my lap and trawling the patio for food scraps and interesting bugs, sprang onto the table. "Butterbud, did you think I forgot to say hello to you? Never!" Mac said. She squatted down to his eye level and drummed her fingers playfully on the tabletop. The cat approached and rubbed his face against her hand.

By then, Jarka had rejoined us. She unmolded the *banista* onto a round platter. The golden brown phyllo had been shaped into a coil, and it emerged from the pan looking like a cross between a gigantic shortbread swirl cookie and a magical snail's shell. Jarka cut it into slices, explaining as she served, "Is traditional Bulgarian phyllo and feta pie. Each layer is painted with butter, and then filled with egg and yogurt custard."

"Like spanakopita?" Daniel ventured.

"No, is not like. I never make *banitsa* with spinach to get stuck," Jarka said, pointing as she bared two parallel rows of small, ivory-colored teeth.

My fork cracked through the crisp top layer of the *banitsa* before sinking into the pillowy egg and cheese interior. The delicate, papery crunch of the pastry held a surprising amount of the creamy filling.

"This is damn good," Mac said, polishing off the last of her portion.

Melody pointed with her thumb over her shoulder. "Whose car are you driving?"

"Mine!" Mac squealed and jumped up, startling Butterball into Melody's lap. "I just bought it tonight. I've been showing it off all over town. I wanted to surprise you. Isn't it awesome?"

Melody frowned, cradling the frightened cat, "How did you afford it?"

Mac took another sip of her drink. "Last year's model. Got a great deal and they gave me a good amount for trading in my old Buick."

Melody continued to frown, but didn't press the point.

The next half hour was essentially a Molly McClintock one-woman show. Mac caught us up on the latest from Juice Revolution—the temporary closure, the police search. Nothing I didn't already know, thanks to Capone. She also said she'd had a text from Sam, reporting that Jordan managed to eat a little Jell-O that evening but still felt rotten. Mac told every anecdote with a zinger of a punchline and shared every tidbit of information as if she were making us privy to the world's juiciest gossip. She focused attention on each person in turn, complimenting, flattering, and generally making us feel grateful to bask in the reflected glow of her personality. By the end of it all, I almost found myself too caught up in her spell to worry about the way she subtly rested her hand on Daniel's arm or the barely concealed distress on Melody's face.

At last, Mac leaned back in her chair, and looked plaintively at her cousin. "Mel, hon, do you think you could give me a ride home? That Tropical Whatsit packed a punch. I don't want to risk damaging my new car."

"But it's thirty miles each way by the time I go to the farm and back," Melody replied.

Mac stuck out her lower lip and flapped her eyelashes. "You can spend the night. It'll be like when we were kids. Plus, I'll let you drive my new car."

Melody flashed a wan smile and nodded. "Sure, okay. Can we stop by Biz's house, first, though? I want to check on her."

"Won't Biz be sleeping by now? My *abuelita* is in bed by nine," Daniel said, looking at his watch.

Melody, Sonya, and I all laughed in unison. A bout of medication-induced ill health the previous year had caused Biz to be constantly drowsy, often taking hours-long daytime naps and sleeping for twelve hours or more every night. Until we discovered the drugs that were at the root of her problems, I'd feared that she was slipping into dementia, or perhaps even slipping away all together. Now that Biz was recovered, though, her natural night-owl tendencies had returned in earnest. Never a great sleeper myself, when I was young and would come to stay with her, the two of us often cooked up huge feasts into the wee hours, sometimes not eating dinner until after midnight.

"I can walk over and check on Biz," I offered. "I'm not ready for bed yet and the walk would do me good." Although I felt that Mac was taking advantage of her cousin's people-pleasing nature, I also didn't want her getting in the car if she felt even the slightest bit tipsy.

"I'll come, too. Keep you company," Son said.

Jarka glanced at the sky. "Bring umbrella. It will rain tonight."

"With my luck, it'll rain all week. I'll go put this beast away and grab a couple umbrellas," I said, lifting Butterball from Melody's lap.

In pairs and trios, we took our leave and went our separate ways: Melody and Mac heading off in Mac's new Mustang; Daniel, Jarka, and Rabbit going to their homes; and me and Sonya walking down the shore path toward Biz's lakefront cottage.

"Thanks for coming along," I said to Sonya. "The thought of walking on the path alone tonight was making me a little skittish for some reason."

"Really? Maybe it has something to do with a guy dropping dead right in front of you yesterday." She put her hands in the pockets of her dress. "Not that I'm suggesting the invincible Delilah O'Leary would be affected by anything like that."

I chuffed her on the shoulder. We walked in silence for a few moments.

When I'd first moved to Geneva Bay, I'd taken a walk on the shore path, the twenty-plus-mile pedestrian track that encircled the lake, nearly every night after service. Despite traversing people's yards, the path itself was a public right-of-way, making it a popular way for tourists to get a close-up tour of the lifestyles of the rich lakefront homeowners. Night on the path meant no sightseers gawking at the big mansions, and no playing Dodge 'Em with dogwalkers wielding tangles of leashes. Just me and the gentle whooshing of the waves against the shoreline.

Even though Sonya didn't know the half of what was worrying me, she, as usual, was spot-on about my emotional state. The shocks of the past few days were affecting my nerves. From what Capone told me, it seemed more and more likely that a murderer was on the loose.

"Speaking of skittish," Sonya said, "I think all that talk about Graham Ulrich the other day got in my head. Ever since I found out he was going to be coming, I keep thinking I see him around town. I have this feeling of impending doom."

I bit my tongue.

"I even thought I saw Renee Ulrich coming out of that old warehouse," she continued. "You know the empty one right on the edge of downtown?"

"The brick one by the elementary school?"

She nodded. "Bananas, right? Even if Graham showed up in town way early for the contest, I can't imagine

Renee would've come with him. I heard she filed for divorce right after he found out about the . . . thing with me and her. Last I heard, she was back home in London."

I knew Sonya well enough to sense a warning beacon in her slightly frenzied tone. I shined my phone's flashlight on her face. Her glittery plum-colored lips sparkled. "Is that new lipstick?" I asked.

She thrust her lips into a pout. "Do you like it? It's called Amped Vamp."

"How many lipsticks did you buy today?"

Her gaze fluttered briefly to the ground before meeting my eyes. "Four. They had buy one, get one."

I slowed my stride. "Any hair dye?"

"I thought maybe I'd do some blue streaks." She ran her fingers along the front edge of her bob. "Just, like, a few little pieces here to frame my face."

Makeup shopping sprees. Impulsive personal grooming decisions. The classic signs that all was not well in Sonya Land.

"Have you been looking online at shelter dogs who are up for adoption?"

"No," she replied.

"Any new tattoos?"

"No." Seeing my skeptical look, she repeated. "*No*, okay? I know what you're thinking, but I can rein it in. The Ulrich thing has thrown me off-kilter, but I'll be fine. He'll be here for one day. What's one day? I'll just hide in my house on the day of the contest. I'll shut the blinds and watch *Gilligan's Island* reruns until it's over. Knowing Graham, he'll probably fly in and out on the same day, and turn up late, just to show off how important he is."

I furrowed my brow. "So this person who looked like Renee was definitely going into the brick warehouse near the elementary school?"

She nodded. "Why do you look like that? Oh my god, you don't think it was really her, do you? I don't think I could handle running into her. It's bad enough that Graham will be here."

I hadn't had time to fill Sonya in on what Capone and Auntie Biz discovered about Rocco Guanciale's property holdings. Usually, Sonya was my closest confidante, but now didn't seem like the right time to get into it. The Renee Ulrich thing clearly had her rattled, and I didn't want to add to her distress. She didn't know that Graham Ulrich had come to the restaurant looking for her, and I wanted to keep it that way. Still, I was unnerved by the potential connection between the Ulriches and the warehouse that Rocco's shell company had owned. Homicides seemed to go hand in hand with Rock Co. Enterprises' former holdings. There was already more than enough cloak-and-dagger going on with the Ulrich situation.

"I'm sure it wasn't her," I soothed. "Like you said, why would she be in Geneva Bay? I was just thinking that I heard a brewpub is going in that space. One of those big national chains. Hopefully they won't steal any of our clientele. We can't afford to lose any business."

We filled the rest of our walk with the usual chat about recipe ideas, Son trying to help me troubleshoot the issues with a spinach salad recipe I'd been kicking around. I thought wistfully about how close I'd come to perfecting the bratwurst cheddar pizza for the contest. Now, I wasn't sure I could even add it to the menu for fear that it might remind Sonya of our lost chance and further wrack her with guilt.

We passed a stand of cypress trees, and my aunt's cottage came into view. The tiny structure was built around 1910 as a summer house for the inhabitants of the large

Greek Revival mansion up the slope, a convenient lakeside spot where they could change out of their swimming
suits or eat lunch without having to make the trek back
up to the main house. The house's current owners resented how my aunt's ramshackle and slightly down-at-
heel home squatted directly in the path to their dock, and
thus they had built a formidable wall of landscaping to
protect their view.

Sonya sniffed the air. "Is that smoke?"

Even as she said the words, the smell hit my nostrils.
In the moonlight, I could make out a white wisp curling
from my aunt's chimney. "Why would she have a fire
going?" Despite the breeze that had kicked up, the temperature couldn't have sunk much below 80 degrees,
and the air was still thick with humidity. Not to mention
that it was getting on toward midnight.

We quickened our pace, cutting through the screened
porch. I let us in with my key.

We found Biz crouched in front of the fire in her small
dining room, fire poker in hand.

The lights were on, the table covered with what looked
like financial papers. A used spool of paper spewed out
of a dinosaur-era adding machine, most likely a leftover
from Biz's teaching days. Auntie Biz hurried toward the
table, still clutching the poker. She wore her slippers but
was otherwise fully dressed in gray slacks and a plaid
blouse in a size I'd probably grown out of when I was nine.

"Hey, Biz," Sonya called.

I fingered the spool of adding-machine ribbon, noticing the series of red, negative balance numbers near the
bottom. "Is this another project for Capone?" I asked.

"It's private," she said, snatching the ribbon from my
hand. She frowned as she gathered the papers into a stack
and tucked them into a manila folder, then whisked the

folder and adding machine into a drawer. Even though I'd suggested it, the likelihood that this was an assignment from Capone seemed low. I'd taken his involvement of Biz in the property research as more of a one-time opportunistic thing rather than an ongoing mission. Capone seemed to be growing to trust us, but he was still a by-the-book kind of cop.

"What are you two doing here?" she said, more an accusation than a question.

"Melody had to drive her cousin home," Sonya explained. "We wanted to swing by to see if you needed anything."

"You think I'm helpless or something? Senile?" Biz snapped.

"Of course not." Sonya held up her hands, surprised by Biz's testiness.

In an irrational way, I was glad to see someone besides me end up on the sharp end of Biz's bad temper. Biz and me bickering was nothing new, of course. Our personalities were too similar—no-nonsense, stubborn, quick to fly off the handle. Type A and then some. But Sonya, with her more mild-mannered style and wry wit, had never passed a cross word with Biz as far as I knew. Whatever was going on was bigger than the perpetual O'Leary women conflict.

Biz gave us a hard look, but then gradually lowered her hackles. "You hungry?" She eyed me. "Bet you haven't eaten a real meal all day."

Of course, she was right. Other than the slice of *banitsa*, I'd simply snacked on whatever seemed like easy pickings and stuffed down bits of food on the fly.

"I was just getting ready to fix a tomato sandwich," she continued. "Got some ripe heirlooms from my garden this morning." Food: the traditional O'Leary peace offering.

Sonya tipped her head to one side. "I could eat."

Biz pulled an oblong loaf of bread—homemade sourdough by the look of it—from the bread bin and put it in front of Sonya, along with a serrated knife. She plunked two large wooden cutting boards on the table, along with two baseball-sized red tomatoes. Sonya sliced the bread as I cut into the luscious flesh of the tomatoes, inhaling the sweet, grassy scent of them.

Biz added a thick layer of mayonnaise to the bread slices and layered them with torn basil leaves before sprinkling salt on to the sliced tomatoes. She finished assembling the sandwiches and plated them, then popped open the tops of three bottles of Leinenkugel's Summer Shandy.

I sat in the chair closest to the fireplace and tucked into my sandwich. The dining room fireplace was one of the charming original features I loved about Auntie Biz's house. When the building was constructed, it was comprised of one men's and one women's dressing room—which had been converted into bedrooms—a bathroom, and a large, lake-facing "lounging parlor," which had been subdivided into a living room, dining room, and kitchen. The brick fireplace, built to warm boaters and swimmers who'd braved the often-chilly lake water, was retained during the renovation, even though its grand scale no longer matched the partitioned room's small proportions.

The familiar atmosphere soothed me, and I savored each bite of my sandwich. It embodied everything wonderful about Wisconsin summer produce—voluptuous, robust, and bursting with the explosive flavor imparted by the short growing season. The bright notes of the locally brewed beer meshed perfectly with it. Despite my training in classical French techniques that often relied on layered flavors, marinades, and sauces, I knew that garden-fresh tomato sandwiches needed no adornments other than a pinch of salt, the basil, and a good dollop of mayo.

"These will be the last for the year," Biz said, indicating two baskets laden with squashes, tomatoes, peppers, and eggplants.

"Really?" I asked. "I'd say we've got a month or more before the first frost, given how hot it's been."

"I'm digging up the garden next week," she replied, taking a small, precise bite of her sandwich. "Plowing everything under. I'll put up some cans, and then that'll be that."

"O-kaaay," I said slowly. Sonya and I shared a look. Biz was a fabulous gardener, a living farmer's almanac. If she said the season was over, who were we to argue?

We shared a pleasant hour of eating, drinking, and conversing, no one mentioning the earlier discord. It was only after Auntie Biz had gone to bed, and Sonya and I were on our way back to the restaurant, that I realized I'd seen no fire in the fireplace, just a few fragments of ash. The room, too, had been cool. Yet I was sure I'd seen smoke coming out of the chimney, and Biz had been holding the fireplace poker. What had she been burning?

CHAPTER 12

When Butterball woke me up just after five a.m. with an aggressive campaign of meowing and swiping at my face, I felt like my head had only just hit the pillow. The storm that had been threatening the previous evening finally broke loose at some point in the wee hours, and Butterball spent the duration of the downpour lying across my neck, cowering in terror. Wearing a sixteen-pound cat like a mink stole made for a hot and suffocating night. Although I'd barely slept, as I prepped my cat's breakfast—egg whites, fish oil, powdered vitamins, chicken livers, and bone meal, all formulated according to Sam's spreadsheet—I was glad I was being forced to get an early start.

Seeing Biz's mysterious financial records put my restaurant's ongoing financial predicament back on the front burner. I opened the accounting program on my laptop and stared again at my projected income and expenditures. Despite the chaos of the previous few days, we'd taken in money hand over fist. But even if we somehow had full houses and sky-high bar tabs every night for the rest of the summer season, I couldn't see how we were going to build up enough of a reserve to make it through the winter until next May.

When Sam and I split, he'd offered to let me stay in

the building rent-free until I could afford to pay him. After all, my business plan had been predicated on having the giant cushion of his cash padding me until my start-up costs were recouped.

I slumped down onto the floor next to Butterball, who was finishing up his breakfast, licking his bowl to make sure there were no hidden morsels in the nooks and crannies.

"Why didn't I just take Sam up on his offer?" I asked him.

He sat back on his haunches and tilted his head to one side.

"That's right, my stupid pride insisted that I pay him the exorbitant market rate for lakefront commercial property rentals," I continued. "Did you know I actually demanded that I pay additional rent on this apartment? Jordan is living in my dream house, probably rent-free. And because I had to prove how independent I am, you and I are spending money we don't have on this shoebox."

Butterball's tail swished from side to side like a metronome.

"Of course I wish I could ask for his help! But you know I'm constitutionally incapable of going back to him with my hat in my hand, especially now. Can you imagine him involving Jordan in the discussion—'My ex, you know, the one with the jacked-up chi who dresses like a hobo and is a terrible cat mother? She's asking for a loan because *her* business, unlike yours, is floundering.'" I shook my head. "No way. I'd rather sell a kidney."

Butterball took a few steps forward and nuzzled his face into my leg, feathering my pants with his orangey fur. He rested his head on my thigh, looking up at me with jade green eyes. I petted him in long strokes, starting at his head and running my hand all the way to his tail.

I sighed. "You're right. I had my chance. He's with Jordan now."

I texted Sam, asking for an update on his girlfriend.

He replied immediately, saying she was improving—an excessive number of exclamation points proclaimed his happiness and relief.

I texted back a series of happy emojis.

Wasn't there some saying that if you really loved someone, you wanted them to be happy? And with Sam, I truly did. I glanced at Butterball, then back at the phone. Yeesh, did that mean I really loved Sam? A little late to be contemplating that.

My early start allowed me to get a jump on the day's ordering and prep, so I was able to peel off on a covert mission before Sonya arrived. Ever since she had mentioned potentially seeing Renee Ulrich the previous night, I'd been unsettled. Graham Ulrich had a reputation for being petty and vindictive, so it hadn't surprised me that he might agree to judge the contest solely to get back at Sonya. However, he was also incredibly busy, with a successful restaurant, a TV show, and a bestselling cookbook to promote. It was one thing for him to show up for one afternoon, blindside Sonya, and embarrass us at the contest. But why was he hanging around Geneva Bay almost three weeks early? And why make a point of coming to my restaurant and tipping us off? Surely, he didn't have endless time to spend trying to intimidate his enemies. And now it seemed that Renee Ulrich—supposedly split up from Graham—might be in Geneva Bay, too.

I decided I had to get to the bottom of whatever was going on with the Ulriches, so I set off toward the warehouse building where Sonya said she saw the "imaginary" Renee—the same building that had until recently been owned by Rock Co. Enterprises.

Long before Renee met Graham Ulrich, she'd built an international reputation as an interior designer for restaurants and hotels. In fact, the two of them met when she designed the award-winning space for Graham's first restaurant. I'd crossed paths with both of them over the years and had been on reasonably friendly terms with Renee, who, thankfully, was not cut from the same odious cloth as her husband. I was vaguely aware that during their marriage, she'd given up her own practice, working exclusively on his brand. If they'd split, though, it wasn't at all farfetched to think that a successful national brewpub chain would hire her for a build-out in a tony area like Geneva Bay.

If the Renee sighting was genuine, it seemed like the best place to start.

The parking lot was filled with the usual pickup trucks and white vans that characterized an active building site. One car stood out, though— a Geneva Bay police cruiser. My heartbeat quickened. It had rained heavily overnight and the gravel parking lot was pitted with deep puddles. I picked my way quickly but carefully around them toward the door of the large red brick box of a building. There, I practically collided with Julio, my former contractor, coming out, accompanied by Harold Heyer.

"Miss O'Leary, what brings ya' by?" Julio asked.

"Looking for an old friend," I replied, peering over the two men's heads to try to get a look inside the building. "Are you working on this project?"

"Uh-huh, I gotta finish this one up and then your, I mean Mr. Van Meter's, kitchen is next."

I glanced toward the police car. "What's going on?"

"A break-in overnight. Nothing was stolen, but there was some vandalism," Julio explained.

"Isn't it awful?" Harold said, pressing a notebook to the front of his plaid vest-covered chest. He looked shaken, but still considerably perkier than he had the last time I'd seen him in the aftermath of Wong's death. "Such a shame," he continued. "I'm going to write up a little piece on the opening of the new brewpub for the next edition of *On the Water*, right alongside the spread about the winner of the Taste of Wisconsin contest. Of course the break-in won't go in the story. It doesn't reflect at all well on Geneva Bay."

Two uniformed officers emerged from the building. I recognized Capone's colleagues, Laura Rettberg and Lee Stanhope.

"Ms. O'Leary," Stanhope said, doffing his cap to reveal his thinning gray hair. "How ya' been?"

"Good, good," I said. "I'm sorry to interrupt. I didn't realize you were in the midst of an investigation."

"Just finishing up. Probably some juveniles with too much time on their hands," Rettberg said with a firm nod of her angular jaw. Her mousy brown hair was drawn into a compact knot at the nape of her neck, all stray strands tamed with a phalanx of bobby pins. "They forced entry and destroyed some property inside."

Stanhope agreed. "Definitely kids. Pros would've taken the tools or pulled out the old copper wires to sell." He gestured back toward the building. "Just finished taking statements. None of the workers saw anything unusual."

Julio opened his mouth to speak, but stopped.

"You don't seem convinced," I observed.

"It's too crazy," he said, waving his hands.

Rettberg drew a tiny spiral-bound notebook out of her pocket and cocked an eyebrow. "You have something to add?" She struck me as a sharp cookie, eager to advance, but I knew she had little experience with criminal cases.

"Well, you know Graham Ulrich? That British chef from TV? I saw him here yesterday, talking to Miss Kessler out back," Julio said. "She's our interior designer. They were too far away for me to hear anything, but Ulrich looked like he was yelling like how he does on TV, and Miss Kessler looked real upset."

"Surely Graham Ulrich wouldn't be involved," Harold said. "He's a celebrity."

Stanhope scrunched his face. "Graham Ulrich? Why would a famous guy like that risk jail time just to smash up a construction site? Didn't like the paint color she picked out or something?"

"See?" Julio said, twirling his finger beside his head. "Crazy."

I swallowed. "Kessler is Renee Ulrich's maiden name. She and Graham are going through a bitter divorce."

"Oh," Rettberg said, her ears coloring slightly.

"Dearie me, I hope there isn't any truth to that. It wouldn't be good publicity for the Taste of Wisconsin contest," Harold said.

Stanhope scratched his head, looking at Rettberg. "I guess maybe we'd better get CSI to come in and take a gander at the scene?"

"They're still tied up processing the scene at Juice Revolution. Probably wouldn't be able to get over here until later today or even tomorrow," Rettberg said.

Julio frowned. "Don't tell me you gotta shut down my site to dust for prints or whatever. Repairing the stuff they wrecked is already going to set us back a week." He shook his head. "It was probably just some dumb teenagers, like they said. I shouldn't have said nothing about Ulrich."

Stanhope looked at Rettberg, clearly not liking the idea of shutting down the site or of having to question Graham Ulrich. I'd liked Stanhope from the moment I'd met him, but unlike the young, ambitious Rettberg, he was nearing retirement. I got the impression he'd be happiest corralling drunken tourists and tracking down lost labradoodles until he could start cashing a pension check. He was the senior officer, so how they'd proceed would probably be his call. I didn't envy him, picturing the almighty wrath that Ulrich could bring down on the Geneva Bay PD. As I knew from my own limited experience, if you were going up against someone like Ulrich, you'd better come heavy.

At last Stanhope sighed and said, "We should question everyone again."

"And talk to Renee Kessler when she gets here. See if she wants to make a complaint or file a restraining order," Rettberg added.

"I suppose I should get out of your hair," Harold said, unconsciously running his hand over his own bald pate. "I hope Graham Ulrich's name is cleared. Can you imagine the scandal? I'd have to find a new judge, redesign the whole magazine. The Chamber of Commerce hates scandal." He pressed his fingers to his lips.

"Don't worry about it for now," I said. "It could all blow over."

"I have the title for the article ready to go: 'The *Beer* Necessities Are *On Tap* with Geneva Bay's Latest Drinking and Dining *Hop-tion*.' If this gets ugly, I won't be able to use it." He looked like a child who'd just lost a balloon.

"We should know more soon," Julio assured him, patting him on the shoulder. "It's a good title. I like the 'hop-tion' part."

The two police officers scurried back inside, looking a little sheepish, while Harold headed away toward town.

"Was there much damage?" I asked Julio, once we were alone.

"Naw, just looked like somebody knocked some holes in the wall, threw stuff around, that kind of thing." He scratched his chin. "Now that I think about it, it could've been done in anger. Usually with kids you'd find beer cans and whatnot." He cut his eyes toward the door of the building. "Not that I'd say that in front of the cops. Shouldn't have said nothing in the first place."

"I know the feeling," I mumbled. "Renee's not here is she? I actually came here to talk to her."

Julio shook his head. "She usually gets here about now, though." Pointing up the road, he said, "Matter of fact, that's her car."

A pearl-colored Mercedes eased into the empty space next to where Julio and I stood. Renee popped out of the car, wrapped in a fog of jasmine perfume and cigarette smoke. Her bouffant of reddish-purple dyed hair, reminiscent of cotton candy, was held at bay by a beaded headband. She wore a smock dress that looked like it was cut from a medieval tapestry, accented with chunky acrylic jewelry. If I tried wearing that ensemble, it would look like the Salvation Army thrift store threw up on me. On her, it was the epitome of style.

She rushed over and air-kissed both sides of my face. "Delilah O'Leary, it's been donkey's years since I've seen you." She drew back, straightening her thick-rimmed glasses. "Is that a police car? Has something happened?"

"A break-in," Julio explained.

Renee clutched her chest. "Oh my. Do they have any idea who did it?"

"I don't think so," Julio said.

Renee looked around warily, as if the perpetrator might be hiding in a nearby bush.

Noticing her stiffened posture, Julio said, "Don't worry, nobody's hurt or nothing like that."

"Well, that's a relief." Renee's expression settled slightly. "I suppose our completion date might be pushed back, though?"

"A week at most," Julio replied. "Nothing major."

"Not ideal, but I suppose it could've been worse." Composing herself, Renee turned to me. "Delilah, dear, I only just heard you'd relocated to Geneva Bay. I can't believe what a small world this is. I had you pegged as a Chicago girl through and through."

I'd assumed she'd kept tabs on Sonya, and by extension, me, but her face signaled genuine surprise.

"I always spent my summers here when I was a kid. I decided to bring a little Chicago here with me. Son and I opened a deep-dish pizza restaurant earlier this year."

Her animated face froze. "Sonya? Sonya's here?"

I flashed a tight smile at Julio. "Okay if I steal Renee for a minute?"

He waved his hand. "Sure, sure. I gotta run to the hardware store anyway."

As Julio departed, Renee looked a little wobbly, so I guided her over to a stack of empty wooden pallets and sat her down. She pressed her fingers to her lips. I thought she was going to cry, but instead she drew in a shaky breath and said, "Sorry, I don't mean to be a ninny. I'm sure Sonya told you things between us ended in a rather dramatic fashion. It's a bit of a shock to find out she's here."

"You didn't know?"

She shook her head.

I sat down next to her. "Honestly, Son hasn't told me

many details about what happened, other than the whole demi-glace-over-the-head thing."

Renee winced. "I'm so sorry about that. Graham can be . . . Well, you know."

"I *do* know. He came to my restaurant yesterday," I said.

"He mentioned it. Said you foisted a pizza on him." She smiled weakly. "He tried it, of course, and had to admit it was excellent."

I was struck dumb, not quite believing that one of the world's top foodies, known for his genre-busting dishes, exacting standards, and cutthroat competitiveness, despite being my sworn enemy, had not only eaten my pizza, but deemed it excellent.

Seeing my expression, she added, "You're surprised? That's one thing about Graham. He's brutally honest. I think that's why the television people love him. He can say the most vicious things, because in some twisted way, they're true."

Recovering from my shock, I asked, "Julio said Graham was here yesterday? Is that when you spoke with him?"

She nodded. "We've barely spoken since the day he found out about me and Sonya. We had the most tremendous row about it the night of the infamous demi-glace shower. He was very, very ugly. Beastly, really."

"I'm sorry," I said.

"Seeing him the day he found out was like that film, *The Matrix*, where that chap Keanu Reeves sees how his whole world is an illusion. I saw the film on a plane once. Very exciting. Anyhow, I realized Graham had gradually become someone I didn't know at all. More akin to that egotistical, ill-tempered version of himself he plays on the telly than to the man I married." She took a cigarette from an old-fashioned cigarette case and lit it. "I know what I did to him, my infidelity, was dreadful. As I said, he values honesty above all things, and I betrayed that."

She smoked in silence for a moment before continuing. "I'm not trying to make excuses. Well, I suppose I *am*. But I'd become terribly desperate, you see? There's only so much 'honesty' one wants from one's spouse. Sonya is such a dear, such a good listener. She can tell the truth with kindness, and she knows when the truth is better kept to oneself. I cared about her very much. I still care." She grimaced. "After my row with Graham, I got the next plane home to England. That very night. I've only just stopped hiding like a whipped dog and begun to reclaim my moxie a bit. So here I am. As well as taking this commission, I'm going to finalize our divorce."

"Is that why Graham came to see you?" I asked.

"Quite." She frowned. "He's not having a bit of it, you see. He has some foolish notion of winning me back." She sniffed. "Really, though, it's nothing to do with his devotion to me. He simply can't stand to lose something he thinks of as his."

"Did he tell you that he tried to talk to Sonya when he came to the restaurant?" I asked.

"No, but I'm not surprised. In fact, it all makes loads more sense now you've told me she's living here. He thinks she and I are back together. Must've assumed I knew she was in Geneva Bay and had come here to be with her. He mentioned going to your restaurant, and then told me he knew why I was here. I told him I had no idea what he was on about. I should've connected the dots to realize that Sonya would be here with you, but I didn't. You telling me just now is the first I've heard of it. Of course he'd never believe me about that. Not after what I did." She took a shaky drag of her cigarette. "I suppose since he hasn't been able to persuade me to call off the divorce, he had to go after her. Assert his dominance like some kind of lowland gorilla."

"How angry was he?" I paused, but realized there was no delicate way to ask my question. "Do you think he could've trashed the renovation to get back at you?"

She gasped. "No, I shouldn't think so. He was never a physically violent person."

"He dumped a pan of gravy over Sonya and shoved her into the back alley."

She regarded the lit end of her cigarette. "Yes, there was *that*," she said slowly.

"You should make sure the police know. They're inside now," I said.

"I don't suppose Sonya would want to see me?" she asked, biting her lower lip. "I thought she must be terribly upset with me, leaving without a word like I did. She tried to contact me after it all happened, but I'm afraid I was too much of a coward to respond."

"It's a bit touchy still," I conceded.

"Please tell her how sorry I am. She should at least know that much." Her eyes took on a sad, faraway look for a moment before she gathered herself together and stood up. "Well, I suppose I'd best speak with these police officers. Cross as I am with Graham, I really don't think he could be involved in this. Despite what happened with Sonya, he's not the type to go about bashing up a building site in the middle of the night. He's much more"—she paused, her eyes taking on a bitter gleam—"subtle."

I sat for a moment after she left, weighing my next move. I wished I could keep Sonya in the dark about all of this, but it was becoming clear I'd have to tell her everything. Ulrich had convinced himself that she and Renee were back together. There was no guessing how far he might take things. Was Renee right that he wouldn't physically threaten her? Or try to do something even worse? Whatever his plan, Sonya needed to know that silver-haired jackal had her in his sights. And heaven forbid she run into Renee without warning. She'd pass out from shock.

As I rose to leave, my phone jingled, and Melody's name flashed on the screen.

"What's up, Melody?"

"I'm so sorry, chef," she began, "but I'm going to be late for my shift today."

"Everything okay?"

"I've got to stay at the farm. The cow pasture was already a swamp from all the rain, and the dam on our retention pond busted during the storm last night and flooded all the lower fields. So my uncle asked me and Mac to help move the cows up closer to the barn and shore up the fences. It's a mess out here."

"I'm sorry to hear that," I replied.

"I'm hoping to be back before the end of lunch service."

"Do you need a ride?" I asked.

"No, Mac's going to drive me back into town when we're finished." Her voice tightened. "In her fancy new car."

"What's the deal with the car anyway? You seemed a little skeptical about her ability to afford it," I said.

There was a pause, and for a moment I thought the line had gone dead. When Melody finally spoke, her tone was uncharacteristically harsh. "Well, I was wrong about that. She got her hands on all the money she needed."

CHAPTER 13

Torrential rain let loose almost as soon as I got back to the restaurant. Because of the miserable weather, business was slow enough for Jarka and Daniel to handle the front of house without Melody, who had yet to return from the farm. I'd spent the entire lunch shift trying to figure out how to tell Sonya about the Ulriches, but still hadn't managed to find the right moment. Rabbit bustled in and out of the kitchen, bussing tables and restocking the serving stations. Then, just when I'd think we had some downtime, another order would come in. Besides, Son seemed happy, working her way through our usual routine, sprinkling salt over the eggplants destined for our Eggplant Nduja pizza. She hummed to herself as she stirred heaping tablespoons of the fiery nduja, a pâté-consistency cured pork spread from the Calabrian region of Italy, into a batch of slow-roasted tomatoes. I didn't know how I'd be able to bring myself to pierce her contended bubble.

Finally, during a lull toward the end of the lunch service, there was a break in the rain, and Rabbit stepped out back for a smoke. Sonya and I had the kitchen to ourselves. I set down my knife and turned to face her. I had to get this over with quickly, the emotional equivalent of jumping into a cold pool. Just as I opened my mouth, though, Jarka marched into the kitchen, a frown creasing her forehead. Not her usual fatalistic "life is an unrelenting slog, filled with disappointments" frown, either, but an expression that looked genuinely concerned.

"Everything okay?" I asked.

She motioned for me to come over to the swing door that connected the kitchen to the dining room. She cracked it two or three inches and slid her eyes toward a man seated at a table near the window. Through the huge picture windows, the lake view was beautiful and dramatic, even on a day as stormy as this one. But instead of facing out toward the lake as most people would, the man had chosen a chair in the corner, which offered him a view of the restaurant's mostly empty interior.

"This person has been there for over one hour," Jarka said.

Even from a distance, the muscled contours of the man's body were unmistakable. He wore a tight T-shirt that showed off elaborately tattooed arms; a bleach-blond goatee punctuated the center of his face. Cinco Frates. His demeanor creeped me out the first time I laid eyes on him that day at Juice Revolution. Now, with the information I'd gotten about him from Capone, I was a long way past creeped out.

"I remember this man," Jarka said. "Recently before Ronald Wong died, this man was there at the Juice Revolution also."

I nodded. "Yeah, I recognize him, too. Has he done anything? Talked to anyone?"

"Nothing. He watches. He orders nothing to eat, just only Diet Coke," she said. "I remember he comes into the Juice Revolution once on the day Ronald Wong died, and one time also before that day. Both times, he sits there for many minutes, ordering only plain coffee. No one comes to the Juice Revolution for drinking only plain coffee."

"And no one comes to Delilah & Son to nurse a Diet Coke all afternoon," I said.

"Strange that he should have this habit," Jarka said, raising an eyebrow. "Do you also think so?"

Remembering the note with Frates's fingerprints, I asked, "Did he give you anything? A piece of paper, maybe?"

She shook her head. "Why he should give me some paper?"

"I just wondered. That's all."

By now, Rabbit had returned from his smoke break. He and Sonya must've noticed our urgent, whispered tones, and they sidled up behind us, trying to get a peek at what we were seeing.

"What's up?" Sonya asked, standing on her toes to try to see past me. "A celebrity sighting? Is it that first baseman from the White Sox? I heard he bought a place around here."

I gently closed the door and shooed everyone back, not wanting Cinco Frates to catch a glimpse of the entire staff staring him down. Rabbit, though, was already backing away, his face sheet white.

"Cinco," he murmured, almost swallowing the word.

"You know him?" I asked.

"Uh-huh. Everybody at Oakhill knew him." His eyes flitted toward the door, as if he expected Frates to burst through it. "I didn't know he'd got out."

"What do you know about him?" I asked.

"He was the kinda guy . . ." His body tensed. "You tried not to get in his way, if you catch my drift. Cinco had worked as hired muscle on the outside, and that's what he did on the inside, too," he explained. "One of those white-collar guys took him on as a bodyguard. Even with mostly nonviolent offenders, you could still get beat up pretty bad, stabbed even, if somebody had it in for you or people think you're an easy mark. Plus, there were times, like out in the rec yard, where anything could happen. Cons who came in there with no street sense needed to watch their backs."

"What's a guy like that doing here? I know Geneva Bay has a reputation as gangster hangout, but that was a long time ago," Sonya said. "John Dillinger and Al Capone have been dead for, what, a hundred years?"

I remembered then that she was in the dark about not only everything that had been going on with the Ulriches, but also the much more recent criminal events swirling around us. I hadn't told her about Capone and Biz's discoveries about Rock Co. Enterprises and, although she knew about Wong's death and Jordan's hospitalization, she had no idea those incidents were very likely intentional poisonings.

"What should we do about him?" Rabbit asked. "Drinking a pop in a restaurant ain't exactly a parole violation. He didn't do nothing."

"No." I paused, thinking through the options. Usually, if we wanted a customer to move along, we'd tell them that we needed the table for another group. That might be hard to justify today, given the empty dining room. Plus, I didn't want to put my staff in the middle of anything that could turn ugly. "I'm going to tell him we're closing for the afternoon because of the weather. It's dead today anyway, so shutting the doors for an hour or two won't break us. Jarka, can you make sure Daniel knows the deal? I'm not sure if Daniel would've noticed him that day in Juice Revolution, but he should be on the lookout in case Frates tries anything."

Turning to Rabbit, I added, "Would you mind running over to Biz's house and checking on her? With Melody gone, I don't like to leave her alone. Leave through the back door so Frates doesn't see you. He might recognize you from Oakhill and he might not want to be recognized himself."

"No problem," he said, seeming glad for an excuse to put some distance between himself and Frates.

"Son, would you mind waiting for me upstairs? There's something I want to talk to you about." She looked at me quizzically, but made her way out the door after Rabbit.

I couldn't keep delaying. It was cold-pool-jumping time. First, though, I had to dispatch Cinco Frates. I walked toward his table, mentally formulating an explanation about the weather leading us to close. I hoped it would go easily, but to be on the safe side, I held the hilt of my paring knife in my clenched fist, concealing it under my apron.

Jarka and Daniel watched my approach from the bar, doing their best to look busy, even though they were observing us closely. I felt the muscles in my neck tense as Frates turned his coal black eyes on me. He had a pronounced widow's peak, so sharp that his close-cropped white-blond hair came to an arrow point in the center of his forehead.

He watched me without blinking, hardly moving at all, still as a coiled snake. I didn't get a chance to deliver the sham excuse, though. As soon as I got within six feet of Frates's table, he rose to leave, throwing a ten-dollar bill onto the table with a smirk. I hadn't even given him his check. The heavy tread of his feet seemed to echo in the empty dining room. As soon as he was out the door, Jarka marched over to turn the deadbolt.

"You want me to call the cops?" Daniel offered.

"No, I'll text Capone about it later, but like Rabbit said, there's not much the police can do about a guy drinking a Coke." I picked up the bill he'd left and turned it over in my hand. No threatening message. Just a plain old greenback.

"Not a bad tipper. I'll give him that," Daniel said.

"Can you two do the bar inventory?" I asked. "If we're going to be closed this afternoon, we might as well use the hours productively."

I could use the time to get a jump on paperwork, but first, I had to get Sonya up to speed on the situation with the Ulriches. I found her in my apartment sitting on the leather couch under the window, giving Butterball's expansive tummy a rub down.

She looked up at me, her kohl-lined eyes wide. "What's up?"

I launched in, recounting Graham's sinister visit to the restaurant asking to see her and my meeting that morning with Renee at the construction site. Sonya said very little, but I noticed that she'd stopped petting Butterball at some point, and that her hands were now balled into fists.

"Let me get this straight," she said slowly, when I finished filling in the details. "You and basically everyone I know conspired to keep me in the dark about Graham being in town. For days. Then you let me think I was going crazy, seeing hallucinations of Renee when you knew she was here, too."

"I was protecting you," I countered. "And I didn't know for sure Renee was here until this morning."

She exhaled a puff of air. "More like you wanted to be in control."

I crossed my arms over my chest. "Bull. You totally flipped out at the mere mention of his name and you said yourself that you didn't know if you could handle seeing Renee. I was afraid of how you'd react."

She let out another incredulous exhalation. "Afraid of how *I'd* react? I was surprised. I dropped an egg. You and your goon squad physically threatened Graham. That's your idea of a measured reaction?"

"He deserved it. And Capone and Daniel are hardly a goon squad."

"And speaking of goon squads, what about that guy who was here this afternoon? Ocho the Impaler, or whatever his name is? What if Graham sent him here to spy on me? You left me totally unprepared for anything like that." The cat-eye contours of liner around her eyes narrowed into a pair of angry black slits.

Although the thought hadn't crossed my mind, I had to admit it might not be too far-fetched. If Ulrich was serious about trying to win back his wife, he might just rope in some extra muscle to bully her former lover. Still, I reassured Sonya she wasn't in danger. "I'm sure it's a coincidence. Cinco might be mixed up in the poisonings, but I can't imagine he's in league with Ulrich."

"*Poisonings*?"

Oh, right. I hadn't filled her in about that, either. As I ran down the suspicions Capone and I had, Sonya's face grew darker.

"You're just now telling me all of this?" she sputtered, her tone incredulous.

"You were stressed. I didn't think you needed anything else on your plate."

"Don't treat me like I'm some fragile little flower that

you have to protect from the big bad world." She slammed
her balled fist on the arm of the couch, sending Butterball fleeing from her lap into the bedroom to hide. "How
many times do I have to tell you that we're supposed to
be in this together?"

"We are, but . . ."

She stood up and struggled with the knot in her apron.
"I don't want to hear it. I'm going to see Renee."

"Are you sure that's a good idea? She left you high and
dry. Not even a text message for all these months," I said.

"She was upset," Sonya replied.

"I'm sure she was. But at the end of the day, she bore
the greatest responsibility for the mess, and she left you
and Graham to deal with it," I said.

"He doesn't deserve your pity," she snapped.

"What about you, then? She couldn't even check to see
if you were okay? You deserve better than that," I said.

"This isn't about you doing what's best for me. You've
always liked it best when poor little Sonya gets into trouble so Super Delilah can fly to the rescue."

I took a step toward her. "Son . . ."

"Don't 'Son' me!" she snapped, finally getting her
apron knot undone. "I'm going to find Renee."

"What about dinner service?" I asked. Her glare was
so icy that I immediately changed my line of questioning. "What about Graham? He's looking for you. What if
you're right about Cinco Frates? What are you going to
do if one of them finds you?"

"Then they'll get what's coming to them. I can handle
myself." She threw her apron onto the floor just as a thun-
derbolt crashed over our heads, giving dramatic empha-
sis to her words.

A gust of wet air rushed into the apartment as she

stomped out into the storm. The ferocious rain had kicked off again, and it was coming down like a sheer wall of water. Business would be sluggish. Might as well stay closed. After all, at this rate, it wouldn't be long until we had to close our doors forever.

CHAPTER 14

I was sitting at my kitchen island, trying to distract myself with a payroll report. In the past, I'd have been fighting a losing battle to keep Butterball from lying on the computer keyboard as I worked, typing an endless series of *j*'s and semicolons with his butt. Instead, he'd spent the afternoon hiding under the bed and would only be coaxed out to eat. I was just deciding whether to try to lure him out when a knock sounded on my apartment door. I opened it to find Rabbit, looking agitated.

"Rabbit, what is it? Is Biz okay?"

"Yeah, she's all right. It's not that . . ." He took his rain-soaked baseball cap from his head and began twisting it between his hands. "Well, you better come see."

I followed him downstairs through the soaking rain and in through the back door to the kitchen, where we found Jarka and Daniel standing in the middle of what looked like a war zone. A full container of pizza sauce had been tipped over, and the contents oozed down the side of the counter, puddling on the floor. The utensil rack was knocked sideways, scattering spoons and spatulas. Mounds of sliced mushrooms, chopped onions, and shredded cheese that had been neatly stacked in labeled bins were tumbled all over the sauce-smeared floor.

"What on God's green earth," I whispered, taking in the devastation.

"We don't know what happened, *jefa*," Daniel said. "Jarka and I were out front doing the inventory. I thought maybe I heard a crash at one point, but I assumed it was the storm."

"You found it like this?" I asked, turning to Rabbit.

He nodded.

"I'm sure I locked the door when I left in case Frates was still hanging around," I said. "Maybe Sonya came back down here after she left my apartment and forgot to lock it?"

Rabbit shook his head. "No, chef. It was locked. I had to unlock it when I came in."

We'd installed security cameras over the exterior doors when the restaurant was built. I pulled up the app on my phone and played the videos from that afternoon to see if they'd captured evidence of anyone breaking in. The back door camera showed Rabbit leaving for Biz's house. A few minutes later, Sonya had walked straight from my apartment's stairs to her car without going inside. There was no additional activity until Rabbit returned from Biz's. The only other ways into the building were through the front door and the patio door, both of which lead into the dining room, where Jarka and Daniel would have seen an intruder. I suddenly remembered how my bratwurst sample had inexplicably vanished the day we found out about Ulrich. That felt like a hundred years ago, when missing meat was the biggest mystery in my life. That incident had been easy to brush aside, but this? It seemed that someone had found a way to get in and out of my kitchen undetected. Time to call Capone.

"Could Butterball have gotten down here somehow?" Rabbit asked, looking down at the floor as he mopped up splattered sauce. "Maybe slipped out a window? That could explain this mess and how that sausage went missing the other day."

"He was upstairs with me the whole time," I replied. "He'd never go out in this rain anyway."

"Coulda been kids," Rabbit guessed. "My friends and me used to do dumb stuff like that when we were younger."

"The same kind of thing happened this morning at a construction site on the other side of town," I explained. "That's what made me decide to tell Capone about this."

As soon as I'd seen my trashed kitchen, I'd called Capone directly to make the report and alert him to Frates's earlier visit, rather than calling the general police department number. I had to admit I'd secretly been hoping he'd drop whatever he was doing and come. His presence always calmed me. Although each of the strange happenings over the past few days didn't amount to much on its own, taken together it seemed clear that something ominous was taking shape. I was starting to feel more and more like a swimmer in shark-infested waters. I couldn't see the danger, but I could feel it drawing closer to me in ever-tightening circles.

Although Capone listened with concern to what I had to say, he was still wrapped up in the Juice Revolution investigation, interviewing Jordan's suppliers and running down leads on Wong's life to make sure he hadn't missed anything. He couldn't drop a suspicious death investigation for a minor, seemingly unrelated report of vandalism or a sighting of a felon drinking a Diet Coke. He'd sent Rettberg and Stanhope to handle it instead. There hadn't been much they could do other than take our statements and gather what minimal evidence there was. I forced a smile to mask my disappointment and sent them back to the station with jars of our home-made pizza sauce to share with their colleagues.

After they left, I got a call from Melody explaining that the rain washed out the gravel road that led to the family farm, so she'd be trapped there until at least the next day. Sonya, meanwhile, was ignoring my calls and showing no sign of returning to help with dinner service. No hostess, no sous chef, and a trashed kitchen. I took it all as a fur-ther sign that we should remain closed for the rest of the day, and I told everyone they could go home early.

Rabbit, though, insisted on staying behind to help me clean up.

"Yeah, I bet it was kids," he continued, pausing to dunk the mop head into a bucket. "Maybe climbed in a window somewhere. Otherwise why wouldn't they take anything? Just looks like someone was goofing around in here."

"I hope you're right," I said, scooping a handful of bruised mushrooms from the floor and tossing them into the compost bin. "Hey, can I ask you something? You've known my aunt for a while."

He nodded. "Miss O'Leary helped me get my GED while I was inside. I owe her a lot."

"Have you noticed anything strange with her lately?" I asked. "She seems a little irritable to me."

"More irritable than usual, you mean?" he said with a chuckle.

I frowned. "Maybe that's not the right way of describ-ing it. Something seems off with her."

He rubbed at the stubble on his chin. "Now you mention it, I guess I do catch your drift. Other day, I tried to help her out of Melody's car. It was raining and I was worried she might slip and fall. She always lets me help her up the stairs and that, used to ask even, but that time she shooed me away. And same thing when I saw she was struggling to open a jar of olives last week when she was cooking. I popped it open for her—did it without even thinking, and she snapped at me, like, 'You think I can't do things myself?' She seems more sensitive lately."

I had a strange urge to laugh at the word "sensitive" being used in conjunction with Elizabeth O'Leary, but I wondered if he was on to something.

"It's like how my daughter was when she was a toddler," he continued. "Mind you, I was locked up a lot of those years, but I still saw it whenever my mom brought her to visit. Didn't want no help with nothing. Everything was a foot stamp and crossed arms and 'I can do it all by myself!'" He shrugged. "That's life, I guess. You can lead a horse to water and whatnot."

Just then, the back door banged open and I turned, expecting to see Sonya, maybe coming back to apologize. Instead, Sam stood framed in the doorway. His long hair clung to his face and shoulders, and his handsome face was marred by dark circles under vacant-looking eyes.

I hurried over and gently pulled him inside the kitchen, shutting the door against the storm. "Are you okay?"

He shivered like a drenched animal.

"Did something happen to Jordan?" I asked.

"No, no. I'm tired. That's all," he said quietly. "I'm sorry to barge in like this. I just needed someone to talk to."

Rabbit cleared his throat and wrung out his mop. "I'm about finished here, chef," he said, apparently noticing that whatever was going on with Sam didn't need an audience. "I should head home."

"Thanks, Rabbit," I said. "I'll see you tomorrow."

As Rabbit took his leave, I dragged Biz's stool in front of the still-warm pizza oven and seated Sam on it. "Did they find out what caused Jordan's . . . episode?" I'd exchanged texts with Sam over the past few days, but hadn't mentioned what Capone and I had discussed about the possible reason for Jordan's ailment. I wasn't sure how much to say.

He shook his head. "They tested her for a bunch of stuff, but it all came back negative." He looked up at me, his eyes wide and pleading. "Do you think she could have been poisoned? That's what the doctors seem to think, and Capone, too."

"Maybe it was an accident," I ventured. "Those smoothies have a lot of weird ingredients. Maybe something got contaminated."

He shook his head again, more forcefully. "No way. Jordan's a stickler about quality control. She hand-inspects everything, and her suppliers are top-notch. Kind of reminds me of you," he said, looking at me through his eyelashes.

I smiled.

"She had that same smoothie every day with the same ingredients from the same suppliers." He swallowed hard and pressed his knuckles against the sides of his head. "I think someone did this on purpose," he groaned. "To her. If they'd been trying to kill that Wong guy, why go after him in the juice bar? There would be no way to make sure whatever toxin it was went into his exact smoothie."

I couldn't remember ever seeing Sam so distraught. He'd practically built his life around trying to avoid conflict, negativity, and bad vibes. But the vibes radiating off him right then were very bad indeed. Distrust and cynicism were baked into my basic personality, so suspecting people of murder wasn't a huge mental leap for me. In fact, it confirmed my belief that some people were, at their core, nasty little weasels. Sam, however, had an optimism about human nature that bordered on naïveté, a quality that was both endearing and frustrating. It was hard to watch him inhabiting this bleak headspace.

"Jarka or Mac could have poisoned Wong," I ventured. I hated to even raise the possibility. The more I got to know them, the more unlikely it seemed that either one could be a murderer. Still, I couldn't ignore the fact that the two of them had the easiest access. "They made the smoothies, so they could have slipped something in."

"That makes no sense. No one can remember him ever being there before. I'm sure the cops will check his credit and debit card statements just to be sure, and ask his wife." His jaw tightened. "Whoever did this must've been after Jordan. Wong was just collateral damage."

I granted the point. No sense in trying to convince him of something that I myself didn't believe. If it did turn out to be an intentional poisoning, using the smoothie bar to go after Wong would've involved some next-level planning. "Any idea why someone would want to poison Jordan? Does she have any enemies?"

Sam's face darkened. "I've been over and over it in my inner eye, you know?"

"I'm not sure I do know."

"Meditated on it. Really breathed into that liminal space," he added.

I tried to put his yoga-speak into regular people words. "You mean you tried to remember who was there or who had access to the ingredients? The people who knew her routine?"

He nodded.

"And?"

"Harold Heyer," he said.

"Harold Heyer," I repeated, trying to keep the disbelief from my voice. "You think Harold tried to kill Jordan?" I tried to picture a calculating murderer's heart hiding inside that Christmas-elf persona. "He told me they've been friends for years."

"They were friendly, yes, but I don't know about friends. They've known each other since middle school. He's always been a bit . . . Well, you've seen him. Kids can be cruel. Jordan is nice to everyone, and he apparently took that to mean she was his best friend. She tolerated him better than other people did, but I don't know if she ever considered him a friend. Then, a few weeks ago, Jordan mentioned she'd been getting weird vibes from him lately. She wondered if he was jealous."

I thought it through. "I guess I could see him harboring a secret crush on her. Why try to kill her, though? Surely her boyfriend, i.e., you, would be the more-sensible target if he wanted to be with her."

"He's done this before," Sam said.

"Tried to murder Jordan?"

"No, gotten obsessed with her. She worked for his family's department store while they were still in high school. He was clearly infatuated with her, but she was always able to handle it. She was dating someone and when they broke up, Harold took his crush to another level, became obsessive, wouldn't leave her alone. It got so bad that she felt like it was easier just to leave town. That's when she traveled in Asia and learned about holistic dietary healing practices, natural botanicals, and Ayurvedic medicine. She figured that by now, his feelings were all water under the bridge. People do weird things when they're young. She thought that whatever torch he was carrying for her had died out by now, so she finally came back to Geneva Bay. She'd always wanted to start a business here." He leaned toward me. "But what if Harold didn't move on? What if he took it further this time?"

"Then I'd ask again, why not take aim at you instead of her?"

"Maybe he realized that she'd never be with him, no matter if she was single or not. After all, they were both single when she moved back here," he said.

"So if he couldn't have her, nobody could," I finished his thought. I'd always considered Harold to be an equal-opportunity flatterer. The only time I'd ever seen him make what could loosely be described as a romantic overture was his flirtation with Jarka on the day of Wong's death. Overall, his attempts at suaveness had been so ham-handed that I hadn't considered them anything other than harmless irritations. "Did she tell you what happened that first time, when Harold took his crush to another level? I'm not doubting her story, but I want to understand."

"Jordan doesn't like to talk about it."

"Have you mentioned any of this to Capone? He might at least look into it," I said. "See if there's any chance that your theory could be true."

He shook his head. "No way. I wouldn't want to throw accusations at Harold unless we could be sure about him. It wouldn't be fair to him."

That was the Sam I knew. Worrying about the feelings and reputation of someone he suspected might be a murderer.

"I don't know what to do," he said.

Tears began to pool in the corners of his eyes, and I, on instinct, gathered my arms around him. He fell into my embrace, squeezing me tight against him. I shushed him gently and brushed his rain-damp hair from his forehead. Touching his warm skin set off a wave of physical attraction, hitting me unexpectedly, almost like muscle memory. Had I made a huge mistake in giving up the life I had with him? What did I have now to show for all my independence? My failing business, my aunt out of sorts for some unknown reason, my best friend furious with me for an all-too-obvious reason, and an empty bed to go home to at night. I wasn't sure even my own cat loved me anymore. If Sam had asked me to get back together with him, in that moment, I would have said yes. But although he was in my arms, it wasn't me he wanted. Yessiree, sometimes life could be a full-on crotch kick.

CHAPTER 15

After Sam left, I finished scrubbing down the kitchen until everything was in order and not a trace of mess remained. As long as I had a scouring brush in my hand, I could push my problems to the edges of my brain. As I headed upstairs, though, I noted that it was only seven o'clock and a long, empty night stretched before me. I'd urged Sam to take Butterball home with him, thinking he'd be more likely to get some much-needed sleep if he had a warm mountain of purring cat curled at his side. Opening the door to the dark apartment, though, made me regret my gesture. With no cat to scamper over to rub his face against my ankles or even, as of late, stare moodily at me from under a piece of furniture, there was total emptiness. One cat divided by two needy humans—the math didn't compute.

I walked the small circuit around my apartment. I'd been working in kitchens since I was sixteen and never developed any other hobbies. Looking around the apartment, there were no stacks of novels to be read, watercolor paints, or half-finished crossword puzzles. I didn't even have a TV show I was dying to binge. The DVR was full of *Matlock* and *Jeopardy!* episodes to occupy Biz. On my rare off nights, I usually cooked with Sonya or played with Butterball. Now both of them resented me.

My throat tightened. What if I lost the restaurant? What would I have left?

My eyes settled on a photo of Auntie Biz and me, taken at my graduation from culinary school. We both beamed at the camera. It was hard to tell who'd been happier that day.

I grabbed my car keys and headed back down the stairs. I told myself I needed to check on Biz, maybe see if she wanted me to cook dinner for her, since Melody wouldn't be home again that night. I should try to get to the bottom of whatever was going on with her—her crabbiness, the mysterious ashes in the fireplace, and the secret accounting project. Or maybe I'd ask her about Mac, see if Melody had shared any insight about her cousin, something that might have bearing on the poisonings at Juice Revolution. That's what I told myself. But in truth, I couldn't spend another minute alone in my apartment.

The rain lightened into a gentle mist as I pulled down the driveway to Biz's house. Because Biz's cottage had been subdivided from the property of the main house, her plot came with an easement that allowed her access to the main road via the mansion's driveway. The two houses shared an entryway of impressive stone columns and a poured-concrete drive. A little farther down the lane, however, a gravel track abruptly branched off, ducking through scrubby, overgrown bushes before dead-ending in front of Biz's cottage. The new owners had repeatedly offered to pave, landscape, and gate off the intersection of the two driveways—at first as a seemingly generous gesture, which Biz had rebuffed as unwanted charity from

"Richie Riches," and later with an insistence that she spurned as "bullying by snobs who think their money makes them better than everybody else."

Biz's cottage held a special place in my heart and I wouldn't have wanted her to change a single broken screen or cracked porch step. However, the perfectionist in me could understand the neighbors' irritation at having something so ramshackle existing cheek by jowl with their perfectly manicured utopia. I expected they'd buy her property and bulldoze it if they could, but there was zero chance she'd ever sell.

I opened the creaky back door and found Biz at the dining room table, poring over old photo albums. When she heard me come in, she blew her nose, stuffed the tissue in her pocket, and popped up from her chair.

"Didn't expect you," she said. "Rabbit said you closed the restaurant early because some kids broke in?"

"Yeah," I said, glad Rabbit had kept the explanation simple. "And since Melody isn't going to make it back tonight, I thought I'd come see how you're faring." I sat down in the chair she'd vacated and slid one of the albums toward myself. "I haven't seen these in ages," I said. Photos of my sister and me were pasted onto the pages. Biz had every picture captioned and dated with a neat, typewritten label. Shea and I as toddlers in our matching striped bikinis posing on her screened porch; as older kids gathering green beans from the garden into the fabric of our turned-up T-shirts; as teenagers, lazily sunning ourselves on beach towels in the back yard.

The photos our mom had of us, on the other hand, were still in unordered stacks, stuffed into shoeboxes, somewhere in the storage unit we'd rented after my dad died. Our mother hadn't been much of an organizer, always intending to undertake various projects, but never finding the time. And then, of course, her time suddenly ran out on an icy road one winter morning.

"You hungry?" Biz called.

"Not really," I said.

"You should eat some real food or you'll be ravenous and stuff your face with junk like you always do."

"Fine," I conceded, knowing she wasn't wrong. I joined Auntie Biz near the sink. "I can cook if you want to rest."

"Who said I need to rest? I'm perfectly capable of cooking," she said.

"Okay, I'll be your sous," I said, not wanting to touch off an argument. "What are we making?"

"Well, I've got basil and tomatoes coming out of my ears, and I picked up some corn at the farmers market. I'll do a fresh mozzarella, corn, and tomato salad. Rummage around in the fridge and grab the half a roast chicken from the bottom rack. Do a little lemon vinaigrette for that. We'll serve it cold. And chop some of those scallions for the salad."

I set to work, ripping the husk from an ear of corn and running a knife down the edge of a cob to remove the pale white kernels. They dropped onto the cutting board like tiny pearls as their sweet, milky aroma hit my nostrils. When I was finished, Biz scraped the corn into a mixing bowl with halved cherry tomatoes, green onions, and cubes of fresh mozzarella, seasoning them with salt and a few tablespoons of olive oil. Meanwhile, I carved the breast from the chicken in a whole chunk, cut it in thin slices, then fanned the slices out on two china plates. As Biz plated the salad next to the chicken, I whisked up a quick vinaigrette of lemon, olive oil, and garlic, pouring the finished dressing into a little jug to be drizzled over the salad and chicken.

Biz pushed the photo albums to one side of the table and set our plates down.

"Why do you have these out?" I asked, pulling one of the albums back toward me to look through.

Biz took it from my hands and stacked it with the others. "You might spill or splatter. When you're eating, eat."

I'd heard her say that a thousand times. Biz would never dream of eating in front of the TV or paging through a magazine while gulping down a meal. For her, the food was the entertainment.

"This might be my favorite summer meal," I said, hoisting a forkful of salad into my mouth. Little sunbursts of flavor exploded with each bite of juicy corn kernels and tart cherry tomato. "The produce from your garden is unreal."

"It's the soil," she said. "I was composting before all these hippies starting yammering on about it. Took me decades to get it where it is." She looked wistfully out the window toward her garden. I wondered again at her insistence on plowing it under seemingly earlier than was necessary.

We ate in silence for a moment, and then I said, "I've been wondering if I should add that bratwurst pizza to the menu. You know the most recent version we had for family meal a few days ago? If I'm not going to get to use it for the contest, at least I can salvage some of my work that way."

"The recipe's not good enough," she said, not even pausing to consider it.

Although, I, too, suspected I still hadn't hit on the exact right marriage of ingredients, I found myself growing defensive. "The last few iterations have all been good."

She gave a dismissive wave of her hand. "As long as

there's plenty of meat and cheese on it, people will like it. If that's what you're going for."

"What do you mean, 'If that's what you're going for'? What's wrong with making food that people enjoy?" I said, crossing my arms over my chest.

"When you opened, you said you were trying to prove that deep-dish doesn't have to cater to the lowest common denominator, like all the other deep-dish places do. You wanted to go beyond traditional recipes. Why'd you open your own place if 'good' is good enough?"

"Those brats are hand ground from pork from heirloom pigs, the cheese is the very best local cheddar, and I pickle the onion topping myself. How is that the lowest common denominator?"

"You asked my opinion," she said, bringing a forkful of chicken to her lips.

I tried to keep my voice steady. "Why are you always so hard on me? Why can't you ever just tell me I'm doing a good job?"

"What top chef do you know who's a sissy? If I molly-coddled you, how far do you think you would have gotten in this business?" she said. "Do you think you'd have had the chops to go toe-to-toe with someone like Graham Ulrich? To open your own restaurant? I would have killed to have my own restaurant, but that opportunity didn't exist when I was a young woman."

I stood up. "Some opportunity. All I have is that damn restaurant, and it's about to go bust. And I have to handle that all myself because no one can stand to be around me. Sam's gone, Sonya's gone. Did you ever think maybe you wanted me to be a little too much like you? Look at us. What good is a perfect meal if you eat it all alone?"

"Don't feel so sorry for yourself."

I grabbed my plate and let it fall into the sink with a

clatter. "Here, you can do the dishes. Show how strong and independent you are. I wouldn't want to mollycoddle you by offering to help."

I stormed out of the house, letting the screen door slam behind me. Even before I got to my car, I regretted my outburst. I'd come over seeking some sort of solace, and instead I'd ended up yelling at the very person I'd moved all the way here from Chicago to be near. It was my own fault for coming to Biz of all people seeking a salve for my bruised spirit. I was a walking paper cut and Biz was lemon juice.

I fired up the engine of my Jeep, still fuming. As I pulled onto the main road, thoughts of my relationship with Sam flickered across my mind. How many times had I made him feel like he didn't measure up? Said something critical when I could've been kind? And how much truth had there been to Sonya's accusation that my actions toward her had been controlling? Even with Butterball, I knew that he hated going back and forth between Sam and me. Yet I insisted on it because I needed the comfort he provided to me. Everything I'd accused Biz of, I was guilty of, too. I sighed. Deep down, I didn't doubt Biz's love for me any more than I doubted my love for her. But neither of us seemed capable of cutting our loved ones any slack. Maybe someday we'd find a way to go a little easier on each other and on ourselves. But clearly not today.

I was almost back home when my phone rang. I answered it through the car's Bluetooth screen. "Renee?"

"Delilah? Oh, thank god you picked up. Sonya's fainted and I don't know what do." Renee's voice was an urgent whisper.

"She fainted? Where are you? Have you called an ambulance?" I asked.

"No. It's not as straightforward as that." She spoke quickly, her voice slightly manic. "We're at the warehouse, and Graham's here with us."

I swung my steering wheel around, hitting the gas as I headed toward the brewery. "Did he threaten you? Are you safe?"

"That's the thing. He can't hurt us. Not anymore. You see, he's, well, I'm afraid he's quite dead."

CHAPTER 16

Thankfully, the streets of Geneva Bay were empty, because after Renee's revelation, I almost certainly set a land speed record getting across town to the warehouse. I skidded across the wet gravel of the parking lot, pulling in next to the only car there—Renee's Mercedes.

I rushed to the glass double doors, where Renee met me. Her wary eyes scanned left and right before unlocking the bolt to let me in. She pulled me inside, locking the door behind us. Wordlessly, she led me through the cavernous space, which was poorly illuminated with a few foldable tripod lights that cast eerie shadows against the red brick walls. My heart pounded too fiercely to take much notice of my surroundings anyway.

"She's over here." Renee hurried me across the main dining area to a smaller side alcove, where a dazed-looking Sonya was propped against a half-assembled banquette. The only light came from a temporary single-bulb incandescent lamp that hung from an unfinished receptacle on the ceiling. The air, unairconditioned and full of humidity and plaster dust, made the space feel even smaller than it was.

I knelt at Sonya's side and took her hand. It felt as cold and stiff as a metal rod, especially jarring in the warm room. The vivid tattoos that covered her arms stood out starkly against her too-pale skin. "Son, are you okay?"

She swallowed and nodded. "I think so." Her eyes lit up with a sudden horror and her hand flew to cover her mouth. "Oh, god. He's still here, isn't he?"

Renee dropped to the floor and patted Sonya gently. "I'm afraid so, chicken, but I've covered him back up." Her eyes darted to a doubled-over length of plastic sheeting covering the top of a large rectangular box a few feet from where I knelt.

That's when I realized we weren't the only inhabitants of the room. I rose and walked toward the box.

"No, darling, you really shouldn't," Renee protested.

Driven by some inexplicable impulse, I continued to walk toward the box, then drew back the plastic covering. Graham Ulrich's vacant eyes stared into nothingness, his head lolling to one side. His jaw, normally set in a resolute line, was slack, as if the cardboard box were a warm bathtub he'd just eased his body into after a hard day's work. The only real hint that something was terribly wrong was the reddish-brown bloodstain running down his left temple, below his impeccably coiffed hair. I quickly replaced the covering, my hand trembling.

"What happened?" I asked.

"Well, we didn't kill him, if that's the question you're dancing around," Renee said.

Sonya pressed her eyes shut and added, "We found him like that."

"I suppose you'll want the details," Renee said.

"You suppose right," I said.

"Fair enough, since I dragged you into this horror show. Sonya rang me this afternoon. She was so lovely about me having flown the coop like I did. I don't know why I'd been frightened to face her." Renee offered a sheepish smile to Sonya, lit a cigarette, and drew a deep, ragged breath of smoke into her lungs. "We had a chat and then met up at my B and B." She looked at me over the top rims of her glasses. "Just talking. Eventually, she said she wanted to see the project I was working on, so I brought her back here to show her around."

"Was anyone here when you arrived?" I asked.

"No one. It was nearly seven p.m.," Renee said.

"So you took Son on a tour and ended up in here?"

"Yes. We've been using this room to store some of the fixtures and fittings for the final fit-out," she said. "When we walked in here, I realized that someone had taken the banquette cushions from that box and installed them on the benchtop." She pointed to place where Sonya sat. Sure enough, four massive leather-effect cushions had been arranged in their proper places along the bench seat.

"It struck me all of a sudden how odd that was," she continued, "since we always do the soft furnishings as the very last thing so they don't get soiled during construction. Even stranger, I realized the box they came in was still sealed with tape. I wondered where the cushions had come from, if not from there." She squeezed Sonya's hand. "When I opened the box to check, well, we got the shock of our lives. Poor Sonya went down like a sack of potatoes."

"And you called me?" I asked. "Why not call an ambulance? Or the police?"

"I've seen all sorts of American television programs and honestly I don't fancy my chances in your criminal justice system. None of it looks very good for me, nor for Sonya for that matter. Both of us had what you might call a beef with Graham," she said. "So, no, I didn't ring the police. Instead, I stood here for a full minute like an absolute ding-dong, staring at the both of them, not knowing what to do. Then I thought of you. You always did know how to handle yourself in a tight spot. I thought perhaps you could help us work out how to get out of this little pickle we've found ourselves in."

I eyed the box, half expecting Graham to rise out of it like some posh zombie. "How long do you think the cushions were out of the box?"

She frowned, tapping her lips with the butt end of her cigarette. "A day at most. I'm sure I would've noticed it this morning if I hadn't been distracted by the break-in. The police asked us to see if anything was missing or damaged. I suppose I was too caught up by the rubbish thrown everywhere to think about a few neatly arranged cushions."

She gestured to a spot where drywall, pieces of brick, and insultation lay in a messy heap on the floor. "There are places like that scattered around the building. Scaffolding knocked over, paint spilled, wallpaper torn, and all that. I had to spend the day ordering replacement materials."

"Did the police take photos?" I asked. "They'll be able to check if the cushions were out of the box this morning."

"Oh, heavens yes. That female officer was terribly thorough."

"Not thorough enough to find a dead body right under their noses," Sonya muttered. Her voice was quiet, but I was glad to see her sarcasm was still intact.

"They'd have had no reason to open a sealed box of cushions, chicken," Renee said.

We were quiet for a minute. Although I was sure none of us wanted to look, I noticed how our eyes kept flicking toward the box, as if it had some magnetic power.

"Hiding a body definitely looks worse than finding one and calling the cops right away," I said at last.

Renee shook her head. "I'm not entirely convinced that's true. They always suspect the wife, and the wife's lover even more so. I'm not even a citizen. What if I'm deported? Almost all of my professional connections are in America."

Sonya began to struggle to her feet. "I'll call my cousin Seth. He'll know what to do."

Sonya's whole family—mom, dad, uncles, aunts, cousins, babies who weren't yet born—were lawyers. Her cousin Seth and uncle Avi Dokter were particularly well known in greater Chicagoland for their billboards encouraging injured motorists to "Call the Dokters!"

"Do you really want to sit here with a dead body for the hour and a half it takes your cousin to get up here from the city?" I asked.

"We could go get a coffee," Renee ventured.

I glared at her.

"I'm only trying to be practical," she replied. After a pause, she said, "We could dispose of him somehow. Geneva Lake is quite deep, or so I've heard."

I glared at her again and then turned my eyes to Sonya. "Son, I've always joked that I'd move a body for you because that's how much you mean to me." I held out one hand to her and used the other to gesture toward the box.

"And I'd move a body for you, too." Sonya's voice broke and her eyes brimmed with tears. "I hope you know that."

Renee brushed a tear from the corner of her eye and cleared her throat. "This is one of the most stirring, and dare I say bizarre, displays of friendship I've ever witnessed."

"I'm sorry about earlier. I know you were trying to help," Sonya said, putting her arms around my waist.

I squeezed her tight. Despite the dire situation we

were in, I felt better than I had all day. Sonya and I were friends again. The world was back on its axis. "I should have told you sooner," I said. "You were right to be mad."

"You are each other's soulmates," Renee observed.

I drew back and looked at her, raising an eyebrow.

She waved her cigarette and tsked. "Not like *that*. I only mean that the bond you have is special. Anyone who really loves either one of you would have to understand that."

Sonya put her hands over her heart. "That's beautiful, Renee."

Renee reached out, took Sonya's hand, and kissed it gently.

"All right," I said, snapping to attention. "We're veering off course."

Renee nodded. "Quite right. Don't let's fall to bits, ladies. We have to attend to"—her eyes fell on the box—"this. Someone get a hand truck. I'll pull my car round back and open the boot."

I held up my hands. "Whoa. No one's putting anyone in the trunk of their car. There's a '*but*' to all that 'move a body' stuff. I *would* help move a body, but we shouldn't move this one. You're innocent. The longer we wait to call the cops, the worse this looks."

"Not if they never find out," Renee said.

"If we hide what happened," I countered, "in addition to endangering ourselves, we're doing a huge favor for Graham's killer."

Sonya nodded reluctantly and looked at Renee. "Dee has a point. *Someone* killed him. That person shouldn't get away with it. Even Graham Ulrich deserves justice."

"Fine," Renee said, casting a vinegary glance at the box.

I took out my phone and held it up. "Last chance to convince me I'm wrong."

Renee sighed and looked at Sonya. "When they pin this on us, I suppose you and I can share a bunk like in *Orange Is the New Black*. Now that program, I actually like."

CHAPTER 17

I sat on one of the built-in benches in the brewery's main room, across from a very tired-looking Calvin Capone. He'd finished taking Sonya and Renee's statements, saving my interview for last. We'd gone through the timeline backward and forward—the last times I'd seen Renee, Ulrich, and Sonya prior to that night, Sonya's previous relationship with Renee, Renee's phone call summoning me to the scene. Capone was noticeably less relaxed than he'd been in the aftermath of Ronnie Wong's death. I supposed this time the situation was clearly serious right from the get-go. Not much chance that Ulrich accidentally bumped his head and sealed himself into a cardboard box.

"You let Renee and Sonya go," I observed, when I'd finished describing again the events that led up to calling the police. "Does that mean you think they're innocent?"

He reached into his briefcase and held up a U.K. passport. "Renee's," he said. "To be sure she stays where we can reach her. And I know where to find Sonya."

"I can't believe you'd suspect Sonya."

"You told me yourself that her last words to you before she left were that if she ran into Ulrich and he tried to mess with her, he would 'get what's coming to him.'"

I crossed my arms over my chest. "But she obviously

didn't mean *killing* him. This is Sonya we're talking about. I can't even count the number of times she's *kept* me from murdering someone I was mad at. She's a lover, not a fighter. I guess I should know by now that you always suspect everyone." I couldn't control the pinch of bitterness in my voice. I'd just about managed to forget what it was like being in the crosshairs of one of Capone's investigations. With the Juice Revolution case, I'd almost come to feel like he and I were on the same team, that maybe we were growing closer. Now here I was, across the table from him, physically and metaphorically.

"Another word for 'suspicion' is 'keeping an open mind,'" he said.

"That's four words."

He glared at me. "Delilah, are you trying to tell me you *don't* suspect Renee? She had motive, means, opportunity. She could easily have engineered a scenario where Sonya was with her when she 'discovered' her husband's body to help with her alibi. You said yourself she didn't seem especially distraught that Ulrich was dead. I'm not the only suspicious one." He pointed to himself. "Kettle." He pointed to me. "Pot."

"Graham Ulrich had a million enemies," I said. "*You* just had a run-in with him the other night. Are *you* a suspect?"

"You're pretty good at this, you know," he said, pressing his index fingers into the inner corners of his eyes.

"Police investigations?"

"No, making my life hell. Because I let myself get drawn into your feud with Graham Ulrich, I'll have to have an unpleasant conversation with the chief about all of that. He could take me off the case if he thinks it's a conflict of interest."

"You didn't have a choice," I said.

"Look, I stand by my actions with Ulrich one hundred percent. He was threatening you, and I acted accordingly to keep the peace. But I don't like the possibility of having to let someone else handle this case. The murder of a TV chef is going to be big news. It's a lot of pressure for a small department. I've dealt with this kind of thing before when I was in Chicago, but most of my colleagues haven't. Not to show off, but I was brought here to beef up the department's major-crimes division. Geneva Bay doesn't exactly have a deep bench when it comes to murder investigations."

I followed his gaze across the room, where Stanhope was stringing crime scene tape across the room where Ulrich's body had been found. As he looked around for something to secure it to, the roll slipped from his pudgy fingers. It bowled across the floor, leaving a trailing ribbon of yellow tape in its wake. As he scuttled after it, arms flapping by his sides, his resemblance to an emperor penguin was uncanny.

"I hear what you're saying, but would getting taken off this case be the worst thing in the world?" I asked. "You've already got your hands full with the Juice Revolution thing."

"Speaking of which," Capone said, "tell me more about Frates's visit to your restaurant. Sorry I couldn't come and take your statement myself. A lot has been going on."

"You can say that again," I agreed ruefully. "There's not much more to tell. He didn't do anything. Just sat there creeping everybody out."

"Still, I don't like the sound of it." Capone's face darkened.

"Weird, right?"

"More than weird. Do you know how many murders Geneva Bay sees in an average year?"

"Ten?" I guessed.

"Zero. Until recently, it had been three years since there'd been a murder. There are plenty of crimes—drug rings, organized crime, gangs of burglars who target empty houses when the owners are away off-season. But to have two suspicious deaths in less than a week, plus whatever hospitalized Jordan Watts? Something's going on."

"The buildings," I said. "There were three buildings in that trust that Rocco's accountant created—Juice Revolution's, mine, and this one—and two of them have ended up with dead bodies in them. That's got to be the connection. Frates was there when Wong died and when Jordan's smoothie was made. His fingerprints were on the note. Then he comes to my restaurant. He didn't do anything outright, but his message wasn't subtle. He wanted us to know he was there, watching. There's nothing to tie him here, but it doesn't take much to connect the dots between a violent felon getting released from prison and the fact that dead bodies are suddenly popping up left, right, and center."

"There are other connections between the buildings," Capone said. "You, for example."

"Me?" I sputtered.

"You were at Juice Revolution on the day Wong died. You were here, not once, but twice, on the day Ulrich's body was found, and you're obviously at Delilah & Son every day."

"What about Ulrich? He was at my place and here, too, obviously."

Capone smirked. "You think Ulrich killed himself? Sealed his own dead body in a box?" He let out a low whistle. "Houdini's got nothing on Graham Ulrich."

"I'm not saying that Ulrich did it. Just that all this

started when he showed up in town." I thought back to my conversation with Sam. "You know how you said there are zero murders in an average year in Geneva Bay? Could it be that there have always been murders, but the police missed them? Take Wong's death, for example. If you hadn't believed that something was fishy, he'd be tucked safely in his casket and no one would be the wiser. Or the break-ins here and at Delilah & Son. If the cops file it under 'Just some rowdy kids' it never gets investigated as anything more."

"Interesting theory," Capone said. "Where are you going with this?

"We can't look at these things as a series of isolated incidents. There must be a connection. Clearly the buildings are connected, but buildings don't commit murder. There was someone else besides Frates who's been hanging around all three buildings—Harold Heyer."

CHAPTER 18

By the time I finished filling Capone in on the limited backstory I had about Jordan and Harold, the clock was ticking toward eleven. I wanted nothing more than to go home and collapse into my bed. Capone promised to look into the lead about Harold Heyer's possible involvement, although I suspected that it wasn't at the top of his to-do list, given that he'd just been handed a giant box of dead celebrity to deal with.

I groaned when I looked at my phone and saw a series of texts from Melody. Apparently the gravel road on her farm was taking longer to repair than she thought, and she was still trapped there.

Seeing that the most recent text had been sent only a few minutes earlier, I dialed her number. "Any chance you can get back tonight?" I asked.

Given how I'd left things with my aunt, the prospect of having to go back over to Biz's to look in on her again was not appealing. One of the key benefits of the current living arrangement was that I could take some space from my aunt, guilt-free, when I needed to, knowing that Melody would see to her needs.

"The track is in pretty bad shape still," Melody replied. "Lots of muddy spots and potholes where it washed out.

Mac doesn't want to risk it in her new car, and my uncle doesn't want to lend me his truck in case he needs it."

"I'll come and pick you up," I said, climbing behind the wheel of my car. "The Jeep can handle the road, I'm sure."

"Oh, chef, that would be awesome, but I don't want to put you to any trouble," she said. "It's already so late."

"You'd be doing me a favor," I said.

The compact downtown of Geneva Bay quickly gave way to a thin ring of suburban sprawl. Within minutes, I was cruising north along a mostly empty stretch of Highway 12, and bumping down the pitch-dark county road that led through corn and soybean fields to Melody and Mac's family farm. I rolled down the window. The worst of the weather seemed to have passed, but the atmosphere still felt unsettled, like another storm could kick off any minute. Although the farm was only thirty miles outside town, Geneva Bay's glitzy mansions and trendy boutiques felt like they might as well be on another planet.

A worn wooden Schacht Farm sign marked the entrance to the family's acreage. From the road, I could just make out a white two-story farmhouse, a sprawling dairy barn, and two storage silos in the distance. I hadn't seen a single other car for the final ten minutes of the journey, so I was surprised when the headlights of a pickup leaving the farm came into view. The truck reached the turnoff ahead of me and pulled onto the road, heading in the opposite direction.

I headed down the track, unsure who would be leaving the Schacht farm at this time of night. Within seconds, my Jeep was lurching and groaning down the rutted gravel track, moving toward the farmhouse and barn. I'd chosen the Wrangler for its sporty good looks back when

I was still a city dweller, and was pleased to put its practical side through the paces off-road. It was a bonus, like discovering that your hot date also had a good sense of humor. I pulled into the yard next to an aluminum-sided shed, where a mounted light pole cast a circle of yellow illumination over the path between the barn and the house.

I hopped out of the Jeep. The smell of musty animals, wet grass, and fertilizer infused the air with an unmistakable tang of Midwestern farm. Piled against the side of the shed was the usual collection of random agrarian junk—used tires, broken-down feed bins, lengths of old hosepipe. That kind of essential clutter was one of the many reasons I could never be a farmer—even the most well-managed of farms could never be totally orderly. I turned to head toward the farmhouse, but stopped when I heard voices emerging from the direction of the barn. I rounded the corner of the shed to see Melody and Mac walking toward me, deep in conversation. They both wore muddy jeans and tall rubber boots, clearly having put in a hard day of farm labor.

By the tone of their voices, they appeared to be arguing, and they were so engrossed in their conversation that at first they seemed not to notice me.

"You have to tell them or I *will*," Melody said.

"Don't be so uptight. It's not hurting anybody," Mac replied. "Can't you just be happy for me?"

I let out a gentle cough and took a step forward, into the light.

"Thank you so much for coming, chef," Melody called, her voice devoid of its usual verve. Her eyes flitted around nervously.

"Hey, Delilah," Mac called, flashing her megawatt smile. Whatever their disagreement, it seemed to have affected Melody more than it affected Mac. Mac stretched her arms wide. "Welcome to America's Dairyland, or whatever it says on the tourist brochures." She gestured to their filthy clothes. "Majestic, isn't it?"

"Who was that, leaving at this hour?" I asked, pointing in the direction the pickup truck had taken.

"The vet. Two of the yearling heifers are sick," Melody explained. Two parallel worry lines creased the space between her eyes. "My uncle is in the barn with them."

Mac put her hands on her hips and looked back toward the barn. "It's like the friggin' Biblical plagues around here," she said. "First floods and now the cows are ADR."

"ADR?" I asked. I had a lot of experience with cows in their steak and ground beef forms, but I was definitely a city slicker when it came to actual livestock.

"Ain't doin' right," Mac flashed a dry smile. "It's the cow version of 'under the weather.'"

"The vet thinks they got into some jimson weed," Melody said. "We moved them from their usual pasture because of the flooding. The spot where we were holding them while we repaired the fences had some jimson weed growing."

"Jimson weed?"

"Yeah," Melody explained. "It's a flower that grows wild around here. Usually animals won't eat it because they don't like the taste, but sometimes their feed gets contaminated with it or, if they're in poor pasture, they'll experiment with it. Ordinarily, we're careful to clear it from anywhere the cows might get to, but in all the commotion, nobody checked the field. Anyway, if they eat too much of it, they get sick."

Underscoring the point, a series of irritated *moos* emanated from the barn.

"Is it deadly?" I asked.

"It can be, but it usually just makes them bloated and

restless," Melody said. "The vet said they'll be all right. They can't have eaten much. My uncle wanted to be sure that it wasn't something more serious."

"We used to call it 'redneck crack,' do you remember?" Mac said, playfully elbowing her cousin's ribs. "The kids from Deer Creek used to smoke it."

Melody's face showed no signs of amusement. "Just the kids from Deer Creek?"

Mac rolled her eyes, seemingly exasperated with her cousin's reproach. "I tried it, like, once when I was fourteen," she explained. "I got high for a nanosecond and then felt like absolute garbage the rest of the night. I thought my heart was going to bounce out of my chest. Ended up puking into my favorite purse."

"I remember you thought mushrooms were growing out of the walls of our room," Melody said. Her tone indicated that her memory of the event didn't have the same "good old days" gloss as her cousin's. "You almost peeled the wallpaper off. You hallucinated all night that babies were crying."

Mac shot me a comic look, as if to say *Can you believe this goody-goody?* To Melody, she said, "It was ten years ago."

"I was eleven and I didn't know what to do."

"Well, what you can do now is thank me for your own personal 'This is your brain on drugs' public service message," Mac said lightly. "You learned there are better ways to get your kicks than smoking some random plant, and I learned the importance of moderation." She yawned. "I'm bushed, kiddos. I've gotta hit the sack. I'm so glad I've only got a few more weeks of being Franny Farm Girl."

"You're moving out?" I asked.

She nodded. "Yep, just put first and last months' rent down on an apartment in town. I'm counting the days until I can get out of here." She yawned again, and then threw her arms around Melody. "I'll see you in a few days, cuz. I'm going to bed." Melody stiffened in her cousin's embrace, and murmured a feeble "Bye." We followed Mac with our eyes as she walked toward the weather-worn farmhouse.

"Brand-new car and brand-new apartment," I observed. "Big changes in store for Molly McClintock."

Melody stared after Mac, not replying. We stood for a moment, listening to the nighttime sounds of the farm—the chirp of crickets and the wind blowing through the fields.

"You don't have to stay with Biz, you know," I said. "If you'd prefer to live in town with Mac, we'd all understand. You're young, and you shouldn't be tied down taking care of an eighty-year-old."

"I'm happy where I am," she snapped. "Besides, I can't afford Mac's rent."

"How exactly can *she* afford it?" I asked.

"She came into some money," Melody mumbled. Before I could ask a follow-up question, she dusted off the thighs of her jeans and said, "I'm sorry about all this mess. I don't want to get your car dirty. Do you want to come in for a cup of tea while I get changed and grab my stuff?"

"No, I'll wait out here," I said. "I have a phone call to make."

My mind whirred. It seemed that Mac had suddenly and inexplicably come into money. She had experience with, and easy access to, a poisonous plant. Something was going on underneath her easygoing, All-American-girl façade. I waited until Melody moved out of sight and then dialed. Capone picked up on the first ring.

"What's up?" he asked, his voice weary.

"I need you to ask the state lab to run a test on the smoothie sample and Wong's blood. Tell them to test for jimson weed."

CHAPTER 19

A huge pink orb of sunshine peaked over the tops of the evergreens that lined the parking lot of the Grand Bay Resort and Spa. Schmooze-fests weren't my natural habitat, but I was actually looking forward to the monthly Visitors Bureau Small Business breakfast. In the two weeks since I'd shared my suspicions about the source of the poison with Capone, southeast Wisconsin had enjoyed a glorious run of weather, and I'd been up to my elbows at the restaurant trying to keep up with the hectic high-season pace. Wong's and Ulrich's deaths had been pushed to the back of my mind. The breakfast would be my chance to catch up on the scuttlebutt around town.

Despite the giant cloud of uncertainty swirling around us all, life for the Delilah & Son crew had mostly returned to normal. Sonya, thankfully, no longer seemed to be a prime suspect in Ulrich's murder. The coroner pinpointed the time of death to the evening before the body was found. Sonya was working at the restaurant that entire night, surrounded by witnesses, and had then accompanied me to Biz's. We all vouched for her alibi, although Capone double-checked our security cameras, too. *Keeping an open mind*, as he called it.

Frustratingly, the state lab still hadn't finished running

the tests on the smoothie sample or Wong's blood and tissue. Was it poison or wasn't it? Had my hunch about Mac and the jimson weed been right? The whole thing had dragged on for so long it was starting to feel like I'd imagined it all. Besides which, Wong's death had been heavily overshadowed by Ulrich's. Reporters descended on Geneva Bay the minute the news broke, and they showed no signs of leaving.

I heard through the grapevine that the chief of police was overseeing the Ulrich investigation due to its "high profile nature." I suspected it might ostensibly have something to do with Capone's previous run-in with the dead man, but that the real reason might be so that the chief could front the press briefings about the death of the famous chef. Whatever investigating was going on with that or the Juice Revolution inquiry, it was all happening very much under the radar. No arrests, no search warrants, and as far as I knew, no suspects brought in for questioning.

Sam kept me updated on Jordan's recovery, and I knew she was planning to reopen Juice Revolution that weekend, in time for the Labor Day Festivities and the Taste of Wisconsin contest. I was hoping she'd be at the breakfast, and I'd have the opportunity for a private word with her to share my suspicion that Mac could be the source of the poison. There hadn't really been an elegant way to convey the message "I think one of your girlfriend's employees might be trying to murder her" through my text message exchange with Sam.

The main lodge of the resort, despite housing two restaurants, a café, a bar, and several meeting and event rooms, was low-slung, the understated Prairie-style architecture concealing its vast scale. Near the main door, two satellite trucks were parked, looking out of place in a lot full of Audis and Benzes. Luckily none of the news crews that were lurking around town had ferreted out Sonya's close connection to the crime yet, but the possibility was causing her tremendous strain. I sighed. At least they were contributing to the town's economy, paying top-dollar rates for the few available rooms to be had over Labor Day.

I walked through the lobby, passing under the amber-colored arts-and-crafts chandeliers, and up the central staircase, taking my spot in the buffet line in the already busy banquet room. I greeted the fellow small business owners I'd come to know and filled my plate with the resort's signature offerings: a Brussels sprouts hash made with apple, sweet potato, and smoked bacon, alongside brioche French toast topped with vanilla bean custard and fresh berry compote. The resort's stellar menu made the monthly hobnobbing get-togethers more palatable, literally.

I saw Jordan move through the crowd and take a seat. A dark little corner of my soul had been hoping she'd look a little worse for the wear after her ordeal. Maybe some stress-related baldness or a bout of full-body acne. No such luck. Her dark bronze complexion was as flawless as ever, and her choppy bob hairdo didn't seem the least bit threadbare. *You're supposed to be trying to protect her from potential danger,* I reminded myself, *not wishing a pox upon her house.* I spotted an empty seat at her table and slipped into it just as Harold Heyer rose to walk toward the podium.

"I hope he's finally going to tell us where our booths are," grumbled a man I recognized as Bert, the owner of Bert's Burger Barn.

"His plate's been full with all this Ulrich stuff," the poofy-haired salon owner next to him said—Margie

Carson, maybe? Or Marti Larson? I'd met her at least half a dozen times. Networking really wasn't my forte.

"He wouldn't even have this job if it weren't for his father," Bert continued. "Just because his dad owned a department store and was everybody's best friend, now Harold gets a lifetime appointment to the Chamber? Ollie Heyer wasn't exactly an ace businessman. His store folded like the cheap suits he sold."

The salon owner sat back in her chair and crossed her arms under her breasts. The line of her cleavage rose up to her neck like an overheating thermometer gauge. "I won't hear a single bad word about Ollie, God rest his soul. What happened to that store was a tragedy. And I've never met anyone so dedicated to this town as little Harold. Have you? He eats, sleeps, and breathes Geneva Bay. He worked hard to get the job, and he works his tail off to keep things running."

Shut down, Bert turned back to his plate and moodily shoveled a forkful of eggs into his mouth. Jordan, I noticed, remained quietly watchful, following Harold's movements with wary eyes. I also noticed that she wasn't eating anything and had brought her own coffee in a to-go cup. Harold, meanwhile, lowered the microphone to his height and cleared his throat. The room's chatter failed to decrease by one iota.

"Ahem," he tried again. When that, too, failed to gain the group's attention, he clinked his water glass with a fork, his face reddening. "Everybody listen to me!"

The room fell silent.

"Sorry, I didn't mean to shout," he said, looking as if his outburst had surprised even himself. I watched him closely. It was rare to see him as anything other than insistently chipper. Was the attitude shift caused by the stress of the upcoming event and Ulrich's sudden death, or was it a sinister peek into his true character?

"Sorry," Harold said again. "I've got an important announcement. As you know, we're three days away from our Taste of Wisconsin contest. Despite the unfortunate circumstances, we're going ahead as planned. I'm glad so many of our participating restauranteurs have joined us this morning." He clicked a remote to turn on the room's AV system and brought up an overhead view of the town's lakefront park, showing labeled squares that depicted where our assigned booths would be located.

"Here are the booth placements," he said. "Paper copies will be available on the table by the door. I'm sorry to be getting these to you so late."

Seeing Delilah & Son's placement—a prime spot at the intersection of the main path in and out of the venue— gave me less joy than I imagined it would. Juice Revolution would be in the tent next to ours. The exposure would be great, but even with Ulrich out of the picture, I still wasn't convinced we had a viable contest entry. I'd continued to refine the bratwurst pizza over the past few weeks, but it still didn't scream *Winner!* quite as loud as I wanted it to.

Bert's hand shot up. "Who'd you get to replace Graham Ulrich?"

"I've looked high and low, but at this late notice, we haven't been able to get another celebrity judge," Harold said. "One of you was kind enough to suggest that *I* might be an appropriate substitute." He dipped his chin demurely. "Since of course I adore all your fine establishments equally and just want what's best for our town, you can rely on my impartiality. Of course, I'm honored at the suggestion, but stepping into the shoes of someone

of Graham Ulrich's stature would be a tall order for me."
Harold's unintentional height-related humor almost made
me choke on a Brussels sprout. I wished Sonya could be
there. "I wanted to see how you all felt about the idea. Can
we have a show of hands? All in favor of your humble ser-
vant Harold Heyer judging the contest, please raise your
hands."

I looked around the room. Some arms shot up, but most
rose into the air with painful slowness, like plant shoots
struggling toward the sun. What were we supposed to do?
Say no, and then have the man who controlled our fate
know that we'd publicly opposed his appointment as contest judge? I raised my own hand and plastered a smile
on my face.

Harold clutched his chest. "You are all too, too kind.
A unanimous vote. I promise I will make Geneva Bay
proud."

After Harold's self-coronation as the contest judge and
some routine Chamber business, there was a brief pause
to allow everyone time to eat and socialize before the
main program began. This month's guest presenter was a
retired second-string lineman from the Green Bay Packers, sharing "Lessons from the End Zone: Using the Winner's Mindset to Tackle Small-Business Challenges."

I scooted my chair closer to Jordan, intending to broach
the subject of Juice Revolution's reopening, and the small
matter of Mac possibly poisoning her. Despite Jordan's radiant skin and glossy hair, in that moment I pitied her.
Someone close to her had tried to kill her. What must that
kind of mistrust and suspicion feel like?

"He's really something, isn't he?" she said, tipping her
head toward Harold and rolling her eyes. "You know I'm
the one who suggested that he judge the contest? But I
meant it as a joke. He was freaking out about not being

able to get anyone, and I was like, at this point, we just need a warm body, so why don't you do it? He's so oblivious I guess he took it seriously."

"Sam said . . ." I began, looking around to make sure no one was listening in. "Are you and Harold on good terms?"

She pressed her eyes closed briefly. "Sam told me about his conversation with you. He blew what I said way out of proportion. Harold is harmless, just a nuisance."

"But I thought you left the country because of him," I said.

"Indirectly, I suppose," she conceded. "I left because I'd been working for Heyers Department Store while I was still in high school, and stayed after I graduated. The store went bankrupt, so I was out of a job. I wasn't all that heartbroken about it, to be honest. It was a good job, but botanical wellness and holistic nutrition have always been my passion, and leaving freed me to pursue those interests. Anyway, around that same time, I broke up with my high school boyfriend. Harold always had a thing for me, and after the store tanked, he kind of fell apart. His great-grandfather had founded that place, and he'd always expected to inherit it. There were accusations that Ollie Heyer had embezzled from the company, or at the minimum mismanaged it into the ground. Harold started leaning on me for emotional support. It got to be suffocating."

"So you didn't tell Sam that Harold was starting to creep you out again, like he did back then?" I asked.

"I don't know what words I used. But, yeah, I guess Harold had started to get a little too close for comfort. He's backed off, though," she said.

"Did you say something to him? Or maybe Sam had a word?" I pressed.

She let out a sputtering laugh. "Sam? Can you imagine him threatening someone? No, I just made it clear as crystal that Sam and I are a serious item and nothing is going to change that."

You certainly did, I thought bitterly. Out loud, I said, "I'm glad you're recovered. You're looking well."

She blew air out of her lips. "I lost twelve pounds, but as diets go, I wouldn't recommend it. Thank god I was in top shape going into that whole ordeal, or who knows what might've happened. We really appreciate you stepping in and helping with Butterball." She gestured to the projected image of the tent placements on the screen. "Looks like we'll be neighbors."

I nodded and flashed a tight smile. "Game on."

"Always," she smirked. "Actually, I'm glad we have this chance to chat. There's something I wanted to talk to you about." She lowered her voice. "You know you can always ask Sam and me for money if you need to, right? Sam said he thought you were struggling. He still worries about you, you know."

She squeezed my hand briefly and then let go. She might as well have punched me in the throat.

"He's been more than generous," I replied, my voice so brittle I felt like my words were shattering in my mouth.

"He said you'd be too proud to take it, but I thought I'd try," she replied with a sympathetic nod. "I made my own money, too. I respect that kind of independence."

Before I could reply, a pair of energetic fiftysomethings bustled in and took the two empty seats on the far side of Jordan. I recognized them as Tripp and Honey, the proprietors of one of the historic B and Bs in downtown Geneva Bay. Renee was staying with them, and I'd heard from Sonya that they'd provided Renee with her alibi for the night of Ulrich's murder.

"I'm sorry we're late," Tripp said, taking a sip from the water glass at his place. He sported a heavy jawline and teeth so gigantic they reminded me of mahjong tiles.

"Well, I'd say we have a pretty darn good excuse," Honey replied, patting a shiny black hairstyle that bore an uncanny resemblance to a German motorcycle helmet.

Jordan cocked an eyebrow. "Traffic?"

"I wish," Tripp said. "Three police officers knocked on our door in the early hours and brought Renee Kessler in for questioning."

"Who?" Bert asked, joining the conversation.

"Geez, Bert, do you live under a rock?" Whatshername the salon owner said. "You know, Graham Ulrich's ex-wife?"

"Questioned about his murder," Honey clarified. "She's been staying with us while she works on a project in town. The cops barely gave her time to change out of her pajamas."

"Why are they bringing her in for questioning? I thought you two were Renee's alibi?" I sputtered, too shocked to keep my composure. When my statement was met with perplexed stares, I explained, "My friend used to date Renee. She told me."

"Oh, yes, Sonya. She's been by a few times to visit with Renee. She's a sweetheart. She should stay a mile away from Renee, though. That woman's trouble," Honey said.

"But what happened to Renee's alibi? Didn't you tell the police she was there the whole time on the evening of the murder?" I asked.

"Yes, except when she ran out to pick up some dinner around eight thirty or nine," Tripp said.

"We told the police all of that," Honey interjected, pointing at her husband with a gumball pink fingernail.

Tripp nodded. "She couldn't have been gone for more

than forty-five minutes. I was baking a sour cream coffee cake for the next morning's breakfast and I had a timer set. I saw Renee through the kitchen window when I put it in the oven, and she was back before I took it out. Other than that, she was in her room or the guest lounge all night. Forty-five minutes didn't seem like enough time to kill someone."

"We told them that, too," Honey added.

"To kill someone, and also pick up sushi. She had the food with her," Tripp clarified. "But when Honey and I were talking about it just now, forty-five minutes is also a long time just to pick up sushi. Wok n' Roll is only a ten-minute drive from the B and B."

"I can't believe we've had a killer under our roof for almost a month," Honey said, fanning herself with a folded napkin.

I rose so quickly I rattled the dishware on the table.

"You're leaving?" Jordan asked.

"You'll miss the presentation," Honey said.

I barely heard them. I definitely had challenges, but no thirty-minute inspirational seminar was going to help me tackle them.

CHAPTER 20

The clock hadn't even hit eleven a.m. and already the day felt like it had been going for about a century.

"This is very kind of you," Renee said. She wrapped a towel around her wet hair, turban style, and slumped onto the couch in my apartment. "I feel miles better after a shower."

Sonya found out about Renee's predicament shortly after she was taken to the station, and by the time I left the Chamber breakfast, she had already sent up the Bat-Signal to her family of lawyers. As luck would have it, her uncle Avi was staying at his friend's fishing cabin a stone's throw away, and responded to the call, stepping in to represent Renee during the police interview. The three of them had just come from the station, where Renee had been released after questioning, to regroup before deciding next steps.

Sonya pressed a cup of black tea into Renee's hands, which the other woman took hold of with a white-knuckled grip.

"You're a saint," she said, downing half of it in one gulp. "Oh, and you even remembered to add a splash of milk. Honestly, Mother Theresa, eat your heart out," she called to the ceiling. "Sonya runs absolute rings around you in the benevolence department."

"Do you want to lie down for a little while?" Sonya suggested. Turning to me, she asked, "She can camp out here for a bit, right, Dee?"

"Of course," I replied.

On the way back from the station, they drove past Tripp and Honey's B and B and found it encircled by news crews. Since Renee had been awakened in the wee hours and hustled out of the house without breakfast or a shower, she was in need of a place to lie low until she was ready to face the media scrum.

"That would be pure heaven, if it's really all right with you," Renee said with a grateful sigh. "Once I've had a bit of a lie down, I can buck myself up and face those vultures." Butterball leapt onto the couch to join her, no doubt enticed by the prospect of a napping buddy. He nuzzled his face into her hip, and she reached out to stroke him.

"Aren't you a lovey?" Renee crooned. "Graham and I had a Siamese when we were first married. Stroppy old cow she was, but I loved her all the same."

"We'll just be downstairs if you need anything," Sonya said, leaning over to give Renee a gentle kiss on the forehead. She pulled a waffle-knit blanket from the back of the side chair and spread it over Renee's legs, taking care not to disturb Butterball. When I'd quizzed Sonya, she told me that she and Renee weren't officially back together, but they certainly seemed headed in that direction. I wondered if Renee knew how lucky she was. If I needed TLC, there was no one I'd rather have by my side than Sonya. She took mother-henning to the next level.

Sonya and I headed downstairs, joining her uncle Avi at a four-top in the restaurant's dining room. He'd rushed to Geneva Bay from his fishing trip, still wearing deck shoes, a floppy canvas hat, and sunglasses. As we sat down, he removed the sunglasses and set them on the table with a disgusted look.

"Damn things. I forgot to grab my regular glasses, so I had to wear these in that interrogation. I looked like a beatnik. But they're prescription and I'm blind as a one-eyed bat without 'em, so what am I going to do?" He lifted shoulders and eyes to the sky, as if asking the universe for alternative suggestions. None seemed to be forthcoming, so he continued, "Hopefully the cops thought I was playing it cool like one of those Vegas poker players." He set his hat next to the sunglasses, unveiling a mass of unruly white frizz.

"So?" Sonya asked.

"What has she told you about the interrogation?" Avi asked.

"Nothing. I didn't want to give her the third degree, after she just spent all morning in the hot seat," Sonya said. "She said you'd fill me in."

Uncle Avi reached across and squeezed Sonya's wrist. "It's not too good for your lady friend, chickadee."

"The B and B owners gave her an alibi, though. She was in the downstairs lounge the whole night reading and then she went out to pick up some food. She had a time-stamped credit card receipt and the restaurant people vouched for her, too," Sonya said, desperately trying to plead Renee's case. As if we were the ones who needed to be convinced.

"Here's how it is. The coppers were able to get Graham Ulrich's phone unlocked," Avi said. "There was a text from Miss Kessler on it, agreeing to meet him at the brewery on the night he was killed. She never told the cops about that."

Sonya's face somehow managed to grow even paler under its coating of ivory face powder. "She didn't tell me, either."

Avi's bushy eyebrow rose. "Interesting."

Recovering, Sonya said, "One text isn't proof."

"Right," I cut in. "Text or no, she still has an alibi. What changed?"

"Well, security cameras from near the building site caught her car driving past just before nine, around the time the medical examiner said her ex was killed. The same cameras also caught images of Ulrich walking from his hotel to the building site not too long before she drove by, presumably for their rendezvous. They put it to her, and she admitted she went to meet him at the site, but said that Ulrich never showed up. She said she didn't even get out of her car, just saw he wasn't there and skedaddled. Went and picked up her unagi roll."

Sonya inhaled sharply. "Geez, I bet he was inside getting murdered right then. His killer was probably inside with him."

"She didn't see anything strange?" I asked. "No other cars in the parking lot?"

"Not a one. Ulrich was staying not too far from there, so he apparently walked. Miss Kessler didn't check the doors or go looking around for him inside the building. Ulrich would've had no way of getting inside. He didn't have a key."

"Why did she order dinner if she was planning on meeting him? That screams manufactured alibi," I said, thinking aloud.

"I always said you were a sharp one." Turning to Sonya, he added. "Didn't I always say that, chickadee?" In reply, Sonya shot him an impatient glare.

Avi lowered his voice to a confidential tone. "You ever

want a job as a case investigator, you call me, kiddo." His eyes twinkled as he chuffed me on the shoulder. "And you bear in mind that my son Seth's divorce was recently finalized. He's a lawyer, you know. Very successful. Nice condo on the Gold Coast with views of Lake Michigan."

Sonya scowled. "Uncle Avi!"

Avi held his up palms and leaned back in his chair. "All right, all right. Excuse me for wanting to see your cousin happy with your smart, pretty friend who's also a great cook." He cleared his throat. "Miss Kessler said she only planned on staying for a second, just to instruct Ulrich in no uncertain terms about what he could do with himself and the horse he rode in on. When he didn't show, she figured he was just wasting her time, or he decided he had more important things to do."

"He always did that kind of thing," Sonya huffed, pushing her coffee mug away with a look of contempt. "He'd call a staff meeting and then be thirty minutes late or just not show up. Some kind of power trip to show his time was more important than everyone else's."

"Right," Avi said. "I see it all the time with my corporate clients. I tell them, you show up when you want, these hours are all billable. And suddenly they learn how to tell time. Anyway, he wasn't there and so she went and picked up her dinner and went back to the B and B. That's what she told the cops."

"Why did you let her talk?" Sonya said. "You named your dog Miranda, for god's sake. The only dog in existence named after a constitutional procedure. You always told me not to answer questions if I ever got arrested."

He threw up his hands. "So I'm supposed to tackle your lady friend and stuff a gag in her mouth? I told her to shut her yapper. She didn't listen to me. Just like your aunt Ruthie, or little Miranda for that matter. She ate a full tube of your aunt's red lipstick, did your mom tell you? Now I gotta buy new carpet for the rumpus room."

Sonya pressed her palms into the tabletop and let out an impatient groan.

"Why didn't Renee tell the cops about the meeting when they questioned her after the break-in?" I asked, trying to get the train back on track. "Not saying anything then must've looked to them like she was hiding something."

"It's not her fault," Sonya cut in.

"I appreciate your loyalty, chickadee, but Miss Kessler isn't doing you or herself any favors here," Avi said. "You're lucky you listened to Delilah instead of her about that whack-a-doodle idea with hiding the body." He looked at me. "Were they really going to hide the body?"

I grimaced and put up my hands. I thought reason probably would've prevailed, but I couldn't be sure what would've happened if I hadn't come on the scene when I did.

"Renee was scared," Sonya interjected. "She panicked."

Avi squinted at her. "There's panic, and then there's a class 6 felony and making my niece an accessory after the fact. I'm all for being judicious with what my clients share with law enforcement, but I draw the line at encouraging them to toss some poor schmo's corpse into the trunk of a rental car."

"He wasn't some poor schmo. He was an epic jerk," Sonya said.

"Schmo or no, every person deserves a little dignity in death," Avi replied. His tone was mild, but the reproach was evident.

Sonya cast her heavily lashed eyes down at the table. "I was only trying to help Renee."

Avi addressed me as he pointed his thumb at Sonya. "This one. Did you know when she was a kid, she'd refuse to pick flowers because she was afraid she'd hurt them? And don't get me started with all the half-dead pigeons she tried to drag home or, worse, the hard-luck cases she's dated." He reached out and put his hand over Sonya's. "Your aunt Ruthie and I worry about you, kiddo. It doesn't bother you that this lady friend of yours was willing to lie to the cops and drag you into all this mess?"

"What happened with Ulrich—the affair—was as much my fault as hers," Sonya said quietly.

"You weren't married to him," I pointed out. "You didn't take a vow."

"No, but I know right from wrong. I feel like his death is my fault, too. I killed him a million times in my head." Her voice cracked with emotion. "He was so awful to her. I mean, I know he was awful to everyone, but to her especially. Always putting her down. Someone had to be there for her. To tell her she looked pretty. That she's talented."

The room fell quiet. I looked at Sonya, with her sleek hair and pristine mask of bombshell makeup. I knew her look was born as much out of self-consciousness as self-expression. A brilliant chef, she'd never been able to muster the moxie to lead a kitchen. So much love to give, but always managing to find some ungrateful sinkhole of a partner to pour it into. I felt exactly the same protective instinct toward her as she seemed to feel toward Renee.

"I don't know where she gets that big heart of hers," Avi said with a mock eye roll. "Not from my side, I'll tell you that for free." He tapped his chest. "Lump of coal in here. Hard as a granite slab."

An affectionate look passed between uncle and niece.

"So why *did* Renee lie to the police?" I asked, anxious to know if Renee had indeed been hiding something. Otherwise, why would she have put herself and Sonya in this unnecessary jeopardy?

"She said she didn't mention it at the time because she didn't think the two things were related. She thought he was just messing around with her," Avi explained. "Even when somebody raised the possibility that Ulrich could've done the break-in, she didn't believe it, and besides, with Ulrich's public profile, she didn't want everyone knowing their business. And she didn't mention it after they found the body because she thought it would look bad for her." He paused and drummed his fingers on the edge of the table. "She was right."

"But the time still doesn't make sense," I said. "Tripp from the B and B was sure she was gone for almost exactly forty-five minutes. If we figure ten minutes each way getting to Wok n' Roll and back, and maybe five minutes inside to pay and collect her food, that leaves twenty minutes unaccounted for. Are they saying she lured Graham inside, whopped him on the head, and stuffed him into a box all in twenty minutes? It's enough time for a brief detour, like the one she admitted to, but not a murder."

"Exactly what I told them. Doing a murder and concealing the body all within twenty minutes? What was she, trying to set some kind of Guinness record?" Avi agreed.

"Plus, she's not very big," I added. "I've had to butcher sides of beef and pig carcasses. It takes muscle to maneuver a dead body."

"I made the same points myself to the officers," Avi replied. "I told them their case was thinner than my ten-year-old underpants. Mind you, they may have more evidence that they didn't share during questioning. That's how law enforcement normally operates. They'll bait the hook with some damning evidence to try to lure the suspect and get them to bite, but they're not going to give the whole game away."

The door to the kitchen creaked. Over Sonya's shoulder, I could see Melody peeking into the room. She raised her arm and pointed to her wrist. I shook my head and shooed her away with my hand. I knew our eleven-o'clock opening time was fast approaching, and the whole staff had crammed into the kitchen to give us privacy. Biz was directing prep, and Lord only knew if we'd be ready in time. I didn't want to rush our conversation, though, and didn't want to force Sonya into cooking if she didn't feel up to it.

"Who did the questioning?" I asked.

"Some smooth operator named Calvin Capone. Guy's a master of the Columbo technique—make the suspect comfortable and then close the trap. After almost fifty years of doing this kind of thing, I've seen a lot of cops, and let me tell you, this guy's good."

I'd been on the other side of Capone's questioning myself, and I knew just what Avi meant. At the end of ten minutes, I'd have been ready to spill the location of Jimmy Hoffa's body.

"Still," I argued, "bringing her in like that seems premature based on the evidence they had."

"I made a few calls to some old friends I have up here," he continued. "The scoop is that they're turning the screws because of all the media attention. The chief of police was pressuring Capone to get somebody in the slammer before the big Labor Day festival. Doesn't look good to tourists to have a murderer walking the streets."

Sonya bounced her knee up and down so fast it looked like she was trying to jackhammer a hole in the floor beneath her foot. "I can't believe they dragged her into the station like that. She's not a murderer."

Avi toggled his head from side to side, his hair billowing like a field of ripe cotton in the wind. "If you ask me, it's savvy. They got her to cough up information that she'd been holding back, which is good for the investigation. And, optics-wise, this lets them throw some red meat to the reporters without actually making an arrest. Probably bought Capone more time, too. Got the chief off his back."

A knock on the glass door that led to the parking lot commanded our attention. A couple stood outside. The man gestured to the Closed sign and then cupped his hands around his face to peer inside.

I looked at my watch. 11:02. "I'll tell them we're opening late," I said, rising from the table and starting toward the door.

Sonya raised a hand to stop me. "No. The whole team has been working on prep. We can eighty-six whatever they haven't finished and anything you don't think is up to scratch. Between us, we can do this."

"Are you sure? We're going to have to go like gangbusters to catch up," I said.

The man outside the door knocked again, and I raised one finger to let him know to wait.

"It's the Thursday before Labor Day and the weather is spectacular," Sonya said, her voice growing determined. "There's nothing else we can do right now. No sense in missing out on one of the biggest revenue generators of the year just so I can sit here and worry myself to death."

When I continued to hesitate, Avi said, "You heard the woman. She wants to cook." He leaned across the table and rested his hand briefly on Sonya's. "Best thing you can do for Miss Kessler is keep yourself busy. Get a knife in your hand and take your aggravation out on some unsuspecting vegetables. I'll be back later to talk to her. But right now," he said, donning his sunglasses, "I'm going back to the cabin to get my damn glasses."

CHAPTER 21

As I stepped out of the shower the next morning, Butterball awaited me, batting at one of my hair ties as if it had gotten between him and an extra-large can of sardines.

"Friday," I muttered, grabbing my towel from its hook.

I'd had another terrible night's sleep, and even a scalding hot shower hadn't managed to soothe my raw nerves.

The contest would be the following day. When I attended the Chamber breakfast the previous morning, I'd planned to pivot away from thinking about murders and toward figuring out how I was going to win. But with everything that had gone on since then, I hadn't been able to give it more than a passing thought. We'd gotten through service—Sonya pulled herself together like the seasoned pro she was, and between us, we cranked out pies nonstop for twelve hours. In the meantime, Avi took Renee back to his friend's fishing cabin, figuring that was a good place for her to lie low for the time being.

Now we were mere hours from the festival, and I still didn't feel confident in our bratwurst pizza entry. Nothing to do but push ahead. Sujeet and Big Dave had dropped off thousands of dollars' worth of pork brats the previous evening, huge quantities of baking soda were on hand to preboil our pretzel crusts, and a mountain of cheddar stood at the ready. It was too late to change direction.

Delilah & Son would be closing after lunch service to allow us time to stage our ingredients and test the portable ovens we'd rented for the occasion. The whole crew, minus Jarka, who would be staffing Juice Revolution's booth, would be working like demons for the next forty-eight hours. We needed to be a well-oiled machine to serve the thousand plus visitors who were expected to descend on the town's lakefront park.

While I brushed my teeth, Butterball crouched on the sink. Usually, he'd be fixated on pawing the water as it came out of the tap, but instead, his eyes were watchful, his posture tense. He lowered his tail, twitching it from side to side. He laid down, stood up, paced in a circle, and laid down again.

"What do you think, Butterbuns? Did we sleep poorly because you were feeding off my agitation or because I was feeding off yours?"

I gently cradled his face in one hand and ran my other hand over his head and neck, one of his favorite kitty massage techniques. There was definitely more padding around his shoulder blades and ribs. Then again, I'd recently had to move my bra to a looser hook. Maybe it was the stress. Butterball had a checkup and weigh-in scheduled at the vet at nine thirty. Since I was busy with contest prep, Sam agreed to take him and then drop him back off with me after the visit. What if he'd gained more weight? Would I be blamed?

I leaned on the edge of the sink and looked at myself in the mirror. It was about time to face facts—Sam and I had been doing this joint custody thing all summer, and Butterball still hadn't settled into the routine. He'd gone from a content creature, settled in his habits and secure in his routines, to a basket case, his behavior unpredictable, his mood turning on a dime. Sam had more time and a more flexible schedule than I did. Was I being selfish keeping my hold over our cat? I continued to stroke his head, watching his eyes blink hypnotically as he sunk into a purring trance.

"What should I do? Do you want to go and live with Sam and Jordan for good?" My voice quavered.

Butterball screeched, jumped to the floor, and ran to the kitchen.

"I'll take that as a no." I heard his food dish rattling. "Or maybe you're just hungry."

Clearly Butterball wasn't going to help me resolve my dilemma. What to do? My mind circled back to my last encounter with Jordan. With a sinking feeling, I realized that I'd rushed out of the Chamber breakfast the previous day and totally forgotten to tell her of my suspicions about Mac. Juice Revolution was set to reopen that morning and she hadn't been warned. I texted Sam, arranging to drop Butterball off at Juice Revolution at nine a.m. for his vet appointment. The clinic was just around the corner, so that would seem like a natural suggestion. I'd arrive early, which would give me a chance to corner Jordan alone.

As I set down my phone, a text from Melody flashed on the screen.

I think Biz stayed up all night, her text read. She made 5 loaves of zucchini bread & 8 quarts of stewed tomatoes. She pulled every vegetable out of the garden. I found her out there super early this morning, digging it all up.

I tapped out my reply. Does she seem okay?

Not really. She barely said 2 words to me yesterday or today.

My forehead creased. Could my aunt be developing dementia? It seemed impossible, and I certainly hadn't noticed any forgetfulness. But then how to explain the strange behaviors and the moodiness?

Another text from Melody appeared. Maybe she's mad at me for something??? I asked but she said to stop bothering her ☹

That wasn't like Biz. Even with her extra crotchetiness over the past few weeks, sweet, sensitive Melody had been spared her wrath. Melody had more than held up her end of the roommate bargain, and it wasn't fair to let her bear the brunt of whatever was going on with Biz.

I'll be right over, I replied. I thought for a moment and then added, I'll take her to Juice Revolution with me.

It was a busy day, and that would allow me to kill two birds with one stone. I needed to warn Jordan, and I needed to figure out once and for all what was going on with Biz.

My grand plan to have a heart to heart with Biz on the way to the smoothie bar was a resounding failure. I could tell from the moment I saw her that something was definitely off. Her permed white hair was tidily styled, and she wore her usual neat blouse and pants combo, but the muscles of her face were strung tighter than a loaded crossbow. She'd initially refused to leave her house, and then when I ultimately convinced her, my attempts to get her to open up to me backfired.

"Melody says you stayed up all night. Is something bothering you?" I asked. "I know you don't sleep when you're upset."

"You've got Melody spying on me?"

"She's worried about you. I am, too," I said. "You've

been snippy for weeks and doing weird things. Maybe we should make an appointment with your doctor. I'm worried that there could be something wrong."

"Like I'm losing my marbles?" she snapped. "Well, I'm not."

"Why don't you tell me what it is, then?" I demanded, slamming the palm of my hand on the steering wheel.

Silence.

Biz spent the remainder of the car ride staring out the window in a sulk. So much for killing two birds with one stone. I should've gotten Sonya to talk to Biz instead. My "add a lit stick of dynamite" communication style didn't suit this kind of conversation.

As Biz, Butterball, and I came in the door, Jarka called out in her thickly accented monotone, "Welcome to Juice Revolution, your local lifestyle juicery." The café seemed to be doing a brisk business, with Jarka and Mac barely able to take a moment to wave to us as we walked in. I settled Biz, along with Butterball's carrier, at an empty table. Biz crossed her arms and turned away from me like a petulant teenager.

"I'm going to find Jordan," I said.

I didn't even bother asking her if she wanted a drink, both because I was annoyed with her and because I didn't want her to accuse me of trying to poison her. Although right at that moment, that didn't seem like such a terrible idea.

I walked down the hallway past the bathrooms and knocked on the door marked Office.

"Come in," Jordan called. Seeing me, she broke into a wide smile. "Sam said you'd be stopping by with Butterball." She looked at the wall clock. "He's not here yet, though."

"I know I'm a little early. I actually wanted to speak with you," I said.

If she was surprised, she didn't show it. She sat behind an uncluttered maple table, working on a silver Mac laptop. A large potted ficus stood in one corner. Transom windows filtered the gentle, rosy morning light into the space. Her office reminded me of a dentist's waiting room—sleek, soothing, and reassuringly clinical. I thought of my own tiny closet of a work space in the restaurant's back corner. I did all my paperwork in my apartment, so we tended to use the extra room as overflow storage. Today, it was piled high with jars of pickled onions and crates of New Glarus beer.

"Pull up a chair," Jordan said. "How's Butterball doing?"

"About the same," I said. "He's moody."

"Sam's worried that he keeps gaining weight despite the diet. He's got him booked in with a veterinary nutrition specialist at the University of Wisconsin. I keep trying to tell him not to get so wrapped up in the number on the scale. Some of us are just destined to be more heavy set." She smiled. "Putting the right nutrients into your body is what matters, right?"

I leaned back in my chair, cradling my fleshy midsection. I did my best to return her smile. "Speaking of which," I said, "it looks like your business is booming. Lucky that no one was turned off by . . . what happened."

"There's still no proof that it was anything other than a weird coincidence. The notoriety probably helped business. Lord knows this town is full of busybodies who want to play amateur detective." She rolled her eyes. "Anyway, we were doing well before that, too. People want healthy choices," she said. "I'm glad we'll be able to put our offerings on full display at the contest tomorrow. It'll be nice to use local ingredients to show that Wisconsin isn't just sausage and cheese and beer, you know?"

Despite her butter-wouldn't-melt smile, I felt certain every one of her comments was aimed at me. A knot of anger formed in my stomach, and I had to muster all my self-control to keep myself from voicing the snarky retorts that were forming in my head. I was willing to admit that even smelling my brat and cheddar pizza could probably clog an artery. But to me, food was synonymous with pleasure and enjoyment. Surely, when it came down to taste, the cascade of umami flavors in the bratwurst pretzel pizza would win out over whatever combination of kefir, beets, and unpasteurized local farm dirt Jordan Watts could throw into a blender.

A knock sounded on the door, and Jarka walked in without waiting to be asked. Despite the stoic set to her jaw, her eyebrows pressed together in troubled line.

Jordan rose to standing, a look of concern spreading across her face.

"You said I should tell you if we get another one," Jarka said. She nodded toward me in greeting. "Hello, chef."

Jordan flashed a tight smile. "Delilah, would you mind giving us some privacy? Sam should be here in just a minute. Ask Mac to make you a drink. Anything you want. On the house, of course."

"Sure." My tête-à-tête with Jordan would have to wait.

As I closed the office door, I heard Jordan ask, "Another note?"

I paused. No one was in the hallway, nor could anyone in the main part of the café see me. I gently leaned my ear against the door.

"Yes," Jarka replied. "I have found next to register, like

last time. Maybe is time we call police? It could have relation to the death of Mr. Ronald Wong."

"We still don't know for sure that he didn't die of natural causes. Until that's proven, I don't want to stir up trouble. We only just reopened, and I don't need the police forcing us to close and turning this place inside out again." Jordan paused. "Although, after what happened to me . . ." There was an audible sigh. "I just don't know what to do."

"You are the boss," Jarka replied.

"What does the note say?" Jordan asked.

"Note says: 'You thought you got away with taking my money but I don't forget so easy.'"

CHAPTER 22

So, it seemed the note I'd found wasn't the only one of its kind. If someone had been threatening Juice Revolution, why hadn't Jordan mentioned it to the police? As I thought more about it, though, I wondered if I might've done the same thing. Assuming they'd found the first note before Wong died, it could be easily dismissed. It wasn't addressed to anyone in particular, and it didn't seem to have been accompanied by any kind of threatening action. The results of the toxicology tests on Wong's body and Jordan's smoothie were still pending, and Jordan seemed to be holding out hope they would conclude that poison hadn't been involved. Crime and death might hold a certain fascination, but if your customers started to associate your food and drink offerings with poisoning, that had to be terrible for business in the long run. Finally, as far as I was aware, Jordan didn't know about the existence of the note I found on the day of Wong's death, or its connection to a reputed murderer. The note I found had Mac's fingerprints on it, but it was impossible to know for sure if she'd even opened the folded paper to read the threat it contained. I doubted Capone would have said anything about it to Jordan, and I certainly hadn't. Yes, if I were in her shoes, I could see myself downplaying the significance of the notes.

I heard movement inside Jordan's office, and managed to slip down the hallway just ahead of Jarka. As I came back into the main space, my eyes darted around the café. The crowd had thinned out significantly, and there was no longer a line of people waiting for drinks. Jarka walked behind the counter, looking distracted, and began rinsing blender parts in the sink. No sign of Cinco Frates anywhere. Mac, however, was very much present, sitting at the table with my aunt. Mac had taken Butterball out of his carrier and was cradling him on her lap. And Biz was . . . smiling? And drinking a smoothie? I hurried over to the table.

"Hi, Delilah," Mac said. "What's shakin' at D and S this fab Friday? You guys ready for the contest?"

"Uh-huh." I nodded, eyeing Biz's drink with suspicion. Would it be an overreaction to knock it out of her hand?

Following my gaze, Mac said, "Strawberry Kombucha Frappe."

"Did you make it?" I asked, hoping the question sounded innocent.

"Nope, Jarka did. One of your aunt's former students insisted on buying her a drink. Did you know your aunt taught practically every person in Geneva Bay over the age of thirty?" Mac said. She pointed to a customer, a mom sitting with two tweenaged kids. "That lady's the one who bought her the drink, and that other lady over there came over to say hello and thank her for her awesomeness."

Although Biz never would've admitted it, the attention from her former students and Mac's flattery had clearly boosted her spirits.

"She's like a celebrity," Mac continued. She held Butterball up and pressed her forehead to his. "Isn't she, B-man? Plus, she remembers everybody's name." Addressing Biz, she said, "I'm super bummed that you retired before I could take one of your classes. Maybe then I wouldn't be such a dufus about financial stuff."

"You're never too old to learn," Biz chastised. "You're clearly a bright girl."

Mac batted away the compliment. "Mel's the one in our family with the brains. That's why I endeavor to be amusing," she said, putting on an exaggerated *Downton Abbey* accent.

"I should put Butterball back in his carrier," I said, a hint of annoyance creeping into my voice. I'd had enough of a struggle getting Butterball into his carrier at home. Now, because of Mac's presumptuousness, I'd have to repeat the process. In public. Without the nuclear option of the jar of forbidden cat treats. "I don't want Jordan to get dinged by the health department for having a cat running around."

I hoisted the cat from her lap, knelt down in front of his open carrier door, and began trying to coax and cajole him inside. He yowled and dug his front claws into the floor. As I struggled to move him, his body writhed from side to side, somehow becoming at least twice as large as the opening of the door.

"May I?" Mac lifted the carrier and set it so that the entrance to it was positioned on the very edge of the table. She then took Butterball back and dangled him aloft in front of the carrier. "Your chariot awaits, my liege," she said, still using her mock-British accent. The cat pinwheeled his legs for a moment, trying in vain to get purchase in thin air. She moved him slowly toward the carrier. Having no other place to put his feet, he alighted into the carrier and scampered inside, grateful to be on solid ground. She slid the door latch into place behind him.

"Hey, did you teach Jordan Watts?" Mac set the carrier back on the floor under our feet and continued the conversation in her regular voice, as if she hadn't just performed a bona fide miracle. It was possible she was a murderer, but damn it if she didn't have a gift for charming the two most problematic creatures in my life.

My aunt gave a prim nod. "I did. She was an excellent student. Very bright."

"Were she and Harold Heyer in the same graduating class?" I asked, eager to find out if my aunt could recall anything about their relationship.

"Yes, I taught Harold, too," Biz said. "He wasn't the accounting whiz that Jordan was, but he worked hard. He wanted to do a good job so he could take over the department store."

A trio of customers came in the door, and Jarka shouted for Mac, gesturing to the line forming in front of the counter. "Why you are sitting there doing chitchat and I am alone working?"

"On my way, Jark-meister," Mac called. "Great talking with you both," she said to us. She bent under the table. "And absolutely fab to see you, as always, B-man."

"What exactly *did* happen with the Heyers' store?" I asked, once Mac was out of earshot. "I always assumed it was the usual story of big-box stores putting the local guys out of business."

"There was some of that, I'm sure," Biz said, taking a sip of her drink.

"So that wasn't all?" I prodded. Biz hated gossip, but I knew for a fact that the women in her duplicate bridge club did at least as much rumormongering as card playing.

"Old Ollie had mismanaged the company's finances, or so people said," she replied. "There were rumors that he embezzled a significant amount of money."

"I vaguely remember that Harold's father died right after the store closed down. Is that right?" I asked.

"Yes," Biz replied. "His wife died a few months after the store went into bankruptcy, and then he died a few months after that. The shame of it all killed them."

"Poor Harold. That must've been awful."

"Actions have consequences," she replied, her tone devoid of sympathy.

"Losing the family business you were supposed to inherit and then losing both your parents because of it is a pretty rough 'consequence' for Harold, no matter what his father did," I said.

Her spine straightened. "Life doesn't owe anybody anything."

I threw my hands up. "*What* is wrong with you? Why are you so negative?"

"Are you going to start in on me again?" She rolled her eyes.

I let out an exasperated sigh. "There's clearly something going on. You asked me if I thought you were losing your marbles, and frankly, I think maybe you are. You're moody, you're doing shady stuff, burning mysterious documents. What am I supposed to think?"

"Why don't you try minding your own business?" she retorted.

"I wish I could, but this isn't just affecting you and me. You can be mean to me all you want, but you can't be mean to Melody," I said. "She doesn't deserve it, and she takes it to heart. Besides, if you're going to stay living in your house, you need her there." I could feel my muscles tightening one by one.

"Maybe I'm not going to stay in my house," Biz said. She refused to meet my gaze, looking out the window instead. "It doesn't concern you."

"I uprooted my whole life in Chicago so I could live closer to you and make sure you were taken care of," I said. "So, yes, your living arrangements do concern me."

"You came here so you could open a restaurant on the waterfront with your ex's money," she said.

My voice rose in tandem with my frustration. "Fine, live in a box under the highway bridge for all I care. That should be about right since you're acting like a mean old troll."

I crossed my arms over my chest and pointed my face toward the window, mirroring her posture. *What was wrong with her? What was wrong with* me? My chin quivered, and I took a few shaky breaths.

"O'Leary women don't cry," Biz said quietly, giving voice to my thoughts. I looked at her face, expecting to see a reproach. Instead, I was met with a sad smile.

"Well, tell that to my tear ducts," I said, closing my eyes to rein in a tear that threatened to make its way down my cheek. "Because they seem to disagree."

Biz took a deep breath and looked down at the table. "You're going to find out soon anyway, so I might as well tell you." She shook her head. "They're going to take my house away."

I sat up in my chair. "What?" I understood the words, but they made no sense. "Who's going to take your house?"

"The neighbors. Mr. and Mrs. Moneybags," she said. "They're going to take my house."

"What are you talking about? I know your neighbors

would love to buy your property, but they can't. You've told them a million times that you're not selling."

"I owe more than fifty-two thousand dollars in unpaid property taxes, interest, and penalties. I can't pay it, so the municipality put a lien on the house, and next month, they're going to auction off the lien. The notice will be posted in the newspaper next week, and then I'll have thirty days to get the money to them. When the Money-bagses will buy it, no matter how much it costs, and I'll be out on my ear. They'll tear the place down and put in a croquet lawn."

"How could this happen?" I shook my head, as if that could bring some order to my jumbled understanding. "I thought the mortgage company is supposed to pay the taxes on behalf of the homeowner?" Honestly, I had very little knowledge of the financial side of homeownership. I'd lived in rented apartments until I met Sam, and he'd always run all his finances through an accounting firm.

"I don't have a mortgage. I paid the place off decades ago," she said.

"If you own it outright, how can they take it?"

"My property taxes are higher than most people's rent," Biz said. "I own almost two acres in one of the best locations on the lake. Walking distance to town, over seventy-five feet of lake frontage, sunset-facing views over the lake. When I bought it, the upkeep and the taxes were manageable, but the costs go up just about every year, and my pension doesn't. I'm supposed to pay the bill directly to the county since I don't have a mortgage. I started falling behind, and then for the past year and more, I didn't pay at all."

"Why didn't you ask me for the money when I was dating Sam? He would've given it to me, no questions asked," I said.

She crossed her hands on the table. "Did you forget that I spent the better part of last year doped to the gills? I lost track of my finances and by the time I was well enough to figure out what was going on, I owed too much. I could barely afford the minimum payments even before I racked up all the penalties." She swallowed. "The hardest part is realizing that I've known this was coming for years. After I retired, I took out a reverse mortgage to try to stay ahead of the payments. But I knew that there would be a point when I couldn't afford it anymore. When debits exceed credits, you go into the red. Simple accounting. It just came to a head sooner than I thought. I'd hoped I would die before the time came when I'd have to leave, but apparently God wants me around for a couple more years. Now there's no way I can catch up. I've run the numbers a hundred different ways."

"Was that what you were doing that night Sonya and I came over?" I asked, remembering how the numbers on the reel of adding-machine tape gradually trended from black to red.

She nodded. "I burned the tax letters when they came in so Melody wouldn't see them. I knew she'd squeal on me."

"And the photo albums. I thought you were looking at those old pictures of me and Shea, but those were all pictures of the house."

"You girls *at* the house." She pointed to her chest. "I guess I'm a sentimental old lady. But not so sentimental that I'm going to let those bastards bulldoze my garden."

"So you plowed it under yourself," I said.

"What did you think? That I was burying a body?" she asked.

"That kind of thing has been going around lately," I said, thinking of my conversation with Renee and Sonya.

"I loved that garden," she said. "It was my pride and joy."

I put my head in my hands. "This is all my fault. Even when I knew you were sick, I never got involved in your finances. I should've done more."

"Maybe so, but even in that addled state I wouldn't have let you get anywhere near my money, and we both know it," she said. "Over my dead body does somebody else touch my checkbook."

"You said the sale isn't until next month, right?" I said, grasping at a thin straw of hope. "Then there's still time to talk to somebody in the assessor's office and get an extension."

"Don't you think I tried that?" she said wearily. "I even played the senior citizen card, if you can believe it."

I thought back through the catalogue of prickly interactions I and others had had with Biz over the past few months. Every time, she'd been rejecting some insinuation that she was helpless or frail. Given the pride Biz took in her independence, especially in financial affairs, the humiliation of having her house foreclosed on must've been eating her up inside. I couldn't even imagine the shame she'd feel, knowing that generations of her students would see her house listed in the newspaper as a forfeit.

"We'll just have to get the money together, then." I pressed my fingers to my lips. "I can ask Sam for it."

She shook her head. "All that would do is delay the inevitable. I can't afford it on my pension, and that's that. My ship is sinking, but I won't allow yours to go down with it. I know how humiliating it would be for you to be indebted to him. I'd never forgive you if you did that for me. I'd never go begging a man for money and neither should you." She straightened a crease in her sleeve. "It's going to be hard to leave that house, but what's done is done."

I leaned across the table and took her hand. With the other, she brushed a tear from her cheek.

"O'Leary women don't cry," I said. We exchanged quivery smiles.

The bell over the door jangled. "Welcome to Juice . . ." Mac's cheerful voice trailed off.

Capone, wearing his badge on a chain around his neck, led Rettberg and Stanhope inside. They marched up to the counter, laser focused, their expressions humorless. The smile on Mac's face stiffened, then melted away. Her body stood taut and coiled, and for a moment, I thought she would try to dash from the room. Sensing the same thing, the officers positioned themselves at each end of the counter while Capone approached her. He said nothing, merely touched the handcuffs on his waistband. It was enough. She hung her head, slowly removed her name tag, and gave herself over to their custody.

CHAPTER 23

Biz and I stared in disbelief as Mac walked out, her head drooped, her curls swishing forward to hide her face. She slid into the back of Rettberg and Stanhope's squad car, which was parked just outside. The arrest seemed like something that had been spliced in out of the wrong movie, incompatible with the bustling scene of early bird tourists walking past in the sunshine, carrying coffee cups in their hands and newspapers tucked under their arms. Of course, I harbored suspicions that Mac was responsible for the poisonings, but actually witnessing the arrest left me with a sinking feeling. I'd set this in motion, but part of me wished I'd been wrong. With so much going in her favor, what had driven her to undertake such terrible actions?

"What's going on?" Jordan asked, joining the small crowd of customers that had gathered near the window.

"The police have taken away Mac," Jarka said.

"Stay with Butterball," I said to Biz. "I'll be back." I pushed past Jordan, Jarka, and the customers who surrounded our table to watch the arrest unfold through the glass.

"Capone!" I called, rushing to catch him before his

Dodge pulled away. I banged on the passenger window. He pressed the button to roll it down.

I leaned in through the window. After he'd brought Renee in for questioning, I'd been tempted to call him to try to get the inside scoop, but I was wary of pushing my luck. Every time I thought things between us were getting friendly, maybe even leading somewhere good and steamy, he retreated back inside his professional armor. I never felt entirely safe from his suspicions.

"Did you just arrest Mac?" I asked.

Capone raised an eyebrow, an expression that said *dumb question* without actually saying it.

"I mean, okay, you clearly just arrested Mac."

Seeing him after some time apart, I was struck again by his physical beauty. That initial rush of attraction always tied my tongue for a minute.

The squad car containing Mac and the two uniformed officers pulled away. "Do you have time to talk?" I asked. "Just two minutes."

Capone looked around. The street was busy with pedestrians. Seeing how I was jammed halfway inside his car and apparently not going anywhere, he unlocked the car doors. I slipped into the passenger seat.

"I have two minutes. I'll let them get her booked in. I like to give the suspect a little time to sweat it out before I come in." His mouth cocked into a self-deprecating half smile. "What do you want to know?"

"*Why* did you arrest her?"

"Well, you were right," he said. "Again. The tox reports finally came back this morning. It was jimsonweed poisoning. The levels in Wong's samples were off the charts, and it was present in Jordan's smoothie as well. The poison was also found in the seaweed powder sample we collected from Juice Revolution. None of the other ingredients had a trace of it. Someone intentionally tainted that particular ingredient with jimson weed."

"Okay," I said, still not quite believing that my hunch had turned out to be true. "So that narrowed the suspects down considerably. It had to be someone who knew that Jordan was the only person who regularly consumed that ingredient, and someone who was also there that day to slip it into the drinks."

"Right. Jordan said she'd had the exact same smoothie the previous day with no ill effects. Mac and Jarka were busy, but I doubt they were too busy to notice if Frates or Harold Heyer or you, for that matter, came behind the counter and sprinkled something into the kelp powder. Of all the suspects, Mac is the most likely. She had access to the poison from the farm, and she knew its effects. She was also one of the few people who knew about Jordan's daily Maximum Wattage smoothie habit. It's circumstantial evidence, but the sheer quantity of it is pretty damning," he said.

"But why would she want to kill Jordan? It's got to have something to do with the money that seems to have fallen into her lap all of a sudden."

"That's still an open question," he said. "The money's obviously not from a legitimate source. I pulled her bank records. She made a cash deposit just shy of a hundred K all at once a few weeks ago, and immediately started spending it like a drunken sailor—new car, deposit on an apartment, jewelry, shoes—all the things you might expect from a young woman with cash to burn. The family doesn't have that kind of money, nowhere near, so it's not an inheritance or anything like that. I wondered if she could be embezzling from Juice Revolution, but their books are squeaky clean. Plus, the shop does a brisk trade, but it would've taken months if not years for her to skim off that kind of sum unnoticed. The bank still had some of her deposited cash in the vault. The bills were sequential."

"Meaning they were issued all at once, rather than collected little by little over a period of time?" I asked. "So it probably wasn't money she gradually accumulated."

He nodded. "That's right."

"What does that leave? Could she have been blackmailing someone?" I asked.

"Could be," he explained. "Right now, though, I'm looking for connections between her and Frates because of the fingerprints on that note."

I sat up suddenly. "There's another note. I overheard Jarka telling Jordan about it just a little while ago. It said something like, 'You thought you got away with stealing my money but I'm not going to forget it.' That could definitely be some kind of blackmail demand. Same with the first one about 'paying for what you did.' It sounded like they'd gotten at least one other note some time recently that they hadn't reported."

"Mac as a blackmailer would make more sense than Mac as a murderer," Capone said. "I'll get hold of that note before I head back to the station and have it analyzed." He paused and drummed his fingertips on the steering wheel, his brow furrowed. "I've been having a hard time getting my mind around why a person like Molly McClintock would suddenly turn to murder. Her past conviction for shoplifting points to someone who's greedy or envious of what others have, and maybe a little arrogant. But poisoning her boss is several levels beyond what I'd expect from someone like her. Assuming Jordan was the intended target, it's possible Frates paid her to kill Jordan, or coerced her into it somehow. But that still doesn't answer the question of why either of them would target Jordan in particular."

"And if Mac *was* trying to kill Jordan, why would she have used jimson weed?" I asked. "She knew from personal experience that almost no one who uses it actually dies from it." I rubbed the back of my neck, hoping to stimulate some brain waves. "Unless she didn't actually intend to kill anyone? Maybe she was just sending a message, or helping Frates to send one. Same kind of thing as the notes. Threatening notes would be best for when you're trying to cause some action without really taking action yourself. It's very passive-aggressive. If your intention is to see somebody dead, sending a note or using a poison that's usually sublethal isn't the quickest path to that particular outcome."

"You might be on to something there. The toxicologist said that to really do damage, the jimson weed dose needs to be very high, probably using crushed seeds or distilling the essence."

"So mixing it into something like a strong-tasting smoothie would be the perfect way to use it, if you were intending to kill someone," I observed.

"Yes, even then, though, death isn't usually instantaneous. Under normal circumstances, the victim would typically have gone home and started to get sick gradually over the course of a few hours. The reason Wong died in such a sudden, dramatic fashion is probably because of the Benadryl he was taking for his allergies. It interacts strongly with jimson weed."

"Poor guy," I said.

We were both silent for a moment, sending our condolences into the universe.

"Last question," I said, breaking the stillness. Something

had been bothering me. "Why did you arrest Mac with all these questions marks still hanging over the case against her? A dozen people just watched you perp walk her into a squad car. Something like that will permanently ruin her reputation. If you suspect Frates could be behind this, why not go after him?"

The muscles in his jaw twitched. "The only evidence I have against Frates is a couple of fingerprints on a piece of paper. He's beaten murder charges with stronger evidence than that. If he's behind this, who do you think is more likely to flip and come clean, him or Mac? More than that, though, as soon as we got confirmation of the jimson weed, I had to make a move. Would you want me to risk letting a murderer loose on the general public at the contest tomorrow, or allowing her to keep working alongside the person she may have poisoned?"

"Was that the thinking with Renee Kessler, too?" I asked, half holding my breath. I knew I was pushing it, but a portion of my loyalty to Sonya and Melody extended to their loved ones. I owed it to them to get answers.

"Renee is lucky she's still walking free," he said. "She lied to me, and I'm not fond of liars."

"But it still seems unlikely—"

He cut me off. "Look, Delilah, I'm not going to apologize for doing my job. I know you care about these people, but I've got two open murder investigations, and Renee and Mac are prime suspects." He made a show of checking his watch. "I need to get back to the station."

Although he'd answered my questions, his attitude had shifted. We'd been talking easily, but suddenly I felt like an outsider, asking unwelcome questions and wasting Capone's time. On a rational level, I agreed with him about both Mac and Renee—they were prime suspects.

But I couldn't silence my intuition, which was practically screaming that he had it all wrong. Was I going soft, letting my affection for Melody and Sonya cloud my judgment about their loved ones? Loyalty to my friends was one thing. Letting someone get away with murder was something else.

CHAPTER 24

I'd gotten as much information from Capone as I could, and then made the handover of Butterball to Sam. I almost had to laugh when I thought how I'd gone out of my way to warn Jordan about Mac potentially targeting her. Mac's dramatic arrest had sent a clearer message than I ever could have. I supposed I did accomplish the mission of getting to the bottom of Biz's foul humor, for whatever that was worth. Now at least I had time to buy an air mattress so she and Melody would have somewhere to sleep when they got booted out of the cottage in a few weeks.

All told, Biz and I had been gone much longer than I intended, and I wasn't sure what kind of chaos would greet us back at Delilah & Son. Although we'd only be open for a few hours that day, between running lunch service on a busy holiday weekend and festival prep, there was a huge amount to do. Would my team be ready? Yesterday, Sonya found out someone close to her could be locked up for murder. Today, Melody would get the same news, along with finding out that the house she lived in was being auctioned out from under her.

On the drive back to the restaurant, I briefly toyed with the idea of withdrawing from the festival and contest altogether. With everything going on, it seemed impossible that we'd be able to put our best foot forward. When I thought of how much money I'd sunk into the ingredients for our offerings, though, I realized that there was no turning back. I'd have to show up tomorrow and churn out pies, even if I had to run the tent alone.

I approached the turnoff for the restaurant. "Do you want me to drop you off at home?" I asked Biz.

"No," she replied. "Now that the cat's out of the bag with you, I suppose I'd better fill Melody in on what's going on."

I was grateful that Biz was willing to do the dirty work. I also hoped that the Geneva Bay grapevine would already have passed the news of Mac's arrest to Melody. I hated the thought of her sweet face crumpling when she found out what had happened.

Rabbit greeted us as we came through the kitchen door, his green eyes wide and agitated. "That cousin of Melody's . . ." he began.

"We know," I said. "We had front-row seats."

"So, it's true, then," he said, shaking his head as he filled a pitcher with ice water. "I've been on the wrong end of an interrogation table more than once. It ain't a comfortable feeling."

"Where's Melody?" Biz asked. "How's she taking it?"

He grimaced. "She's setting up on the patio for family meal. She's steaming mad, if you can picture that. Throwing down plates on the table like she don't care if she smashes 'em. Daniel tried to get her to take five, maybe go home to the farm and check up on her family. You shoulda seen the stink eye she gave him."

"I can understand why she'd be upset about the arrest," I said.

"That's not what's got her steamed up. She's real ticked at her cousin. Says she finally got what's coming to her."

Biz and I looked at each other. I don't think either of us had realized that anger was even in Melody's emotional repertoire. The three of us walked through the empty dining room toward the patio. We found Melody opening a patio umbrella, her blond curls bursting off her head in all directions as she yanked on the thin rope to raise the canopy. Daniel and Sonya were arranging platters of food for family meal on a distant table, keeping safely away as Melody engaged in an increasingly violent brawl with the uncooperative sunshade. She tugged and jerked, trying to force it open. When it failed to yield, she gave a final, colossal yank of the rope, toppling the heavy umbrella onto the brick patio pavers. She stared at it for a moment, her breath heaving. Then, she swung back her leg and whaled on the contraption, kicking it as if she were trying to extinguish its life force. Once she finished, she stood with her hands on her knees, doubled over. Her pale complexion had deepened to a purply red.

We were all struck dumb. A flock of Canada geese flew overhead. A motorboat zipped across the sapphire surface of the lake. Still, none of us moved.

Rabbit was the first to stir. "I'll go on and throw this in one of the dumpsters out back," he said, gingerly lifting the slain umbrella from its resting place.

Melody brushed a clump of sweaty hair from her forehead. "Sorry, chef," she said. Her eyes followed Rabbit and the umbrella as they disappeared around the side of the building. "You can take that out of my paycheck."

"Feeling any better?" I asked, no stranger myself to the cleansing power of an outburst of intense rage.

She nodded.

"Want to talk about it?" I asked.

She raised and lowered her shoulders and slumped into a chair at the table where Daniel and Sonya had set out the family meal. "I'm probably going to get arrested, too," she said. "Because of Mac."

The rest of us exchanged worried looks.

"Did you kill somebody, too?" Biz asked, cutting to the chase like the human buzz saw she was.

Melody glared at her. "Mac didn't kill anyone. But she stole a bunch of money. I've known about it for weeks and I didn't do anything. She always pulls this garbage," Melody fumed. "When she'd stumble in drunk every other weekend when she was in high school, who had to cover for her?" She pointed her thumbs at herself. "When some jilted boyfriend or girlfriend turned up at the farm all moony-eyed wondering why she ghosted them, do you think she'd even come down to talk to them? Believe you me, she was nowhere to be found. So I had to hold their hands while they cried. Then she goes and tells me she 'found' a pile of cash, but not to tell anyone."

"How do you know she stole it? Maybe she *did* find it," I ventured, taking a seat next to her.

"I guess I don't know for sure. She wouldn't tell me where she got it. But this is just like that time she got busted for pocketing a gold bracelet. She told me it was a gift, but deep down I knew she'd taken it, and I covered for her."

Sonya, Daniel, and Biz took seats around the table. Rabbit rejoined us a moment later.

"She started showing up with new clothes about a month ago," Melody said. "I didn't think much of it at first, since she'd just gotten the new job at Juice Rev. But that night when we were all out here and she drove up in the new car, I knew something was up. I questioned her about it when we got back to the farm, and she said she found some money, but that nobody would miss it, so I shouldn't worry." Her eyes welled up. "She must think I'm a total idiot."

"Then *she's* the idiot," Daniel said, taking hold of Melody's hand. "Because you are one of the smartest people I know."

She gave him a grateful smile.

"Well, she was definitely wrong about nobody missing the money, that's for darn sure," Melody continued. "I found a note in her room that night when I stayed there, written on a dollar bill. It said, 'Better watch your back because thieves get what they deserve.'"

That was yet another threatening message, on top of the notes I already knew about. Jarka and Jordan's conversation implied they'd received an additional note or notes prior to that morning. Was one of those the one Melody saw in Mac's room? Or a different one altogether? Apparently the threatening note I found on the day of Wong's death was just the tip of the note iceberg.

"I'm sorry to ask this," I said, "but is it possible she could have written the note herself? And intended it for someone else?"

Melody thought for a moment. "I really don't think so. I confronted her about it, and she seemed genuinely scared. She said she didn't know who was sending the notes, but that this wasn't the first one. She's a good liar, but not that good. She said she was going to spend the rest of the money as quickly as she could so there would be none left for whoever it was to go after."

Sonya pressed a hand to her own heart. "I'm so sorry, hon. If you want, we can talk to my uncle Avi, and see if he can take her on as a client."

"And me, too, now that I'm an accessory or whatever," Melody said grimly. "They'll probably arrest me next."

"Uh-uh," Rabbit said. "You don't know anything about what she did. Not really. And you didn't do nothing wrong except try to keep your cousin outta trouble."

"We can check with Avi, but I think Rabbit's right," Sonya said. "You didn't take any money. You didn't spend it. You don't even know for sure that it's stolen. There's nothing inherently illegal about money, or knowing someone else has it. For all you know, she found a treasure chest buried under your family's barn. Money's just money unless they can prove it was stolen. It's not like she waltzed in with a brick of cocaine or an endangered white rhino. I don't think there's anything to charge you with."

I sighed. "Whatever you do, don't go turning yourself in to the police today. We've got too much work to do. On Sunday, you can call Capone and tell him what you know, if you think it'll help them get to the bottom of things." I pointed my finger at the rest of my staff one by one. "That goes for the rest of you, too. No murders, no robberies, no confessions. Not today. Not tomorrow."

Melody swallowed. "Honest to gosh, I'm glad to be busy. I'm just so confused about how to feel. Part of me is glad that Mac is finally having to pay a price for all the stuff she pulls. But I know she's not a bad person. Mac's always been there for me, and most of the time she's so awesome. It's like she's my best friend, but also my worst enemy."

"I hear you," I said, thinking of my sister. My very own best frenemy.

"I feel bad, but I told my grandma and my aunt and uncle that I couldn't come home until after the festival because of work," Melody continued, holding up her phone. "They're bugging out. To them, this has come out of the blue because they don't know half the stuff she's pulled over the years. Plus, I've got about a thousand un-answered texts from everybody I've ever known trying to pretend like they care even though all they want is gossip."

"I know that feeling," Sonya said. "People I haven't worked with in ten years are hitting me up for the inside scoop on Renee."

"At least the Delilah and Son tent is guaranteed to draw a crowd tomorrow," Biz said.

"Just like any major car crash," Daniel quipped.

This time, it was me who snort-laughed. Black humor was definitely the dish du jour at Delilah & Son. I looked at my watch. "Well, should we get on with family meal?" For the first time since I'd sat down, I noticed the food arrayed before me. "What is this?" I asked, picking up a bite-sized pretzel nugget from a basket. It was golden brown and dotted with kosher salt, just like the crust from our contest entry. However, it wasn't a pizza. The platter next to me held small chunks of bratwurst, another brimmed with pickled onions, radishes, and kohlrabi. Near the center of the table stood ramekins of velvety orange cheese sauce and a tray containing several varieties of mustard, from sunshine yellow to seed-filled brown.

"Oh, right . . ." Sonya grimaced. "I know you said you wanted me to make one final test run of the bratwurst pizza for family meal, but I couldn't. I just physically could not, Dee. Please don't be mad."

Daniel chimed in. "We all agreed that we could not face it again. It's not even eleven a.m."

Melody lowered her eyes, while Rabbit silently nodded. We always ate family meal at this time, and no one had ever complained about having savory dishes before. Given the few breaks we typically had during service, hearty food was required to power us through until closing.

"So you mutinied?" Biz asked.

Sonya toggled her head from side to side. "'Mutiny' is a strong word. I prefer 'improvised.' I thought we might be able to cope with having it again if I cut everything into small pieces. And I added a few dipping sauces, for variety."

They watched me as a popped the pretzel bite I was holding into my mouth. I let the first burst of salt bathe my tongue and began to chew slowly, until the gluten gradually converted into sweetness. "These are good," I said.

Seeing that a verbal haranguing wasn't in the immediate offing, my team gradually began to fill up their plates.

"That yellow mustard sauce has a nice kick," Rabbit said, gesturing with his fork. "Tastes good with the brats."

"And it's nice to be able to take a little break from the meat, if you just want to dip the veggies," Melody said. "They taste so fresh."

Sonya nodded. "Yeah, I did a very light apple cider and sugar pickling, to brighten them up and cut through the heavier ingredients."

"Vegetarians and meat-eaters could share this," Daniel added, popping a bite-sized chunk of brat into his mouth.

"The size is good, too," Biz said, examining one of the pretzel nuggets. "You could sell this as an app tomorrow along with the mini slices of our usual pizza offerings. They'd be nice and easy for people to eat while they're walking around the festival."

As they spoke, I'd been testing each ingredient and sauce. There were endless combinations in each bite:

unctuous meat and sharp chunks of lightly pickled veggies with sauces that ranged from bright, piquant mustard to luxuriant, mouth-coatingly rich cheddar. Sonya had transformed what had been a forceful, overstated pizza into something fun. Fun and tasty.

"This is it!" I said, my volume increasing with my excitement. "I never loved my recipe. These ingredients were meant to be an app, not a pizza. This could be our entry!"

"How can we enter an app that I just threw together?" Sonya argued. Although her voice contained a note of skepticism, her cheeks flushed with pleasure. "It's not even a deep-dish pizza. Deep-dish is our signature."

"*Twists* on traditional deep-dish are our signature," I said, rising to my feet. "That's why I didn't open just another run-of-the-mill knock-off Chicago pie shop. This place takes inspiration from traditional deep-dish, but we also want to be inspired by local ingredients. I pointed to the table. "Eating this, here"—I spread my arms to the sparkling lake, the trees that ringed it, the infinite expanse of blue sky—"feels right. Besides, what could be more of a twist on the usual pizza pie than a deconstructed deep-dish?"

CHAPTER 25

I got into bed that night feeling hopeful for the first time in days. We'd pushed aside the sucking miasma of murders and poisonings and foreclosures, pulled together as a team, and prepped all of our food offerings for maximum efficiency. Sizable vats of mustard and cheese sauce waited, ready to be portioned out as part of our new contest entry, and the signature pizzas we'd be serving had been baked and frozen, waiting to be reheated on site tomorrow. I couldn't have ordered a more glorious forecast—75 degrees and sunshine all weekend.

Even Butterball's weigh-in had gone better than I'd hoped. Sam had dropped our cat back off with me that evening, reporting that he'd lost an ounce. The vet tech wasn't quite prepared to call it progress, since apparently that kind of reading was within the scale's margin of error. So, maybe not an unqualified success, but at least I didn't have to deal with the unspoken reproach in Sam's eyes that came with each ballooning measurement.

Yes, there was hope. Maybe things could still turn out all right. Maybe Delilah & Son could win this contest after all. Even if we didn't, putting our best foot forward with the festival attendees could gain us new customers and a much-needed influx of cash. Maybe it would be enough.

Considering that I'd drifted off with dreams of svelte cats, magazine features, and cash prizes dancing in my head, I was surprised when my body woke me up in the pitch dark gripped by a heart-thumping panic. I bolted upright and pulled my phone to my face. Two a.m. I cycled through my mental task list, trying to root out the trigger for my anxiety. Had I forgotten something important? Even my exacting psyche couldn't conjure up any lurking dangers. Our signage was printed, ovens tested, timings and roles nailed down. I consoled myself. Of course a current of subliminal stress would be coursing through my dreams. Despite the day's successes, two people in my close orbit were under suspicion of murder. Plus, I hadn't even started to get my head around Auntie Biz's impending homelessness. Yes, that must be it. Perfectly natural to carry vicarious stress. But there was nothing I could do about any of that right now. One day at a time, and for tomorrow, at least, I was ready. I sank back against my pillows, pulling the duvet over my shoulders. I stretched my feet down to the end of the bed and wiggled my toes from side to side.

Butterball wasn't there.

My heart set off hammering again, and I threw the lights on and the covers off. It wasn't totally unheard of for my cat to go on some noisy expedition in the middle of the night, but this was different. The apartment was unnaturally quiet. The air was still. His absence felt almost like a presence.

"Butterball?" I called.

I walked out into the main room, flicking on the floor lamp. "Butterbutt?" No sign of him in the bathroom, either. Repeating my circuit, I checked the closet and his usual hideaways under the bed and the couch. No cat. I removed the forbidden cat treats from the cupboard and shook the jar loudly. Even if he were at death's door or throwing his worst ever temper tantrum, that should've summoned him, but instead, the eerie silence remained. I shuffled on a robe and flip flops, pocketing my cell phone and grabbing a sturdy, metal flashlight from a kitchen drawer. In his younger days, Butterball had been an accomplished escape artist, but looking around the apartment, I couldn't for the life of me imagine how he'd slipped out. No one had come or gone once I'd locked up for the night. All the doors and windows remained fastened. I made one more pass through the house, checking under, over, behind, and inside every stick of furniture. Confirmed. Zero cats.

A chorus of crickets and locusts greeted me as I made my way down the stairs. The relentless humidity of August was finally giving way to crisper autumn air. High above, a fat lump of yellow moon cast a dim glow. I flicked on the flashlight and shined it around the dumpsters. Surely, that would be a hungry kitty's first port of call. But the light revealed nothing but a few of Rabbit's discarded cigarette butts.

I rounded the corner of the restaurant, heading toward the parking lot, the beam of my flashlight tracing arcs back and forth across the ground. I opened my mouth to call Butterball's name again, but was stopped dead in my tracks by the unexpected sight of Mac's brand new Ford Mustang convertible.

"What the . . ." I began. The top was down, and even though I could see no one inside, I approached slowly, shining my light into the empty interior. I pulled my phone from my pocket, and checked for notifications.

Surely someone would've texted me if they'd released Mac? I'd figured that her arraignment wouldn't be scheduled until Tuesday at the earliest because of the holiday weekend. Could the police have decided to release her without charges? Could Melody have moved Mac's car here for some reason? And if she had, why would she have left the top down?

Seeing no texts or voice mails, I opened a message to Capone. I snapped a photo of the car, framing it against the backdrop of the restaurant, and sent it, followed by a second message with a chain of question marks.

As I moved to pocket my phone, a detail of the photo I'd snapped suddenly registered in my mind. An interior light glowed faintly in the darkness. We always left the security lights burning when we closed up, but the illumination I'd noticed appeared to be coming from the kitchen.

"What the . . ." I began again, this time completing the question with a potent expletive.

I marched toward the door. The glass near the lock had been punched through, and the door stood open. I pulled out my phone again, intending to dial 9-1-1. My finger hovered over the keypad. Maybe the call could wait. Although I didn't have the familial bias that Melody did, I, too, couldn't quite make myself cast Mac as a cold-blooded poisoner. If she *had* done it, something extreme must've driven her into the act. A thief? Maybe. If Mac was trying to rob the restaurant, she was going to find herself sorely disappointed. We deposited cash takings every single night, meaning that we never had more cash on hand than what was needed to make change from the register. I was baffled. If she'd just gotten out of the slammer, why would she risk a breaking and entering charge? Whatever her motives, this could be my only chance to get to the bottom of her mysterious cash influx. Instead of dialing the police, I pushed Record on my phone and slipped it into the pocket of my robe.

Cautiously, I nudged the door open, taking care not to step on the broken glass that sprinkled the floor. A muted clattering sound emanated from the kitchen. Switching off the flashlight, I slowly approached the source of the noise. I changed my grip on the flashlight, so I now wielded it like a truncheon. I trusted my instincts about Mac, but not enough to confront her unarmed. I cracked the swing door open just enough to glimpse what was going on inside.

Cinco Frates stood hunched at my usual workspace, poring over a blueprint that lay unfurled on the counter before him. The task light above him cast a demonic downward shadow over his rough features.

The shock of seeing him caused me to recoil. I took five or six careening steps backward until my hip met the corner of the two-top table that stood nearest to the door. My breath caught in my throat as the small, empty flower vase in the center of it teetered. It seemed almost suspended in the air, and for a brief moment, I thought I might still be able to escape undetected. My fantasy evaporated as the vase fell with a clatter onto its side. I reached for it, already knowing I was too late. The next few seconds passed in a horrifying blur. I took off in a dead sprint, pleading with my top-heavy physique to run faster than nature intended. A moment later, I felt myself lifted off my feet and dragged backward toward the kitchen.

The flashlight flew from my hand. It turned itself on as it hit the floor and spun in tight spirals across the length of the restaurant, casting shadows of my struggle like some kind of macabre shadow puppetry. I screamed for all I was worth, even knowing that it would take a miracle for someone to hear me from the restaurant's secluded, tree-ensconced location. Frates forced me through the swing door and on to Auntie Biz's stool. He drew back his arm and slapped me sharply with the back of his hand. Rather than cowing me, the blow fired me up. I pushed against his brick wall of a chest and twisted sideways, reaching out for something to fight back with. The only weapon at my disposal was an empty steel pizza pan. *Damn my excessive tidiness.* My fingers coiled around the pan and I swung it at Frates. It connected with the side of his head, drawing out a percussive groan from deep within his belly. Recovering quickly, he grabbed my wrist and bent it back in on itself, forcing me to my knees. *Damn those lightweight pans, too. Excellent for heat conduction; practically useless for conking an attacker.*

"Sit," he commanded, nodding toward Biz's perch. He pushed me into place with one hand. With the other, he drew a pistol from the back of his waistband.

I glared at him, unable to do anything with my fury except try to project it through my eyeballs at him.

"If you can't hear me, I'll say it real loud," he said, gesturing faintly to his gun. "Real loud."

He spoke in an upper Midwestern accent that far eclipsed Melody's hockey-mom pronunciation. The cheerful Lutheran bake-sale connotation felt completely incongruous on a hulking murderer, whose face was still contorted with the effort of hauling me into the kitchen.

"I'm actually glad you showed up," he said. "Maybe you can help with a little problem I'm having."

I threw an acid smile at him. "My pleasure."

He matched my expression and then stabbed at the blueprints with the barrel of the gun. "Where are the original walls? The plans say there should be a brick wall here, but this is all drywall and studs."

I looked at the enormous piece of paper spread out on the worktop. I recognized it immediately as the architectural drawing Sam and I had submitted to the town when we renovated the restaurant that had formerly been owned by Rocco Guanciale into what became Delilah & Son.

Frates waved the gun at the wall that backed the prep counter and ovens. "*This* doesn't match up with that."

"Those are the original drawings. We had to change the plans when the renovation got underway." I found myself gulping air. I had to make a conscious effort to draw enough breath to get through each sentence. "I wanted to preserve the original brick, but our contractor had to take all of it out. Water damage. The mortar was crumbling. It ended up being a blessing. The layout flows better."

"Who was your contractor?" he demanded.

"Why?" It seemed that I'd been violently kidnapped for a warped version of HGTV.

"I've been watching you and your crew for a while. If any of you has the money that was hidden in these walls, you're doing a damn good job of acting like a bunch of flat-broke losers. So I'm guessing your contractor stole it during the renovation," Frates said.

"How much money are we talking about?" I asked.

"About a hundred Gs." The fact that Frates was so forthcoming about the money felt like a bad omen. His track record showed that he wasn't keen on leaving witnesses.

"If that's the case, then my contractor is doing an amazing job of pretending to work sixty-hour weeks, busting his butt trying to put his two kids through college and support a lot of relatives back in Mexico. I don't think he's taken a vacation in years." I paused. "Could've been one of the workmen. There were dozens. Or maybe it went into the dumpster with the rest of the torn-down wall." Maybe if I blew a thick enough smoke screen, Frates would take his sights off Julio and my team.

"How can you even be sure there was money in the wall?" I continued. I was trying to buy time, hoping God just needed a hot second to organize whatever miracle he was cooking up to save my ass.

"I was a bodyguard for this accountant, Jimmy Krimins, when I was in Oakhill. Got the info from him," he said. "He was the money man for Rocco Guanciale. I suppose you heard of him?"

I nodded. "I thought Jimmy Krimins died in prison. What are you, his next of kin?"

His mouth twisted into a sneer. "Something like that. Jimmy hid some rainy-day cash for Rocco, before they both got put away. When Jimmy found out his liver cancer had spread, he realized he wasn't getting out, unless it was in a pine box. He'd never told Rocco exactly where to find the money. Jimmy had to get a message to Rocco, but Rocco's in the federal prison upstate. By then Jimmy wasn't doing too hot, health wise, so he needed my help to smuggle out a letter."

"Why did he need you to smuggle the letter? Aren't prisoners allowed to send mail?" I asked.

He shook his head at my ignorance. "Not to other prisoners. So Jimmy had me deliver a message to Rocco through some contacts, telling him where to find the cash, for when Rocco got out in a couple years. A hundred grand inside the walls in each of the three buildings that Jimmy had bought on Rocco's behalf." Again, the level of detail made my palms sweat. It was the kind of tell-all you'd get from a Bond villain, right before he sliced you in half with a laser beam.

"That seems naïve of Jimmy Krimins to trust you with the intel about the money. He must've known you'd be getting out of prison before Rocco." I held out my hands. "No offense."

He pursed his lips, granting me the point. After all, he was engaged in betraying Jimmy's trust at that very moment. "See, that's the thing. He thought he was clever. Sent the message written in code, in case someone got their hands on it along the way. Thought I wouldn't know what it was all about. But I have ears, for one thing, and I was around him all the time. Plus, the code he used was just matching up numbers with different letters in the alphabet, with a few substitutions. Half the time I was inside, I was working on those word finder puzzle books, or else crosswords. Anyways, I steamed open the envelope and had it figured out in five minutes. He thought I was stupid." His face broke into a wide smile as he added, "Maybe *he* was the stupid one.

"Still and all," he continued, "even with the info in the note, I had some legwork to do. Jimmy didn't count on the buildings being sold off so quick after he croaked. And with all the renovations, it hasn't exactly been a cakewalk." He leveled the gun at my forehead. "This, for instance, I don't enjoy. Especially killing a good-looking woman. I know everyone thinks I don't mind it, but just because you're good at something doesn't mean it's fun. But that's how it is with a lot of jobs. They've got their good parts and their bad parts."

He raised his shoulders, signaling that his dilemma was a universal one. And in a way, I supposed it was. I didn't especially like ordering and bookkeeping, but it was part of the job of a head chef. He didn't particularly enjoy blowing holes into people's skulls, but that's life, right?

"So," he said, taking aim at me again, "why don't you

tell me the names of the subcontractors who worked on this project, so I can do a little more legwork? Find out if any of them are living on a beach somewhere off of my money."

I thought back to my conversation with Julio about the double-dealing drywall contractor—the guy who Julio said had cut corners, both literally and figuratively. I could reveal his name, but that could throw him under a very large bus named Cinco Frates. The guy had clearly been shady, but there was no indication he'd come into a windfall like the one Frates seemed to be looking for. If he had, why would he be trying to cheat Julio out of a few hundred bucks? Poor workmanship and bad business practices shouldn't result in a death sentence. Besides, I had a feeling that no amount of information I could provide was going to convince Frates to let me walk out of here alive.

"I don't know them all," I said. "I was going back and forth to Chicago, trying to deal with my father's estate, so I wasn't here every day."

"Well, I bet I can convince your contractor—don't worry I'll find out who it is—to give me a list. Although after tonight, I'll have to leave town for a little while, until things cool down. They'll be looking for the person who killed that lady chef in her own kitchen."

My heart jumped into my throat. I had to grit my teeth and swallow to keep it from choking me. "Wait! Let me help you think this through. You've been in this room before, right? Looking?"

His forehead wrinkled in confusion, bringing his widow's peak almost to the level of his eyebrows. "I never set foot in this kitchen before tonight."

Now it was my turn to look confused. "A few weeks ago, somebody smashed up my kitchen. It was right after you paid that 'friendly' visit. That wasn't you, looking for the money?"

He shook his head.

"And I've also had food go missing," I added. "Disappeared in broad daylight."

"Food?"

"Bratwurst."

His expression morphed from confusion to annoyance. "Are you screwing with me?"

"You think with my life on the line, I'd make up a story about stolen bratwurst?" I asked. "I'm trying to get a handle on all of this, just like you are. Like, what if someone else with access to the building has been in here? Maybe someone else knows about the money. Maybe it's still here."

"I don't have time to hang around all night playing 'what if,'" he countered. "This is my last stop, and then I've gotta get out of town for a while."

He seemed to be coming to the end of his use for me, and I was desperate to keep him talking. *Feel free to send that miracle any time now, God.* Frates raised the gun.

"Where did you get that car?" I sputtered. "The white Mustang parked outside. It's Molly McClintock's right?" I had to hope it was a subject that he'd have something to say about.

"I took it as my consolation prize. It was left out back of Juice Revolution after that dumb blond got picked up by the cops. I happened to walk by when I was on my way here, and I seen it out there. She bought it with the money hidden at that juice place where she works, money that was supposed to be mine. So I figured the universe was trying to tell me something. I know a guy who'll buy it, no questions asked. At least that way, I'll get something for my troubles."

My mind, which had been firing off thoughts like a kid with a new BB gun, suddenly stilled. A picture emerged. Mac. The threatening notes. Her sudden influx of cash. Frates had been watching the comings and goings at each of the three Rock Co. Enterprises buildings, and he was no dummy. It would've taken him no time at all to figure out why Mac was suddenly flush with cash. She must've come across the money on one of her forays into the storage cellar.

"So that was you, leaving notes for Mac, trying to get her to cough up the money," I said.

"What can I say?" he replied. "I'm a sucker for a pretty face. Seemed a shame to kill her if I didn't have to. Still, my patience has its limits. She's lucky she's safe inside, because today was her last chance to pony up."

I wondered if Mac realized what a close shave she'd had. Based on what Capone and Melody had told me, I doubted there was much money left to pony up, and Frates wasn't likely to have looked kindly on her spending spree. She'd underestimated her blackmailer, probably thinking whoever it was couldn't get what she no longer had. She'd been proven right, but only by pure luck. Her spending spree had led to her arrest, which had saved her from Frates's wrath.

Before I even came to terms with my first realization, a second, far more horrifying mental picture formed. This wasn't just about stolen money. If Delilah & Son was Frates's "last stop" before skipping town, I doubted he was leaving with only his "consolation prize" car. Mac had spent the money from Juice Revolution, and the money from Delilah & Son was AWOL, which meant Frates probably already had the money from the brewery renovation site. He must've gotten it the night Ulrich was killed.

"Oh my god," I whispered. "The break-in at the new brewpub. That was you, wasn't it?"

His face darkened. "Smart *and* pretty." He clicked his tongue against the roof of his mouth. "It really is a shame. I wish I could at least guarantee you'd leave a nice-looking corpse, but . . ." He waggled the gun.

I steeled myself, getting ready for one last frantic escape attempt. If I died here, the truth about Ulrich's murder might never be known. Renee could rot in prison for something she didn't do. I hoped my phone was still recording, that Frates would somehow overlook it, and that the recording would end up in the right hands. Assuming he'd leave my body somewhere it could be found, that is.

My eyes darted around the room. The space within arms' length was devoid of anything that could be turned into a weapon, but just beyond where Frates stood, there were knives, a fire extinguisher, any number of heavy cans and jars. Could I catch him off guard? Knock him into something sharp? Or were these frantic heartbeats to be my last?

As my mind worked through my options, I asked, "So, what? Did Graham Ulrich walk in on you while you were knocking holes in the wall? Or maybe he saw you trying to cover your tracks by making it look like a break in?"

"I don't like to go into detail about my work. Let's just say I should change my name from Cinco to Seis, and leave it at that." His tone was flat, almost sad. I guess he was telling the truth—he didn't enjoy killing. He probably wasn't going to enjoy murdering me. Not much consolation in that. "Sometimes people like Graham Ulrich end up in the wrong place at the wrong time," he continued. "Kind of like you."

"*Seis*? With Graham Ulrich, isn't it already *siete*?" I asked, buying as many precious seconds as I could.

"There's Graham, plus the guy you poisoned in Juice Revolution, plus your original five. That makes seven."

"I had nothing to do with that. In fact, that threw off my whole game," he said. "I'd been closing in on the Mc-Clintock girl, about to get her to hand over the money or else shut her up for good. But after that guy dropped dead, I had to lie low for a while because the cops were crawling all over the place. Meanwhile, she blew through a huge pile of my cash."

"Why did you run away then, when he collapsed?" Every word felt more and more like the last thing I'd ever say. Should I have chosen something profound instead of asking a question? Prayed a Hail Mary maybe?

"I'd have been stupid to stay. I've seen guys die before. Lots. And I knew from the jump that's where that situation was headed. It wasn't in my interests to stick around and enjoy the show. Just like I'd be stupid to stick around here any longer." He regarded the gun as he raised it toward my head. "Huh, I guess with Graham Ulrich and now you it'll be *siete* after all. Funny thing is, I don't even speak Spanish."

CHAPTER 26

The air inside my chest turned to ice. Impossible to breathe. Impossible to move. Six-foot-five and three hundred pounds of violent assassin stood before me, aiming a gun at my head. My brain screamed *Fight!*, yet my body sat rooted to Auntie Biz's stool. The only movement I could manage was to shut my eyes. I could refuse him at least that victory. Refuse to let the last thing I'd lay my eyes on be Cinco Frates's merciless face. Instead, I summoned an image of the lake from my childhood. The pure blue, welcoming crispness of the lake. Me and my sister, running along Biz's dock and vaulting headlong into the deep water.

Crash!

My eyes flew open. The sound hadn't come from my mental image, but from somewhere very real, and close behind me. The gun in Frates's hand wavered as his gaze flitted to the floor. I didn't turn to see what had distracted him. Instead, my body finally complied with my mind's command. I barreled forward, plowing straight at the arm that held the gun. A shot went off next to my face with a deafening blast. The flash of the muzzle lit up the dim space, momentarily blinding both me and Frates. I didn't need to see, though. I knew my kitchen like the back of my hand. I rushed past Frates, grabbing a colossal cast-iron griddle pan from the stovetop. Taking high aim, I connected it with the side of his face.

Every chef knows the importance of choosing the right pan for the job, and this time I'd gotten it very right. Frates groaned and slumped to his knees. For good measure, I took a second swing at his kneeling figure. The sound—like the collision of two enormous billiard balls—almost made me gag. Frates, out cold, didn't brace for the fall as he hit the floor face-first.

That's when I saw what had captured his attention in the crucial second before he pulled the trigger. A stack of metal prep bowls lay scattered across the floor. Butterball cowered on the undercounter shelf where the bowls had been stored, peeking out to see if the commotion and noise had come to an end. I gingerly reached my toe out to nudge Frates's still form. Not even a twitch of movement. Still, I gripped the pan tightly as I picked my way over and around his large, prone body and knelt at shelf level in front of my cat. I kicked the gun away from Frates with my bare toes.

"It's okay, bud," I soothed. I set down the pan and reached for Butterball, but he refused to be held, instead stretching to grab something with his mouth. Once he had the object firmly grasped, he leaned into me, allowing me to pick up him and his prize—an entire fully cooked bratwurst.

Before I could even begin to contemplate how Butterball had teleported himself into the kitchen, the sound of crunching glass and footsteps caused my heart to race anew. Did Frates have an accomplice? I shifted Butterball on to my hip and grabbed the pan with my free hand.

"Delilah?" a voice called. Capone's voice. I rushed out into the dining room, still clinging to the pan, Butterball, and his treasured sausage.

In the dim illumination offered by the security lights, I could see Capone moving toward me, his eyes scanning the room, one hand on the holster of his service weapon. Capone flicked on the wall switch, bathing the dining room in a warm glow. The area near the kitchen looked like the epicenter of a mini earthquake. In the flurry of Frates grabbing me, I'd had only a vague awareness of knocking into chairs and tables. One of my flipflops lay on the floor, ripped off during the struggle. I hadn't even noticed.

"He's in there," I panted. "Frates."

Capone rushed past me, already unholstering his weapon. I followed him into the kitchen a moment later to find him crouched next to Frates's body, checking the pulse in his neck.

"Is he . . ." I began.

"He's breathing. Out cold, though." He picked up Frates's gun from where I'd kicked it and tucked it into his waistband. Then he knelt across Frates's wide back, rotating the unconscious man's meaty shoulders in order to cuff his wrists together. "But just in case." Without turning to look at me, he called, "Are you okay?"

"Uh-huh."

Capone drew out his radio and relayed the request for an ambulance and backup officers. With the urgent matters attended to, he rose and crossed the room in two steps, enfolding me in his arms—Butterball, pan, bratwurst, and all. For a split second, I thought I might fall apart and start sobbing messily against his chest. By all rights, the bullet that was lodged somewhere in my kitchen ceiling should be in the back of my skull. But as the earthy, vanilla smell of Capone's body washed over me, my turbulent emotions calmed.

He began to stroke my hair while I nestled my face into his neck and just breathed. Without conscious thought, I pressed my lips against the skin next to his Adam's apple. He responded by pulling me tighter, his strong fingers pressing into the small of my back. His body heat radiated through the thin material of my pajamas, warming my insides to a melting point. When he whispered my name, my knees almost went out from underneath me.

Butterball broke the spell, shifting within our cozy huddle and allowing the bratwurst to drop from his mouth to the floor with a splat. "*Mew*?" he asked looking from me to Capone.

"I don't know, buddy," Capone replied, gently releasing me from his embrace. His lips formed a smile. "I just got here. Why don't *you* tell *me* what happened?"

I reluctantly pulled away from Capone. With Butterball's interruption, the mood had changed, and we were back to reality. I said, "I guess I can probably let go of this pan now."

"Probably," he agreed.

"How did you know I was in trouble?" I asked. I pulled my robe tight around me.

"When I saw your text with the picture of Mac's car, I knew something was up," he said. "I didn't want to wake up the whole department in the middle of the night if it turned out that a friend had a spare set of keys and had moved it or something innocent like that. But I also didn't want to leave you on your own if it turned out to be something more."

"Thank god you came," I said. I looked up at the ceiling, realizing that my desperate prayer for a miracle had been answered in the form of a ravenous cat and a work-aholic detective.

I felt disembodied over the next hour, watching from some floating space outside myself as the paramedics and other officers arrived. Only with help from Capone were they able to shift Frates onto the gurney for his ride to the hospital. With Butterball resting in my lap, I gave my statement, the details of my encounter with Frates echoing strangely inside my ears. *Did that really just happen?* Finally, somewhere toward sunup, the frenzy of activity eased and I began to settle back into myself. Besides Capone, only Officer Rettberg remained, her always-serious face looking even more resolute than usual. She'd shown up to the scene with her perfect, slicked-back bun intact, despite the ungodly hour. I wondered if she slept with her hair like that. Capone and I sat in the dining room, while Rettberg stayed in the kitchen, taking evidentiary photos.

"What time is it?" I asked, watching through the windows as the first pink tendrils of morning began to curl around the edges of the lake.

Capone looked at his laptop screen. "Six twenty."

I ran my fingers through my hair. "The festival is today. Rabbit's going to be here in an hour with the rental van to get the last of the stuff loaded. We're meeting everyone else at the park to get set up. I better get in the shower."

"You've been through a lot. I'm sure they'd understand if you need to call it off," he said.

I lowered my chin and fixed a dismissive look on him.

He held out his palms. "Okay, I should've known better."

"So this solves Ulrich's murder," I said. "Renee's off the hook."

"I'm just glad I was able to keep the chief from arresting her." Capone sighed. "One less mess to clean up."

I was surprised at how quickly Capone and I had reverted to our usual back-and-forth conversation. Now that the overhead lights were on and the immediate danger had passed, the intimacy of our embrace evaporated like dewdrops in the sunshine.

"So, Graham's murderer is behind bars, assuming you can make the charges against Frates stick this time," I said. A thought occurred to me. "I'm going to have to testify, aren't I?" I pulled my robe a little tighter around my body, chilled by the knowledge that Frates had a track record of eliminating threats against him.

He shook his head. "You recording his confession was a stroke of genius. We'll make sure Frates knows that we have hard evidence so we don't need your testimony to nail him. There would be no point in him going after you."

"What about to get revenge?" I asked. "He's not going to be very happy with me when he wakes up."

"Yeah, I'd say you're probably off his Christmas card list."

I tried to smile.

Capone reached across the table and touched my arm reassuringly. "He's a contract killer, not a sociopath. You told me yourself he said he doesn't enjoy hurting people. Killing is a means to an end for him."

"Let's hope so," I said. "What do you think about the poisonings? Frates had no reason to lie to me when he said he wasn't involved. Did you get anything out of Mac?"

"As a matter fact, yes. We got a near perfect corroboration of what Frates told you. She admitted that she found the money in the basement of Juice Revolution. That part of the building wasn't really touched when the upstairs was renovated. You know those weird little half doors you find in old buildings?"

I nodded. My sister and I had one in our room when we were kids. She used to tell me a troll lived in there and that if I was very quiet, I'd hear him breathing. I don't think I slept for the whole year we lived in that apartment.

Capone leaned back in his chair. "Out of sheer curiosity, Mac opened the little door one day when she went down to get something out of storage. Inside, there was a suitcase of cash, hidden behind some old junk," he explained. "She said she thought about telling Jordan, but then figured, finders keepers. She held on to the money for a week or two to see if anyone would ask about it, and when no one did, she started spending it. But then a note showed up. Jarka found it next to the register and showed it to both her and Jordan."

"Did Mac know it was meant for her?" I asked.

"Absolutely," he said. "It was something like 'I know you took the money and it's payback time.' Not exactly subtle. But she played it cool in front of Jarka and Jordan. The note you found was apparently the second one."

"And there was a third one as well," I explained. "Melody said that Mac brought it home. Melody found it the night I picked her up from the farm, when I called you about the jimson weed. It said, 'Better watch your back because thieves get what they deserve.' Mac must've known that was meant for her, too, so she hid it."

"Sounds like there were at least four notes in all, then. The one you found at Juice Revolution, Mac admitted she'd seen right before Wong collapsed. She planned to destroy it, but didn't have time with all the commotion. Apparently those Juice Revolution tunics don't have pockets. When she went back to pick it up, it was gone. She had no idea where it disappeared to. After that, she ramped up her spending. I think she was hoping if the money was spent, that somehow made the problem magically disappear."

"So we know she took the money. But how does that connect to the poisonings? Without a motive to kill Jordan, is a circumstantial case going to be enough to convince a jury?" I asked.

"I'm not sure she realized it, but the true story of how she came by the money helps paint a better picture of her potential motive. If she thought Jordan knew about it, or that she might find out about it and claim ownership, that could've been threatening to her." He held out his hands, as if inviting me to offer a more plausible scenario. "For the time being, I can hold her on a larceny charge. The law is pretty clear that holding or possessing property that you know doesn't belong to you is illegal. You have to prove you made a reasonable effort to find the rightful owner, which clearly Mac didn't. If this does turn out to be Rocco's money, it technically belongs to the government, although who knows if that'll ever be proved," he said.

Rettberg poked her head out of the kitchen door. "Sir, you need to come and check this out," she said.

Capone raised an eyebrow and closed his laptop screen. I held Butterball in my arms as we followed the prim junior officer into the kitchen.

Rettberg knelt on the floor near the spot where I'd found Butterball earlier and withdrew a flashlight from her tactical vest. We stooped down beside her. She pushed aside the mixing bowls and blender parts and shined the light along the wall at the rear of the shelf. "See that?" she said. Sure enough, at the bottom of the wall, there was a run about a foot wide where no baseboard had been installed. The drywall hovered a few inches off the floor. She played the light along the gap, revealing a spot where a large, chipped brick had been pushed out from the inner wall. "I think I might have solved at least one breaking and entering," she said. "Clearly, this is the work of a skilled cat burglar."

Rettberg cracked only the slightest smile, and it took both Capone and I a full second to realize she was joking and burst into laughter.

"Here's further evidence," she said. She jiggled another loose brick and pulled it away from the wall, and then reached into the gap. Laying her upper body on the shelf, she was able to get her whole arm inside all the way to her elbow. "I think it's a tunnel," she explained.

Capone patted Butterball's hefty midsection. "You're lucky you didn't get stuck in there, big guy."

Out of the hole, Rettberg pulled a dusty, ragged object. As she brought it out into the light, it was revealed to be a hunk of bratwurst, very much worse for the wear.

Capone wrinkled his nose. "That's nasty, Butterball."

The cat stirred in my arms, whether at the mention of his name or the smell of slightly rancid meat, I couldn't tell.

I reached past Rettberg and took hold of one of the loose bricks she'd dislodged. It was crumbling and worn with age. "This is so strange. Julio, my contractor, told me they had to remove all the original brick from this wall and replace it with breeze block."

"Well, apparently they missed a few. If I had to guess, I'd say you'll find the other end of this passage somewhere in your apartment," Rettberg said, dropping the bratwurst into the trash can. "That would explain how your cat got down here."

I lifted Butterball and held his face up to mine. He refused to meet my eyes, as he always did when he knew a reproach was coming his way. "You little stinker," I scolded. "No wonder he hasn't lost any weight." I lowered the cat to the floor. "I bet he wrecked my kitchen that day when I thought we'd had a break-in. Probably knocked something over and then scared himself into a frenzy. He's done that before." Butterball hopped on to Auntie Biz's perch and began daintily licking his paws, daring us to prove that he'd been responsible for ransacking my restaurant and squirreling away questionable meat inside the wall. I shook my head at his chutzpah. "All those times I thought he was hiding under the bed, he was probably down here in his secret bratwurst passageway."

Rettberg took out her notebook and pen. "Victim reports that suspect repeatedly penetrated her bedroom tunnel with a large sausage," she narrated. Her sober tone and expression didn't change, but her eyes twinkled ever so slightly.

The color rose in Capone's cheeks. He cleared his throat and said, "I think we're done here."

CHAPTER 27

The morning sunlight sparkled on the lake's surface as Rabbit and I off-roaded our rented van through the grass toward our assigned tent. Although it would be several hours before the Taste of Wisconsin opened to festival-goers, the town's lakefront park had already taken on a carnival-like atmosphere. On one end of the park lay the town's public beach and Frank Lloyd Wright–style library; on the other, the public marina. White vinyl food and beverage tents ran in parallel lines, interspersed among the park's mature trees and walking paths. The shore path marked the south boundary, beyond which lay the lake. A stage and concentric semicircles of chairs had been erected at the west end of the tent rows.

"Sure you're up for doing this today, chef? I don't think I would bounce back from a run-in with Cinco Frates that quick," Rabbit said. "There's guys I did time with, and I'm talking hard-core guys, who get weak-kneed if you mention his name."

While Rabbit and I were loading up the van, I'd given him a very superficial account of what had befallen me during the night. Frankly, I would have preferred not to talk about it at all. I just wanted to get through the day. However, there'd been no avoiding the topic. I hadn't had time to clean up the mayhem in the kitchen and dining room; the broken glass in the front door also demanded an explanation.

"I'm fine," I assured him. "Let's just concentrate on today."

There was certainly plenty to concentrate on. With a picture-perfect forecast of pleasantly warm, sunny weather, the festival was expected to draw a sizable crowd. As always, the festival itself—including live music, a sailboat regatta, and kids' entertainment—would be free to attend, with Taste of Wisconsin food available for purchase separately. Each food vendor would offer a curated selection from its regular menu as well as smaller "Taste of" portions of its contest entry for five dollars each. The setup allowed attendees to try a dozen or more dishes without risking nuclear levels of indigestion. Opening at ten o'clock, the festival would culminate with the contest judging and winner announcement just before seven p.m. If I could just push through until seven, there would be sleep. And wine. And kitty cuddles on my couch.

Rabbit pulled the van in alongside our tent, where Melody, Sonya, and Daniel were already unpacking the supplies we'd stashed in Sonya's car the previous day. The three of them came over and greeted us. They all seemed energetic, although Melody's expression looked decidedly downcast. I supposed Biz had broken the news about the imminent sale of the cottage. Or Melody was worried about her cousin's plight. Or both. I was glad she'd showed up. If the festival was as busy as predicted, we'd need all the help we could get—even if we risked the possibility of losing another patio umbrella to a fit of unbridled rage. She and Daniel went to the back of the van to help Rabbit unload. I moved to join them but Sonya intercepted me, taking hold of my arm. She steered me a little ways away from the tents to ensure we couldn't be overheard.

"Melody just told me about Biz losing her house. How awful," she said.

"I know." I shook my head. "Did Melody seem okay? Biz can move in with me if she needs to, God help us. I can handle sleeping on the couch if it keeps her from going into some kind of subsidized assisted living place. She'd absolutely hate that. But there's no way I can put Melody up for more than a few nights. I feel terrible."

"I wish I had the space for her," Sonya said. Since she moved to Geneva Bay, she'd been renting a guest house in town while looking for something affordable to buy. With her modest budget, finding a suitable place was no easy task. "Maybe once I find a house."

"I'm sure she can move back to the farm if it comes to it. It's just that it was going so well with Biz," I said.

Sonya clicked her tongue. "It's terrible all the way around." She paused, her gaze drifting toward the impressive mansions that ringed the opposite shore. From this distance, they looked like delicately crafted dollhouses.

"Those places probably have twenty spare bedrooms apiece," I said wistfully.

"You had no idea what was going on with Biz?" Sonya asked.

"I knew she was out of sorts, but I had no idea why. I should have, but I didn't," I admitted. "Biz is so private about money and she's always been such a whiz with finances. Even last year when she was clearly struggling, I thought it would insult her if I asked to get financial power of attorney. Her caregiver was supposed to help with anything she needed, but of course that backfired spectacularly." I turned to look down the shore path in the direction of Biz's cottage. "It's really going to hurt to lose that place."

Sonya's eyes widened as she took notice of the side of my face, which had been revealed when I turned my head. "Geez, Dee, you've got a huge bruise. What happened?" She reached out to place her fingers delicately against my cheek.

I'd tried to use makeup to camouflage the welt that rose on the spot where Frates belted me, but Sonya's expert eye saw right through my poor disguise.

"First off, great news," I replied. "Cinco Frates confessed to Ulrich's murder, so Renee is out of the crosshairs."

Her eyes lit up. "I knew she was innocent! I have to call Uncle Avi." She reached into the pocket of her cherry red swing dress and took out her phone. She took a few steps away, but froze mid-stride. "Hang on. What does Cinco Frates's confession have to do with your face?"

"Long story," I began. I tried to get my mind around how to summarize the saga of Rocco, his accountant, the hidden stashes of money, the buildings held in trust, the secret jailhouse message, the accountant's death, Mac's illicit windfall, Ulrich's murder, last night's break-in, my near-death experience, Butterball's timely appearance, the sausage tunnel, and the reason our best cast-iron grill pan was temporarily impounded as evidence by the Geneva Bay PD. Instead, I said, "We can talk about it tonight, over a bottle or ten of rosé."

While I'd been talking to Sonya, I noticed Jordan and Jarka arrive at the adjacent tent and begin arranging vats of liquid and containers of ingredients. Out of the blue, Sam rounded the side of the tent hauling a crate of lemons. He set it on a table and hailed me.

"You go call your uncle," I said to Sonya. "I'll catch up with you in a minute."

"Okay, but before we open to the public, I'm coming at that bruise with some foundation and powder," she said. "We can't have our head chef looking like she moonlights as a streetfighter. This is the one day when you and me are on full display instead of socked away in the kitchen." She swept her hands along her body, highlighting the knotted polka-dot scarf in her hair, her flawless makeup, and the fifties-style dress she'd swapped for the chef's uniform she usually wore during service. "*Some* of us made a bit of an effort." She walked off toward the lake, already talking excitedly into her phone.

I headed to the Juice Revolution tent, which lay only a few steps away from ours. "What brings *you* here this morning?" I asked Sam.

"Lending a helping hand." He picked up a lemon and threw it into the air, popping it off his bicep before catching it in his hand again. "Without Mac, Jordan's short-staffed, so I sailed over with her on the boat this morning." He paused, frowing. "What happened to your face?"

"Accident in the kitchen." I touched my swollen cheek. "How's Jordan taking Mac's arrest?" I asked, moving on quickly. "It must've been a shock to have someone so close to her under suspicion for trying to kill her."

"Oh, for sure." He looked over his shoulder, presumably to make sure Jordan wasn't nearby. "I wonder if Mac was jealous of her. Jordan is an ambitious woman, and some people find that threatening." He smiled his sweet, boyish smile. "You were never intimidated by other strong women. Or men, for that matter. You two have that in common—confidence in your ability to stand on your own two feet."

In a lightweight Patagonia sweatshirt, with his long hair free, he looked casual and healthy, beautiful and pure. Every detail of his appearance married with the stunning scenery that formed the backdrop to the festival. I could picture him helming his boat, Jordan at his side, leaning into the wind—a readymade cover for *On the Water* magazine. Clearly, his life had returned to its well-ordered status quo—good had triumphed over evil. His loved ones were safe. God was in his heaven, and all was right with the world. Magic.

I longed to say, "Hey, man, thanks for the 'standing on my own two feet' pep talk, but I've been to hell and back, so can you just write me a check for a hundred grand so I can save Biz's house and my restaurant?" He would've done it, I had no doubt. Instead, I said, "Uh-huh," and flashed a tight smile. "Can I ask you something?"

"Sure thing," he said, resting the lemon he held on top of the others in the crate.

"Do you remember anything about the wall they had to replace in the restaurant kitchen during the reno?" I asked.

"Uh, yeah, actually I do. Why?" He looked slightly taken aback.

"It seems like maybe the work wasn't done right," I said. "It's not like Julio to condone shoddy work."

Sam ran his hands through his hair and glanced off toward the lake. When his gaze returned to me, he'd taken on a sheepish expression. "I was kind of hoping you'd never find out about that. You were in the city, dealing with your father's estate, and I didn't want to bother you with minor details. Julio was away from the job site for a week—do you remember when his daughter had that emergency appendectomy?"

I nodded.

"The drywall guy told me they'd found an issue, an old chimney that would be hard to take down, and asked if I wanted him to just box it in with plasterboard. I told him I was fine with whatever. I found out later that Julio had explicitly told him to wait and take care of it properly. By the time I found that out, though, the work had already been done. I felt bad for the guy and I didn't want to get him in trouble, and I didn't want to delay the project by having to rip it out and start again. So I covered for him."

I closed my eyes briefly, trying to tamp down my annoyance. I didn't want to go into the whole saga of Frates's search for the hidden money and Butterball's adventures inside the wall, so I said, "The work wasn't done properly. There's a gap between the drywall and the brick. The opening runs all the way up to my apartment. I'm going to have to get a structural engineer to look at it to make sure it's safe."

"Geez, I'm sorry. It'll be fine, though, I'm sure. Just send me the bill for any remedial work that needs to be done," Sam said. "I'll pay, of course."

"Sam, thank you, but that's not the point. That guy was ripping off Julio. Stealing. Julio ended up firing him."

"I'm sorry," Sam said again. "I didn't want to create a problem."

"And you didn't want to be the bad guy," I muttered under my breath.

"Huh?"

"Nothing," I said, turning up the volume on my voice. Sam had so many good qualities—his kindness, his generosity, his tranquility. He lived a charmed life, and I'd loved being a part of it for a time. But there was too much Chicago in me not to chafe at that kind of willful ignorance.

Jordan peeked around the side of the tent. Seeing me, she waved.

"Hey, Delilah, good to see you. Babe," she called, turning to Sam, "I'm sorry to interrupt, but can you help Jarka put together some more to-go sachets of the gut microbiome super-cleanse powder?"

Before I could restrain it, a horse-like bray escaped my lips.

Jordan's black baby doll eyes opened wide, inviting me to share the joke with her.

I shook my head, trying to turn my inelegant laugh into a cough. "Sorry, allergies."

"Well, gotta go," Sam said to me as Jordan moved back into the tent. He picked up another lemon and juggled it from hand to hand, pausing and regarding the oblong fruit with a troubled gaze. He took a step toward the Juice Revolution tent, but stopped and turned back to me. "I have to say, I really thought Harold was involved somehow, in the poisonings."

"Jordan seems to think his crush on her was harmless," I replied.

He shook his head. "It's not just that. Do you remember the drink orders that day? Jordan said you needed a One in a Melon to control your bile. She ordered a Maximum-Wattage Anti-Tox Mocktail for herself, and the same for Harold, to balance his chi. She and Harold had the same thing."

I finished his thought. "But Harold didn't get sick."

"Yeah. Weird, right? So I was wondering, did he not drink his because he knew it was poisoned?"

"No, he definitely drank it," I replied. "I remember seeing him down it while he was talking to Jarka." I couldn't believe that inconsistent detail hadn't occurred to me earlier.

"Oh, well, that's what I get for second-guessing the cops." Sam shook his head and tossed the lemon back into the crate. "Anyway, I've gotta get to work."

I stood fixed to the ground for a moment. My conversation with Sam stirred up the sediment that had been resting at the bottom of my brain. Something, some messy detail, floated there, but I couldn't see it clearly.

From the moment the festival opened, the day passed in the kind of busy, foodie blur I was born for. Even in the unfamiliar confines of an open-sided tent, with rented equipment and an altered menu, my team worked like an experienced naval crew. Daniel and Melody, with their top-notch customer service skills, handled the registers. Sonya and Rabbit, cool under pressure at the prep tables at the back of the tent, assembled ingredients and shuffled pizzas in and out of the ovens. I shuttled back and forth between them, expediting and packaging, keeping the ship running smoothly. Everyone knew their stations and performed their roles beautifully. Order, fire, pickup, repeat. Take the money, serve the food. Restock, wipe down, ring up, smile.

As chef, I usually didn't get to hear diners' reactions in real time. Typically, compliments came in the form of licked-clean plates or repeat customers asking the waitstaff to pass on their good wishes. Being in an open-sided tent allowed me the rare opportunity to bask in the "ooh"s and "aah"s as people tried our offerings.

It wasn't until I heard Harold Heyer's familiar, trilling voice that I realized how late it had gotten. "Greetings, my deep-dish dynamic duo," he called, sidling up to our tent. "Just making the rounds of the tents to give you your ten-minute warning. All the contest entries need to be labeled and in the judging tent by six p.m."

"Oh my gosh, I could *eggs*-plode with *eggs*-citement," Sonya said, coming up alongside me. "We'll get an *eggs*-tra special portion of our entry put together for you."

"That sounds exquisite," Harold said.

"*Eggs*-quisite," Sonya agreed, nodding solemnly.

"Don't tell me anything about your entry," Harold continued. "I'm going to judge all the entries blind so I can be as impartial as possible. I made scorecards to rank them all in terms of appearance, execution, taste, and most importantly, Wisconsin-ness."

"How important is *eggs*-ecution to the overall score?" Sonya asked, resting her chin earnestly on her fist.

I kicked her ankle and said, "I'm sure it's all very important. How many entries are there?"

"Over two dozen. The most we've ever had," Harold replied. "My father would be so happy. He loved this festival." His voice filled with unexpected emotion as he looked toward Main Street, where his family's store used to stand.

"You and Jordan worked at Heyers together, right?" I asked.

He nodded. "Oh, yes. Dad thought the world of her. She was such a whiz with accounting. Only two years out of high school, and she was promoted to head bookkeeper."

"I didn't realize that she had such an important position," I said.

"Heavens, yes. Dad was never very good at finances. I suppose you've heard about all that." Harold's tone was muted. An intense sincerity had taken the place of his trademark carpet bombing of optimism. "He never would've hurt the company on purpose, I'm sure of it. If there was anything wrong with the accounts, it was an oversight. He loved Geneva Bay too much to do anything that would hurt it."

"I'm sure you're right," I said, giving him an encouraging smile.

He clapped his hands, as if trying to spark his internal combustion engine into motion. "Well, much as I'd love to remain in your delightful company all day, duty calls. I must press on and alert the other entrants. I see the ever-radiant Jarka Gagamova over there. What a vision she is." He cast a longing glance in the direction of the Juice Revolution tent.

Once he moved away, I turned to Sonya. "You're terrible. He was trying to share his feelings."

"I know. He was really coming out of his *shell*, don't you think?" she replied.

I rolled my eyes. "I've got a joke for you. Knock knock."

"Who's there?"

"You better help me put together our contest entry or I'm going to *knock* you upside your head," I deadpanned.

"Is that an *eggs*-ecutive order?"

CHAPTER 28

Still shaking my head at Sonya's string of terrible egg puns, I pushed her toward the prep area at the back of the tent. Together, she and I assembled our pretzel bites, pickled veggies, sliced brats, and assorted dipping sauces into a contest-worthy plate. We stepped back to admire our work. We'd managed to make bratwurst, if not exactly beautiful, at least highly appetizing.

"Well," Sonya said. "Here goes nothing."

"More like here goes everything," I replied. Would this be enough to bring home the contest prize for us?

"Do you want me to take it to the judging tent?" Melody asked, regarding our finished masterpiece. "Seems like the crowd's thinning out. I guess everyone's starting to head over to the stage to get seats for the announcement."

"I'll take it," I said. "I could use a little walk."

I made my way down the path toward the judging tent, weaving carefully through the cuddling couples and balloon-clutching kids. I fell into step behind two amateur gourmands doing their own unofficial judging of the dishes.

"To me, the contest is between that pretzel thing from Delilah & Son and the rosewater and pistachio frozen

custard from the Turkish place," I heard a middle-aged
Indian woman in a sherbet orange sari say.

"No, no, no," her husband replied. "How can you even
consider the frozen custard? Did you dip the little pret-
zels in the cheese sauce?"

I beamed inwardly, hoping that Harold would agree
with the couple's verdict. The judging tent was the only
one in the park fully enclosed by white vinyl sides. All
the vendor stalls stood open at three sides so customers
could watch as their food was cooked. I imagined Harold
inside this sanctum, surrounded by flavorless sorbets and
unsalted crackers to cleanse his palate between tastings.
Maybe he'd never come out, choosing to appear from now
on only as a holographic floating head, like the Great and
Powerful Oz. I wanted to be angry that my fate was in
the hands of someone without any culinary credentials,
but somehow I couldn't summon even a flicker of rage.
Sure, Graham Ulrich had the name and the resumé, but
he couldn't have cared less about this town or our contest. Harold, on the other hand, had spent his entire adult
life as the town's cheerleader-in-chief. I had no doubt that
he'd roll every last cheese curd and butter burger and bite
of booyah stew around his taste buds trying to determine
which best exemplified the terroir of his beloved little corner of Wisconsin.

A trio of event volunteers flanked the tent's entrance,
cataloguing the entries and ferrying them inside to be
judged. I handed our deconstructed deep-dish over to one
of them, a middle-aged woman with shellacked blond
hair and the expansive bosom of a Wagnerian soprano.
"Lori-Anne" matched my dish against its preassigned
number card, cooing, "Ooh, that cheese sauce looks so
scrummy, I want to just dive right in and take a bath in it.
I'll get this right inside."

I smiled at her and headed back toward our tent. Our destiny was in God's hands and upon Harold Heyer's tongue. We could take a few last orders while Harold sampled his way through the contest entries, and then it would be time to start packing up and making our way to the stage for the verdict.

Ahead of me, I saw the familiar contours of Capone's muscular physique. In his arms, he cradled a little bundle of cherub-cheeked cuteness—his two-year-old granddaughter, Audra. Next to them walked a lankier, darker-skinned version Capone. The resemblance between the two men left no doubt—it had to be Audra's father, Calvin Capone Jr. Capone's son had been widowed shortly after Audra's birth, and now Capone and his jazz singer mother did the lion's share of childcare during the week so that Calvin Jr. could concentrate on his med school studies. The act of juggling one toddler between three adults seemed to work well for them, since Capone, his son, and his mother were all on complimentary schedules.

"Delilah," Capone called, catching sight of me.

"Hi," I replied. I felt uncharacteristically shy seeing Capone with his family, under a cloudless blue sky. Virtually all of my interactions with the elder Capone since I'd first met him had revolved around murder investigations. Now, here we were, running into each other outside our professional roles, divorced from our natural habitats. I'd seen Capone only a few hours earlier, of course, when I'd fallen into his arms, a disheveled, traumatized mess. Our shared world centered on roasting-hot kitchens and blood-spattered crime scenes, not family outings and a cavalcade of well-dressed day-trippers gliding by in flashy yachts. I felt exposed, as if we'd been having a clandestine affair that had suddenly been revealed.

"Oh, hey," the younger Capone said in greeting.

)

"You're the chef, right? Dad's mentioned you." The corner of his lip curved upward as he shot a sidelong glance toward his father. "A few times."

I blushed. Embarrassment—another emotion not in common use for me. Capone, too, looked like he wanted to melt into the lush grass beneath our feet. Calvin, by contrast, seemed perfectly at ease, clearly relishing our junior high school levels of mortification.

We made small talk for a few minutes. Me, enquiring politely about Calvin's medical school studies; him, asking about the restaurant and the nature of the food contest. Audra, whose vocabulary had expanded by leaps and bounds since I'd met her a few months prior, provided comic relief by trying to pronounce my name.

After cycling through "Dee-lah and Die-lie, she finally settled on "Dolly."

"It's a tough one," I granted, laughing. "Tell your daddy and your granddad to bring you to Dolly's restaurant sometime. I'll make you any kind of pizza you want, and you can play with my kitty cat."

"If there's pizza and a cat, you can bet we'll be there," Calvin Jr. laughed. "If you can somehow get Elsa from *Frozen* to be our server, she'll never leave."

"We should let you get back," Capone said. "The big contest announcement is coming soon."

Calvin swept his daughter into his arms and blew a raspberry on her chubby cheek. "And I promised this little monster she could get her face painted like a mermaid angel. Whatever that means. We better be quick if we're going to get there before they close. Say bye-bye to Miss Delilah," he said.

"Buh-bah, Dolly," she called, flapping her tiny, dimpled fingers as they turned to walk away.

Names, my brain whispered. *The names*. Some clue,

some crucial bit of information floated past me like the wisp of a dandelion seed. But even as I reached for it, it drifted away.

Instead of moving off with Calvin and Audra, Capone stopped in front of me and peered into my face with a concerned look. "Everything okay?"

"Yeah, yeah," I said, giving my head a little shake. Calling to Calvin, I asked, "Could I steal your dad for a minute?"

"Not sure what you'd want with a janky old geezer like this," he said, stepping back toward us and giving his dad a good-humored slap on the back, "but go ahead and take him." Turning to his dad, he said, "We'll catch you by the stage later on."

Capone and I watched the pair for a moment and then set off toward the Delilah & Son tent.

"What's up?" he asked.

"I'm not sure. Something Sam said earlier has been bothering me," I explained. "About the poisonings. He pointed out that Harold had the same smoothie as Jordan, but he didn't get sick. I remember her prescribing it specially for Harold to balance his chi. Mac told me that Jordan's usual smoothie, the one Harold had, wasn't officially on the menu. It had some kind of extinct seaweed in it."

His forehead creased. "Extinct?"

"Never mind. What I mean is the kelp powder was a special add-in. Jordan was the only one who used it regularly," I explained.

"I know. Presumably, that's why the killer targeted that ingredient. To be sure Jordan would be on the receiving end of it. If he or she had poisoned something more commonly used, half of the customers would've gotten sick or died," Capone said.

"Right, and Wong couldn't have had the same drink as the other two. He couldn't have ordered a special off-menu item because he'd never been there before, and I don't think Jordan would have prescribed that add-in for him. I didn't see them talking," I said.

"No, he definitely ordered something different," Capone said. "The register at Juice Revolution creates a sticker with every order, so the name of the patron prints out along with their drink order. They stick that on the cup to keep track of the orders. I checked the register, and Wong ordered something called the Verdant Hills Super Juice."

"So how did the poison get into Wong's drink?" I asked.

He cracked his knuckles and looked off toward the lake. "I wish I knew. If we're working on the assumption that Wong was collateral damage, then some kind of mix-up with the ingredients or equipment contamination is most likely. The killer wouldn't have sprinkled the kelp powder on at the very end of the preparation. They'd want it mixed in thoroughly. That argues for one of the staff being the guilty party."

I tapped my fingers on my lip, thinking. "Did you test the blenders and stuff?"

"We did, and one of them showed trace amounts of jimson weed, which supports the equipment-contamination theory. But you have to remember that we didn't process the scene until the following day. Unfortunately, everything had been cleaned, the trash taken out, pretty much all the physical evidence compromised or destroyed. According to the ticketing system, your drink was made before the others, which explains why you didn't get sick. Harold's came next. Then Wong's. Then Jordan's. Maybe the killer slipped the jimson weed into the kelp powder right after Harold's smoothie was made, thinking that Jordan's would be next. Or maybe they didn't care if they killed an innocent bystander, as long as they killed Jordan, too." Capone stopped walking and fell into a thoughtful silence. "Did you say Jordan 'prescribed' smoothies? What did you mean by that?"

"She looks at your aura or something and tells you what kind of drink will be best for you. Apparently, I have an imbalance of my bile, so she told me to have something with cumin, to cleanse my liver," I explained.

"So she told people what drinks they should have?" he asked. "Nobody mentioned that."

"I don't think she did it for every customer, but she did it for me and Harold. Mac said she did it quite a bit," I replied.

By now, we'd drawn level with the Juice Revolution tent. Jordan and Sam commanded an industrial-strength blender each, while Jarka barked out the customers' names over the noise of the whirring machines. "One in a Melon for Juan."

"Did you say Gwen?" a tall woman with high cheekbones and a nasal voice yelled.

"No, *Juan*," Jarka repeated, enunciating slowly. "J-U-A-N."

The drink's intended recipient, a wiry Latino man, emerged from the crowd to claim his beverage.

"So Jordan chose *your* drinks," Capone murmured distractedly, clearly chasing some rabbit of an idea down its hole, "but not Ronald Wong's."

"What did you just say?" I asked. My attention, too, had wandered, but now it snapped back to Capone.

Not wholly listening to me, he continued speaking, half to himself. "Jordan chose the drinks."

I took him by the shoulders. "No, you said *Ronald* Wong. Did the order sticker say Ronnie or Ronald?"

He thought for a moment. "Ronald. When I interviewed his family and business associates, I got the impression that only his wife called him Ronnie."

I rushed to the front of the Juice Revolution line, drawing annoyed murmurings from the people I cut in front of. "Jarka, what smoothie did you make for Wong?" I asked.

"I made no smoothie for Mr. Wong," she said, nodding her head vigorously. After a moment of recalibration, I remembered about the Bulgarian custom of nodding to mean *no*, and realized she was answering in the negative. "That day, I made Maximum-Wattage Anti-Tox Mocktail for Harold Heyer."

"But I saw you put the smoothie on the counter and call out Wong's name," I responded. "I remember him coming up to collect the smoothie right after you called him." I hadn't been paying particularly close attention at the time, but that part of the memory was clear in my brain. Jarka had placed a smoothie on the counter and Wong had brushed past me to collect it.

While the three of us were speaking, Jordan and Sam drifted from the blenders to the register, drawn by our urgent voices and the disruption to the flow of orders.

"Everything okay?" Jordan asked.

Jarka didn't answer her, and instead repeated, "No, I was making smoothie for Harold Heyer. I put on the counter and I say 'Harold.'"

"Jarka, say that name again," I requested, the gears in my brain whirring.

"Harold," she parroted.

"Jarka, can you say 'Ronald,' please?" Capone asked, his voice imbued with a steely calm.

She complied, using a similarly guttural "hr" sound at the start of each name. Her forehead creased as she sought to understand the nature of this command performance. Suddenly, the muscles of her face fell slack, and she repeated the names again.

"Jarka, what's going on? Will someone tell me what's going on?" Jordan asked, her voice rising in pitch. She took hold of Sam's hand, her gaze flitting nervously from person to person.

Capone looked at me, his eyes fixed and serious. A shared understanding hung between us, so solid it was almost visible. What if it wasn't the ingredients that got mixed up, but the names? With the noise of the blenders, Jarka's accent, and the chatter of customers in the background, the two names would have sounded indiscernible. That kind of thing has happened to all of us at some time, in a Starbucks line or a crowded room. This time, though, rather than sucking down an unasked-for peppermint latte or enduring a moment of social awkwardness, the consequence had been death. Jarka had called out "Harold," but Ronald Wong misheard. He drank the poison that was intended for Harold Heyer. The Maximum-Wattage Anti-Tox Mocktail that had been specifically prescribed for Harold by Jordan Watts.

Even as I was mulling this new understanding, Jarka gave voice to my thought. She'd been a beat behind, but now she, too, caught on. "The smoothie I made for Harold Heyer was poison. Someone was trying to kill him? But who would want to kill Harold Heyer? He is so kind to everyone and he has the most beautiful soul."

"Jordan." I spoke her name instinctively, before I was even aware of thinking it. Words began to tumble out of my mouth, half-formed ideas that gained clearer contours as reality chiseled them into shape. "The pot rack in Sam's kitchen. You didn't just thrash around and hit it, did you? It was fastened into the ceiling so securely, and you're so small. It must've taken all your strength to knock it hard enough for the pots to fall off that morning when you drank the smoothie. You needed to be sure Sam would hear you, so he'd get you to the hospital right away. You knew you'd ingested a low dose, but you weren't taking any chances."

Jordan's eyes, usually brimming with intelligence and vitality, were instead wide with fear.

"But you had to go through with it," I continued. "Because that was part of the plan from the beginning. Even when Wong died instead of Harold, you knew that getting sick yourself would be the best way to throw off suspicion. But why? Why try to kill Harold?"

As I'd been speaking, Jordan was slowly backing away, as if increasing the distance between us might blunt the force of the accusation. She turned to Sam, pleading for understanding. "Harold threatened me," she said. "The notes. He knew I took the money from the Heyers' store. He wanted to kill me." Her mouth hung open, and for a moment, I thought she would spill the whole story. Instead, I watched as her petite, athletic form vaulted over the table and took off, sprinting for the boat dock as if her heels had grown wings.

CHAPTER 29

Jarka, Capone, Sam, the half-dozen customers who'd been gathered at the Juice Revolution tent, and I froze for what felt like eons, but was probably closer to five seconds, watching as Jordan skirted the rows of tents and dodged around pockets of festivalgoers.

"The smoothie!" Jarka gasped, coming around the table to the outside. "Our contest entry. Jordan insist to make it by herself. With *special ingredients,* she said."

"Go!" Capone ordered her. "If Harold drank any of it, get him to the hospital. And preserve it so it can be tested."

Without another word, Capone took off after Jordan, opening into a full sprint. I'd been impressed by Jordan's speed, and Capone's sporty physique clearly wasn't just for show, either. If anyone had a chance of catching her, it was him.

Sam and I, lacking the kind of emergency training Jarka and Capone shared, remained in place a few moments longer, staring slack-jawed at each other. His face cycled through a discordant mix of emotions—blame, confusion, hurt, anxiety. I suspected my expression was just plain confused. How had we all missed it? Once we'd decided that Jordan must've been the killer's target, we all fixated on finding out who poisoned her, never allowing ourselves to consider the possibility that she could have done it to herself.

I tried to piece together her motive from her disjointed semi-confession. After last night's events, I knew with certainty that the threatening notes had been sent by Frates to shake down Mac. Jordan, though, seemed convinced Harold sent the notes, that they were meant for her, and that they had something to do with Heyers department store.

I played back the tidbits of history I'd picked up over the past few weeks. Jordan had been a financial whiz, top of my aunt's accounting class, leading her to be promoted quickly to the Heyers store's head bookkeeping job. No doubt she held a position of trust and considerable responsibility for the company finances, especially given Ollie Heyer's reputation for not being particularly adept with numbers. If Harold's father was anywhere near as oblivious as his offspring, embezzling the store into the ground was probably a cakewalk for someone smart and unscrupulous. Apparently, Jordan had gotten too greedy, though, and milked her cash cow to death. Then she skipped town. *I made my own money*, she'd told me. Maybe she stayed away long enough to believe that locals wouldn't question where her nest egg had come from. Harold hadn't pursued charges for all those years; she must've thought the coast was clear.

She would have wondered, though. Wondered if anyone knew. If Harold suspected. If he blamed her for his parents' deaths and the destruction of his family's business. And then, right after her return, the notes began to arrive, referencing the theft of money. *It's time to pay for what you did*. All of the notes said something about stolen money, either directly or indirectly, and ended in a threat. Had Jordan considered going to the police about the harassment? I guessed not. If anyone started digging into the notes' origin, it could lead back to Harold, and her past criminality could have been exposed. The carefully curated life she'd built would crumble.

I'd never been much for English class, or reading in general, but Edgar Allan Poe's story *The Tell-Tale Heart* had clung to the inside of my skull since my sophomore year of high school. The parable of a man who becomes so paranoid, so consumed by guilt, that he reveals a crime he would otherwise have gotten away with.

"Oh my god," Sam whispered. He was peering into my face, watching my expression as I conjured the series of events that had led to today, the strength of my conviction growing as each detail fell into place.

"It's true?" he continued. "*Jordan* put the poison in the smoothies?"

I nodded, wishing I could shield him, knowing I could not. "I think so."

He looked utterly broken, and I remembered what Renee Ulrich said about her husband. One day, she'd "seen through the Matrix" and realized she'd been living with a monster.

Sam moved to follow Capone's retreating form toward the dock, which snapped me back to the present moment. Not knowing what else to do, I headed off in Jarka's wake, running across the park toward the judging tent. Soon, however, a chest-crushing breathlessness and piercing back pain slowed me to a jog and finally to a race-walking pace. No amount of adrenaline could counteract my innate biology and the laws of gravity. Gasping as I reached the judging tent's opening, I silently vowed to get into better shape and purchase more supportive bras. This was the second time in less than twenty-four hours my lack of running ability had proved to be detrimental.

Luckily, Jarka was in better shape than I was, and she seemed to have covered the distance without breaking a sweat. However, rather than being inside the tent rescuing Harold, I found her outside, arguing with three officious-looking women wearing Event Volunteer badges. They seemed fervent in their determination to keep her out.

A woman with a heavy jaw and pair of half-moon-shaped reading glasses perched on her nose held her arms wide, barring entry even as Jarka tried to push past. "As Lori-Anne told you," she said, gesturing to her ample-chested companion whom I'd met earlier, "Harold was very clear that he should not be disturbed during the judging, especially by any of the competitors. He wants a fair process."

The third member of the well-heeled door bouncer gang—a compact, precise-looking woman wearing a beige fedora—waggled her phone in front of Jarka. "I don't want to have to call security, but I will," she warned.

"Please, I must speak with Harold Heyer now. Is very urgent," Jarka said.

Although her expression and voice were more animated than usual, I could see how, to someone who didn't know her, Jarka's terse, impassive demeanor might fail to convey the life-or-death stakes involved. And, in the eyes of the doyennes of Geneva Bay, Jarka's unfashionable magpie outfit, regrettable dye job, and indecipherable accent probably made her seem untrustworthy, possibly even not wholly sane.

"You are killing Harold Heyer," Jarka pleaded, making another attempt to push her way into the tent. Clearly her bony frame was no match for the likes of the surprisingly stalwart Lori-Anne and Co. I had to hand it to the middle-aged ladies of Geneva Bay. They might lead cushy lives, but they were no softies. When they volunteered to do something, they committed, body and soul.

"Out of the way, Lori-Anne," I said, throwing my elbows out and barreling right through the makeshift game of Red Rover. Finally, my size and shape could be of some use. I grabbed hold of Jarka's wrist and pulled her through the breach.

"I'm calling security!" the fedora lady yelled.

"Good!" I yelled back. "Call an ambulance, too, while you're at it."

Dark, humid, and mostly empty, the interior of the tent had an almost womblike quality. Although thin vinyl sheets were the only thing separating us from the rest of the festival, the tent felt infinitely quieter. Three catering tables stood in the middle of it. Laden with Dutch apple and white fudge Oreo pies, traditional German potato salad, golden cheese curds, hearty beet soup, and fried walleye—the supreme offerings of Geneva Bay's finest food purveyors—the tables resembled a Día de los Muertos altar.

Behind this cornucopia sat Harold, eyes closed, mouth hanging open, his huge bald head lolling backward. A sickening gurgling noise rose from deep in his throat.

"Oh no," I whispered.

Jarka and I screeched to such a sudden halt that Volunteer Lori-Anne and her posse, who trailed in after us, rammed into our backs.

"Harold Heyer!" Jarka shrieked. Her voice cracked with emotion as she broke free of the scrum and hurtled across the empty space that stood between us and him.

At the sound of his name, Harold's eyes flew open and he leapt up in surprise. A fine spray of fluid spewed from between his lips and he began to choke. He doubled over as his body was wracked with coughs. I flashed back to the final moments of Wong's mighty struggle against the effects of the jimson weed, my heart skidding in my chest at the memory of that horrific scene. I searched the table, expecting to find the dregs of the tainted Juice Revolution offering. When I located the cup amidst the array of plates and bowls, though, I was shocked to see it next to last at one end of the table, wholly untouched astride its assigned number. My own deconstructed deep-dish lay next to it, also untouched.

"He didn't drink it yet!" I called to Jarka, practically shedding tears of relief as I lifted it into the air. "It's still full."

Jarka rubbed Harold's back and encouraged him to breathe.

A red-faced Harold waved one hand, the other still braced on his knee. "I'm okay. I'm okay." Another round of hacking followed before he straightened his back and rose to standing. "You surprised me."

"Sorry, Harold Heyer," Jarka soothed. "We thought you were dying of poison."

"Poison?" Harold's eyes scanned our faces, trying to determine if we were joking.

"Poison?" One of the women behind me repeated. "What on earth are you talking about?" She pivoted to the woman behind her. "Lori-Anne, did you call security?"

"You were choking . . ." I said. "Your head was rolling backward."

"No, no, no." Harold clicked his tongue. "There must be some silly mix-up. I was gargling with deionized water. I read online that it helps to clear the palate between tastings. I want my tongue to be in tip-top condition for each dish. When you came in, Jarka called out my name and I sat up too quickly and choked."

"Do you know these women?" Lori-Anne asked Harold, stabbing her finger in our direction.

"Of course," Harold replied, recovering some of his usual pep. "This is the fantastic pizza prima donna Delilah O'Leary of Delilah & Son, and this is the beautiful and talented physician-server-barista Jarka Gagamova." The bridge of his snub nose wrinkled in confusion as he turned to Jarka. "Why would you think I'd been poisoned?"

"Well," I began. There was nothing for it but the truth. "Because Jordan Watts is trying to kill you."

CHAPTER 30

A speedboat skimmed across the lake past Delilah &
Son's patio, towing an inner tube that held two squealing
teenage girls—the final revelers of the Labor Day weekend. It was Tuesday afternoon, and most of the tourists
had departed the previous day, heading back to Milwau-
kee or the Chicago suburbs, back to school, back to the
grind. Within a few weeks, the boats would be in dry
dock and the summer houses would close up for the long
off-season. I'd made the preservice family meal, and invited Renee, Harold Heyer, Uncle Avi, and Auntie Biz to
join us as special guests. I'd asked Sam along as well, but
he wasn't up to facing the world just yet, still smarting
about the revelation of Jordan's true character.

"It's a shame about Sam's sailboat," Melody sighed.
She put her napkin into her lap and looked wistfully after
the inner-tubers as they retreated into the distance. "Almost brand new and now it's wrecked."

Jordan Watts's escape attempt had been the talk of the
town for days. With the head start she'd gotten, Jordan
managed to reach Sam's boat and zoom away using the
outboard motor before Capone could catch up with her.
He'd radioed the lake police to intercept her, and the en-
suing chase played out like an action flick, with crowds

swarming the beach to watch. The excitement ended in dramatic fashion, with the police corralling Jordan into a narrower and narrower strip of water until she crashed the boat into a floating dock. Cell phone videos of the incident had already pushed the Ulrich murder from the top slot on the evening news.

Jarka, who'd been arranging chairs around the long patio table as our guests arrived, stopped what she was doing and reached out to take the hand of Harold Heyer, who was seated in front of her. "How can you worry about sunken boat when that woman tried to kill Harold Heyer two times?"

Harold gazed adoringly at Jarka and squeezed her hand. The two had been inseparable since Harold's close call with death. Physically, the couple made no sense. He was round, awkward, and neatly-groomed; she was angular, nimble, and eccentric. Moreover, their personalities seemed totally incompatible. I thought back to that long-ago conversation about Melody's grandma hopping on the back of Rocco Guanciale's motorcycle. As Biz had wisely observed, you never really knew what drew two people together.

"Jordan tried *two* times?" Daniel repeated Jarka's assertion. "Was it confirmed that the smoothie at the contest was poisoned?"

"Not the smoothie," Uncle Avi interjected. He waved away Sonya, who was applying aloe gel to his sunburned nose.

She set the bottle down on the table and glared at him. "Aunt Ruthie is going to kill you if you get melanoma."

"I can't decide which would be a worse way to go," he quipped.

"Wait," I said, placing the heavy pan of pizza I'd been carrying on the table next to the aloe. "What do you mean the smoothie wasn't poisoned? I heard that she confessed."

"Oh, she tried to poison him at the contest, all right," Avi explained. "But my friend in the DA's office told me she slipped the poison into one of the other entries. Some kind of pretzel thing. Distracted the ladies who were checking in the entries and put a little toxic cocktail into the cheese sauce. She wanted to throw suspicion off because I guess she was smart enough to realize that the cops would test everything if Harold croaked." Avi turned to Harold, who'd gone pale as a ball of fresh mozzarella. "No offense."

"That lying little troll," I hissed. "She was going to bump Harold off with *my* dish?"

"Maybe can we please stopping say about murdering Harold Heyer?" Jarka said. "Is upsetting to him."

"Sorry," Sonya said, passing a bowl of spinach, green apple, and goat cheese salad to Harold and giving him a pat on the back.

Renee smiled as she reached for a napkin. The cloud of suspicion around her had lifted, and she would be finishing up the brewery commission and heading back to London at the end of the month. Although Sonya put up a good front, I knew she was taking it hard, having approached the possibility of a reunion with her usual all-in, goo-goo-eyed zeal. Renee, however, had made it clear that she needed time and space, and had no interest in pursuing a long-distance romance. Alas, Sonya's perfect record of heartache would remain intact a little while longer.

"On the positive side," Melody said, "the Twenty-Fifth Annual Taste of Wisconsin Cook-Off was certainly the most memorable."

Renee held out her wineglass for Daniel to fill. "Yes, it rather seared itself into one's brain, didn't it?"

It had been one to remember for sure. Despite the notable omission of crowning a contest winner, I felt confident that it would be many years before anyone would forget the day. While the insanity had been happening out on the water, the police swooped in to the judging tent where Jarka, Harold, and I were holed up, summoned by the repeated calls of the Lori-Anne crew. Officer Rettberg, first on the scene, had insisted on confiscating every one of the contest entries as potential evidence. I thought it was overzealousness at the time, but after learning how close I'd come to being framed for Harold's murder, I was grateful for her thoroughness. After that, the festival ended abruptly, in confusion and chaos.

Rabbit came out of the restaurant carrying a second pizza and set it down next to Auntie Biz. He cut into a piece with a triangular spatula and lifted it. The cheese stretched into a preposterously long string as he moved it from the pan onto Biz's plate.

Though Biz had at least a month until the foreclosure proceedings on her cottage would take place, she had summoned me to come over after service that night to begin clearing it out. I argued that there was still hope; we still had options we could pursue. She refused to even consider waiting and praying for a Hail Mary option to emerge. "Better to rip off the Band-Aid," she told me. Typical Biz, demanding to be in the driver's seat, even if the car was heading straight for a brick wall.

"Pizza?" She looked at me. "I thought you never did deep-dish for family meal."

"Special occasion," I said.

"It's Eggplant Nduja," Sonya explained. "Harold's

favorite. Since he almost . . ." She stopped herself. "Delilah just thought he deserved something nice."

Harold beamed.

Sonya patted him on the shoulder again, and returned
his smile. I noticed she had steered clear of any egg puns.
Sure, Harold would probably continue to be irritatingly
peppy, and I didn't expect him to develop a sudden gift
of self-awareness. But we'd both realized that someone as
sincere and trusting as Harold Heyer needed our protection, not our ridicule. I wished someone had done the
same thing for his father to prevent Jordan Watts from
wheedling her way into his life.

I looked around the table, watching my team as they
passed dishes and served our guests. Jarka, our quirky,
no-nonsense new addition; hard-working, reliable Rabbit; sweet, neurotic Melody, with her tender heart;
Daniel, my loyal, confident consigliere; and Sonya, my
soulmate. Would I be able to hold on to this place, support these people, now that my hopes of winning the
contest prize were dashed?

"Are we waiting for Detective Capone?" Daniel asked,
calling me away from my musings.

"He couldn't make it," I replied. "He's got his hands
full after Frates's and Jordan's arrests, but I told him I'd
bring some pizzas over to the station when I drop Butterball off with Sam."

"Can you see if he'll let you say hi to Mac from me?"
Melody asked, her voice quivering a little. Melody was
still angry with her cousin, but mostly she just wanted her
best friend back. While Mac was waiting to find out the
consequences she'd face for the theft of Rocco Guanciale's money, she was being held in one of the jail cells at-
tached to the station, rather than transferred to the larger

county lockup. A small kindness, although I doubted Mac would find much to be grateful about.

Uncle Avi reached across the table and patted Melody's wrist. "Don't worry, kiddo. I'm going to get those charges dropped for your cousin. She'll be out by the end of the week, you'll see. Nobody wants to see a young kid like her get put through the wringer over a stupid decision."

We all fell quiet for a moment. I couldn't know what anyone else was thinking, but my mind went straight to a comparison with a young Jordan Watts—pretty, personable, quick-witted. And greedy. And dishonest. I wondered if Mac's latest escapade would be enough to scare her back onto the straight and narrow, or if her character flaws were too deeply ingrained. Maybe her getting arrested was a blessing. Jordan almost got away scotfree from her past crimes, and look what it had done to her.

"I'm going to bring Butterball down to join us," I said, rising from my seat. "He hates to miss out on a social occasion, especially when there's a chance somebody might drop food."

I mounted the stairs and found Butterball snoozing on my bed, bathed in a rectangular shaft of sunlight. After I returned from the festival on Saturday, I spent some time tacking sheets of heavy cardboard over the two entrances to the infamous "sausage tunnel." As Officer Rettberg theorized, I'd found the other end under my bed. The bed was now pulled to the other side of the room, waiting for the police to send someone over to scope out the interior of the tunnel for potential evidence before a structural engineer came to fix it. Capone said it would be a few days at least, given the veritable crime wave the town's small force had to contend with.

Butterball leapt off the bed when he saw me. Instead of coming to greet me, he made his way to the cardboard-covered opening and began to paw at it. Our relationship had improved marginally now that he wasn't spending so much time sneaking down to the kitchen, but he was still far more aloof than he used to be. Tuesday was the restaurant's short day, and I'd promised to drop the cat off at Sam's before we opened for dinner service. I knew that he'd go ballistic as soon as I got his cat carrier down.

I eased myself onto the floor next to him. "What do you think, babe?" I asked, reaching out to stroke his spine. "Is it time we talked to Sam about ending this joint custody arrangement? He's really heartbroken, and I'm sure he'd appreciate having you around more. And Biz is going to be moving in here soon. It'll be tight quarters and you two don't always get along, so this will be better. Maybe when you go to Sam's today, we could bring all your things and you could just stay there . . ." I couldn't finish my thought, although I knew the word I was looking for was "forever."

I knew in my heart that staying in one place would be best for Butterball. Given my demanding schedule, Sam had more time to devote to him. Butterball had been Sam's cat before I'd ever met either of them. Given the choice between cutting my baby in half or seeing him happy with Sam, I knew what I had to do. My body felt heavy with grief. If I was going to go through with this, I needed to get it over with, no turning back. I'd thought Biz was being overly callous about cleaning out the cottage, but it turned out I knew exactly how she felt.

As I'd been weighing all of this, Butterball stopped pawing the cardboard and sat up prettily with his head cocked to one side, as if considering my proposal. Out of nowhere, he reared up and brought the full weight of his front limbs down on the top edge of the cardboard, ripping if off the wall. He leaned his head and shoulders into the blackness.

"B-man," I groaned, pulling him away from the opening. "I'm trying to have a heart to heart with you, and all you care about is bratwurst."

I lifted him into my arms, intending to carry him downstairs to join family meal. On a whim, however, I released him and laid down next to the tunnel. I grabbed a heavy stone candleholder from my nightstand and began to bash the drywall. I pulled pieces of Sheetrock and insulation away with my hands until I'd created an opening that spanned the width between two wall studs and rose about twelve inches off the floor. I reached inside and felt around. Turning on my cell phone flashlight, I pressed my face into the hole.

"Well, I'll be damned," I breathed.

CHAPTER 31

I teetered into Capone's office, carrying a box containing a piping hot, deep-dish pizza. Over my shoulder, I'd slung a grimy, stuffed-full duffle bag. Even though civilians weren't usually allowed to wander the halls of the police station, gaining entrance had been a snap once I bribed Stanhope with the three other pizzas I'd brought. Capone looked up from his computer as I entered. The office contained six desks, the sum total of the department's criminal investigative division.

"I told her you were busy," Stanhope said, shadowing me into the room, carrying the other pizza boxes. "But she said you'd definitely want to talk to her. And she brought pizza, so . . ." He shrugged.

Capone waved me in. "I need a break anyway," he said. "I'm going cross-eyed from filling out reports." He took off a pair of gold-and-black-rimmed reading glasses and rubbed his eyes.

"Those pizzas are to share," I called after Stanhope as he closed the door to leave.

The office was sparsely furnished and utilitarian, with the exception of a surprisingly healthy row of African violets lining the windowsill and an enormous Green Bay Packers flag stretching across one wall. Definitely not Capone's. He, I knew, hadn't surrendered allegiance to the sports teams of our native Chicago. A pair of framed degrees—undergrad from Loyola, Master's in Criminal Justice from Chicago State—flanked Capone's desk, which, although relatively clean compared with his officemates', held an array of take-out coffee cups that hadn't yet migrated to the trash can. He rose and came around the desk to clear off a chair for me to sit on. Then, he shifted aside a stack of folders and a picture of his granddaughter so I could set down the pizza and duffle bag.

"What do we have here?" he asked, giving the duffle bag an exploratory poke with his pen.

"One hundred thousand dollars in cash," I replied. "Oh, and a Red Hot Mama pizza with extra hot sauce. I know it's your favorite."

Capone's face went slack. For this first time since I met him, I'd managed to genuinely shock him. "Rocco's money?"

I nodded. "Either that, or somebody used very unorthodox materials to insulate the walls of my building."

Capone took a seat behind his desk, his face turning serious. "I seem to recall telling you to seal off the opening to the wall. Once again, you're coming between me and a clean chain of custody."

I opened the lid to the pizza box, releasing a delicious burst of scent. "Do you have any plates around here? And a fork and knife? I'm starved."

"Don't think you're going to distract me with pizza," he snapped. "All I asked you to do was to keep away from that wall for another day or two until I could free up a CSI to get over there. We both knew there was a possibility something like this was in there, and that it needed to be collected and documented properly. Since you know how much money is in the bag, can I assume you opened it and counted it, and therefore compromised it?"

I nodded.

"Now any chance of obtaining evidence to prove that Rocco's accountant put that money there is probably out the window," he grumbled.

While he'd been chastising me, I located a stash of disposable paper goods in a basket on top of one of the filing cabinets and served us each a piece of pizza. I cut into mine and lifted a forkful into my mouth. The toppings hit my taste buds first, the lemony funk of blue cheese and the cooling drizzle of the buttermilk ranch sauce. The layers of flavor started to build as I chewed. Gooey mozzarella. Rich, buttery crust. Then the signature blend of spicy paprika and red pepper–infused sausage Sujeet and Big Dave had developed for us, and finally, the crescendo—the blissful, fire-roasted heat of the tomato sauce.

"Here's the thing," I said. "I need that money like crazy. Fifty-two thousand would buy Biz's house out of her neighbors' clutches. The other forty-eight could see me and my staff comfortably through the winter. Without it, the restaurant will probably fold by March. I need that money so bad I could cry just talking about it." Instead of crying, though, I let out a very unladylike open-mouthed cackle.

Capone's eyebrows knitted together. If he was concerned that I'd come slightly unhinged, he wasn't far off base. Having a pile of illicit cash fall into my lap just when I needed it most, but knowing that keeping it would probably ruin my life? I must've done something epically awful in a former life.

"Even now," I continued, "I'm thinking what a fool I am for turning it in. I could've gotten away with it, I bet."

I chewed another bite of pizza, and then another. "But then I think about Mac, and how she thought she could get away with stealing pre-stolen money. And also about how Frates might not be the only bad guy who knows this is out there, and do I really want to look over my shoulder for the rest of my life?"

Capone said nothing as I picked up the crust and stuffed it into my mouth, cramming my cheeks full, chipmunk-style. I'd always been a person who ate my feelings. Based on how famished I was, these feelings might merit an entire pizza all to themselves.

"Do you have a Coke?" I asked, spewing crumbs.

He walked over to a mini fridge in the corner and pulled out two cans of pop.

"So there you have it," I continued. "Once I knew for sure the money was there, I had to get it away from me as soon as I could, before it could become my tell-tale heart."

"Your tattle-tale what?" Capone asked. Apparently, the Poe reference was garbled by my stuffed mouth.

I chewed and swallowed. "Never mind. I'm not expecting you to be happy about what I did, but I do need you to know that I did the best I could." I ran my finger along the zipper of the duffle bag. "Man, doing the right thing sure feels a lot like destroying your life, doesn't it?"

Together, Capone and I polished off a small Red Hot Mama and a couple Cokes, not saying much. I wasn't sure Capone would forgive me, but I felt like he at least understood that I'd stared down a duffle bag of temptation, and I'd ultimately done the right thing. Well, right-*ish*. After I left the police station, I hurried across town to drop Butterball off at Sam's house before the start of service.

As I drove down the familiar curving driveway, I drank in the view of the spectacular Queen Anne house fronting an even more spectacular view of the lake. Yet another thing that could've been mine if it weren't for my scruples. If only my relationship with Sam had worked out, I'd have been living on easy street. But I'd never use a man for his money. I'd never do that to Sam. He deserved someone who loved him only for himself. Now that Jordan's greed and duplicity had been exposed, I wondered how long it would take for him to trust someone again.

When Sam didn't answer the doorbell, I walked around to the back of the house, awkwardly supporting the cat carrier in my arms. The porch wrapped around three sides of the house. In the back, it opened onto a wide set of stairs that led down to the lawn, the boat dock, and the fenced pool area. I found Sam sitting on one of a pair of Adirondack chairs positioned under the sturdy old oak in the middle of the lawn.

"Oh, sorry," Sam said, rising from his seat as he noticed us. "I must've lost track of time." Glancing back at the house, he asked, "How did you know I was out here?"

"You always commune with nature when you're feeling down." I gestured to the tree and the lake.

He nodded, his eyes cast downward. "Thanks for bringing B-ball over," he said, taking the carrier from me and easing it to the ground. "It's been lonely around here the past couple days."

I leaned down and opened the tiny wire-mesh door of the carrier. Instead of running free like he used to, though, our cat cowered inside.

"It's okay, bud," Sam cooed.

"I've been wanting to talk to you about Butterball," I began, taking the seat next to Sam. "I thought you might want to have him around more often."

Time to rip off the Band-Aid. I was on a roll as far as

sabotaging my own happiness to do the right thing. Why stop now?

"I wanted to talk to you about the same thing," Sam interrupted. "This joint custody has been a disaster, hasn't it?" Sam crouched down and gently extracted an aggravated-looking Butterball.

"It really has," I agreed.

"He doesn't like it," Sam continued. "By the time he gets reacclimated, it's time to switch again. I feel like he never settles."

I nodded. "You're right. I haven't wanted to bring it up. I was . . ." I dug my fingernails into my hands to keep from breaking down. "I was afraid you'd realize that he was miserable and take him away from me."

Sam shook his head. "I'd never do that. I know how much you two love each other."

"I just want what's best for him," I said.

Sam petted Butterball and then set him down on the grass. "It's okay, bud," he said. "Go explore." Instead, Butterball scampered under my chair.

I dropped to the ground and started waving a piece of long grass for our cat to pounce on. Butterball took a few tentative steps toward it. He lifted his paw and shrank back.

"Here's my proposal," Sam said. "He should stay here, full-time."

I nodded again, perilously close to bursting into tears. It had been one thing when I'd planned to make the same suggestion as a noble sacrifice. But now that Sam had beaten me to it, I wasn't sure I could hold my emotions in check. My instinct to fight for a piece of my cat, even if it was a small, damaged piece, threatened to overwhelm me.

"With you," Sam said.

"With *me*?" I asked, not sure I'd heard him.

"Yeah. I want you and Butterball to live here," Sam explained. He moved off his chair and sat down on the grass next to me, cross-legged. His voice quieted. "I've decided to go away for a while. I'm not sure how long. I've got an offer to work with some venture capitalists in Palo Alto. We're talking about starting a new company focused on wellness apps. I can't spend my whole life trying to find my bliss in new gadgets or hot yoga." His voice grew still quieter as he added with a sad smile, "Or in another person." He took in a deep breath. "It's time I did something productive."

"I can't live in your house, Sam," I said. "I'd be happy, so, so happy, to have Butterball full-time, for as long as you need. But we can't live in your house."

"It's *your* dream house," Sam protested. "You did all the design work. I bought it for you, and you should have it."

"I can't. It was bought with your money. I didn't earn it," I said.

"Listen, Dee. I know you need the space. Sonya told me what's happening to Biz's cottage. Are the two of you really planning to live together in a one-bedroom apartment?" He shook his head. "If that's the plan, I should call Detective Capone right now, because there's going to be another murder." He flashed the charming, slightly lopsided smile that caught my heart the day I'd met him.

"We'll figure it out," I said. "I'll lock up the knives or something."

"I went over there yesterday, to Biz's, and tried to give her the money to pay the taxes. Did she tell you?" he asked.

"No," I replied, taken aback.

Sam and Biz had always been polite to each other, but never close. I certainly hadn't expected this, especially knowing what Sam had been through over the past few days. Sam tended to mind his own business, never wanting to "interfere" or put anyone in an uncomfortable position. He gave liberally to good causes, but always anonymously. He didn't like the power dynamics of overt generosity. Now, he'd gone out of his way to get involved, even though he must've known his chances of success were next to nil.

"She wouldn't take any money from me," he said, "not even to save the house we both know she loves. I tried everything. I told her she could think of it as a loan and pay me back if it made her feel better. I said I'd buy it as an investment property and rent it back to her. Nothing doing. Plus, she said she'd never speak to me again if I tried to pull anything behind her back." He chuffed me on the shoulder. "Stubbornness must be genetic."

"It was really nice of you to try." I reached out and squeezed his hand.

He looked up the hill toward the house. The early afternoon sun sparkled off the windows, reflecting disconnected slices of the lake back to us—a rectangle of the dock in the kitchen windows, a rectangle of a passing sailboat in the windows of the yoga room; in the dining room's bay window, a triptych of shimmer-leaved trees.

"You and Biz and Melody and Butterball would all fit here very comfortably. It would be nice to know that the place is full of life."

"We can't, Sam. That's so generous, but we won't do it. You're right that O'Leary women are stubborn. Plus, we're allergic to charity."

He leaned his elbow on the seat of the chair where he'd been sitting, and brushed his fingers through the grass.

"Well, suck it up, because you don't have a choice," he said. "I'm giving you notice on your apartment. I'm the landlord, and it's my right. You can still use the apartment over the restaurant as an office, if you want, but you have thirty days to move out. You can't live there anymore. The letter is already notarized and in the mail."

"What?" I dropped the frond of grass I'd been using as a cat toy.

"I knew the two of you would rather cram into that tiny apartment than accept the house as a gift. So I'm not giving it to you. My lawyer is drawing up papers right now giving the house over to Butterball. But as his caretaker, I expect you to live here, in *his* house, with him, rent-free. I'll pay the utilities and upkeep. Not having to pay rent should buy you a little breathing room on expenses while you get the restaurant off the ground."

"How dare you . . ." I began, rising up to a kneeling position and clenching my fists. Did he think just because he had money and I didn't that he could control where I lived? Tell me how to run my business? That he could hold my cat as a hostage?

"If you don't want the job as Butterball's live-in caretaker, I can hire someone else," he teased. "I hear Melody needs a place to live. I'm sure she'd like not having to worry about scrimping on rent money to save up for tuition."

I crossed my arms over my chest, not amused. I wasn't going to let my affection for Melody or my feeling of responsibility for her plight force me into going along with the plot Sam had hatched.

Sam reached out and gently uncrossed my arms. He took hold of my hands and pulled me up to standing, hooking his arm around my waist and turning me toward the lake. While we'd been arguing, Butterball finally ventured out from under the chair. He'd made his way over toward the fence that surrounded the pool, and he was now darting in and out of a butterfly bush, chasing bumblebees. No doubt this would end badly, like most of his encounters with the great outdoors. Always on the cusp of another vet visit, that one. Still, I couldn't deny that he seemed happy, doing what he loved. Sam's yard was definitely a healthier environment for him to hang around than the dumpster behind the restaurant. Here, he had endless space to explore and fewer neighboring cats to brawl with. Maybe with all this space to run around in, he'd finally lose some weight.

"He'll be happy," Sam said. He leaned his head on my shoulder, speaking softly into my hair. I remained taut, refusing to soften into his embrace. "I know you want what's best for him. And I want what's best for both of you."

"So you think you know what's best for me?" I demanded.

Sam spread his long, elegant fingers and waved his hand slowly in front of us as if casting a spell. "Think about it. Waking up to this view every day. You and Biz, cooking one of your epic feasts in that glorious kitchen you designed. And better still, there's enough space here so that you can sulk in different wings of the house when you inevitably piss each other off."

I grunted and nudged his head off my shoulder, turning so that I faced him. "I appreciate what you're trying to do, Sam. It means a lot. But it wouldn't be fair for me to accept this."

"Fair to who?" His eyebrows shots up. "I designed an app a million years ago, made a boatload of money, and it led to all this. Is *that* fair?"

"I just . . . I just . . ." I sputtered. I'd run out of objections, but I couldn't figure out how to yield.

He let out a little chuckle.

"What's so funny?" I asked, still rankled.

"I know you think I'm clueless sometimes and that I just drift along through life. Did you ever consider that I'm not the only one who has some character flaws to work on, though?" He asked. "Pride is practically your middle name."

"I thought Wrath was my deadly sin," I mumbled, allowing myself a tiny smile.

He poked his finger playfully into the soft curve of my waist. "You can have more than one, you know."

RECIPES

MAXIMUM-WATTAGE ANTI-TOX MOCKTAIL (MAC'S NO POISON VERSION)

Guys! Molly McClintock aka Mac aka Mickey Mac aka Molly Olly Macintolly here. This is the first time I've ever written a recipe, and let me tell you: I. AM. STOKED. Like, super stoked. Anyhoo, Delilah helped me take Jordan's original recipe and strip out some of the not-so-delish ingredients, like the extinct seaweed (and the poison, duh, obvs.), and then we added a few new things to achieve, you know, next-level awesomeness. And for the record, at Juice Revolution a "mocktail" is a smoothie. So is an "infusion" and a "blast" and a "juice fusion." They are literally all just different words Jordan made up to mean "smoothie."

The basic smoothie philosophy is super simple: 1½ cups liquid, 1 cup greens, 1½ cups fresh or frozen fruit. You can get fancy with spices and smoothie boosters and nut butters and protein powders, but if you stick with that basic ratio, you probably won't make a vat of liquid garbage that makes you *wish* your smoothie was poisoned. . . . Too soon? OMG. You guys have no sense of humor.

Preparation Time: 10 minutes
Yield: 1 serving

Look at me over here, writing "Yield: 1 serving" like I'm Betty Freakin' Crocker. Lolz.

Ingredients

- ½ cup baby spinach leaves, tightly packed
- ½ cup kale leaves, tightly packed (Kale adds a more intense earthy flavor, so if you want a milder taste, forget the kale and use another ½ cup spinach instead.)
- 1½ cups almond milk, either plain or vanilla-flavored
- 1 cup frozen banana, cut into rough chunks. (That's, like, 1 large banana, BTW.)
- ½ cup frozen mango chunks
- 1 tablespoon chia seeds
- 1 teaspoon grated fresh ginger
- ½ teaspoon ground turmeric

Okay, so basically you whack the greens into your blender along with the almond milk and, you know, blend it. You can add more or less liquid to get the consistency you like. You'll need a decent blender for smoothie-making to ensure you don't end up with big, gnarly spinach chunks in there. After you've got the greens and almond milk well blended, add everything else and blend until smooth. Then drink the heck out of it.

BANITSA, A BULGARIAN CHEESE PIE

I am Jarka Gagamova. Here is this recipe. You must read it so you can make traditional Bulgarian cheese pie.

Time you should be preparing this pie: 20 minutes
How long you should cook this pie and how
hot should your oven be: 30 minutes at 175°
Celsius.*
How many people this pie should feed: 6 people
*Sonya says that because I live in America now
I must tell to you that it is 350° Fahrenheit.
Everyone in the world is using Celsius except
for America. You have ounces and inches and
what in heck are even yards? To measure this
way makes no sense.

Ingredients
- Oil or butter, for greasing the pan
- 3 large eggs
- 250 grams natural Greek yogurt (1 cup)
- 7 grams baking soda (1 teaspoon)
- 400 grams finely crumbled feta cheese (2 cups)
- 10-15 phyllo pastry sheets, defrosted if frozen
- 115 grams unsalted butter, melted (8 tablespoons)

Instructions
Preheat your oven to 175°C/350°F. Make greasy a 9-inch pie plate with a little oil or melted butter.

Crack the eggs into a medium-sized bowl and beat them not too hard.

Add the yogurt and baking soda. Mix until foamy. Stir the feta cheese into the mixture.

Unroll the phyllo pastry, then paint the melted butter on one phyllo sheet. Then, put two or three spoonsful of egg-and-cheese mixture on top of this phyllo sheet, leaving about 3–5 centimeters of space all around the edges. Spread the mixture around the center of the pastry dough. Gently for this, like you are stroking the cheek of very small, small baby, or else you will rip the dough.

Roll loosely the sheet of phyllo pastry up like a log, starting from long side. Beginning from center, place each filled log next to each other on your pie plate. Little by little, this will form spiral shape like magnificent snail.

Keep doing this until you have done this with all of your pastry or you cannot fit any more pastry.

If you have left any melted butter, brush it on top of the whole pie and bake for 40 to 45 minutes, until golden.

Leave to cool for 20 minutes before you cut the pieces. Serve with extra yogurt for the side, and also have a glass of fruit liqueur such as *rakia*.

EGGPLANT NDUJA DEEP-DISH

Feeds: 4–6 people
Prep time: 1.5 hours (including rising the dough)
Bake time: 30 minutes

Every time I think Delilah is being a pain in the ass, calling "Son, taste this" for the bazillionth time, trying to get a recipe just right, she comes up with a stroke of genius like this, and I have to admit that the woman knows what she's doing. The mysterious, seductive umami flavor of the spicy prosciutto spread known as nduja makes our customers fall in love at first bite. Eggplant provides a mellow backdrop, and the hearty crust lets the nduja-infused sauce shine.

The Recipe

This recipe will fill a 12-inch round deep-dish pan and will feed four to six people. If you don't have a pan that big, you could do some hard math and cut this recipe down by about one-third for a 9-inch cake pan, or, save your brain cells and just keep the leftover dough and sauce for another purpose.

Here's a rundown of all the ingredients. At the restaurant, we make the eggplant chips *en masse* the night before. They'll keep for a day or two in the fridge. You can also make the sauce in advance. The spiciness will mellow if it sits for a day.

Dough

- 3 cups flour
- 2 tablespoons cornmeal
- ¾ teaspoon sea salt
- ½ teaspoon sugar
- 2¼ teaspoons (1 sachet) instant yeast

Did you notice that we're using instant yeast, not active dry? Okay, good.

- 3 tablespoons melted unsalted butter
- 3 tablespoons corn oil
- ¾ cup warm water (about 110°F)
- Oil, for greasing

Eggplant Chips

Makes 40 to 50 chips.

- 5 small or 3 large, unpeeled Asian eggplants (or another variety of long, thin-skinned eggplant), trimmed and cut into ½-inch rounds

- 3–5 tablespoons olive oil
- 2 teaspoons garlic salt
- ¾ cup finely grated parmesan cheese

Sauce

- 2 tablespoons butter
- 1 small onion, diced extremely fine, or better yet
  zhuzhed in a food processor for about a minute
  (should yield about ½ cup)
- ¾ teaspoon salt
- 1 teaspoon dried oregano
- 1–2 teaspoons crushed red pepper flakes
- 4 ounces nduja sausage*
- 2 garlic cloves, minced
- 28-ounce can crushed tomatoes
- 1 teaspoon sugar

*We're fortunate to have Sujeet and Big Dave,
our meat guys, who make this killer spread for
us. If you don't have a private butcher at your
disposal, the next best thing is the mail-order
nduja from La Quercia Cured Meats. You will
want to eat it on scrambled eggs, mixed into
sautéed zucchini, or just slathered on a chunk of
crusty bread. You'll need to adjust the amount
of red pepper flakes depending on the spiciness
of your nduja and your own preferences.

Toppings

- 4 cups (16 ounces) shredded (or sliced) low-
  moisture mozzarella
- Eggplant chips
- Fresh basil leaves
- ¼ cup grated parmesan

Step 1: Make the Dough

Combine the flour, cornmeal, sea salt, sugar, and instant yeast in a large bowl or the bowl of a stand mixer and give everything a little how-do-you-do with a wooden spoon. Then add the melted butter, corn oil, and warm water, and stir again until the dough just begins to come together. Pop the dough hook onto your mixer and let that sucker spin on medium-low for about 6 minutes.

Quick tip: If you don't have a stand mixer, you can do all of this by hand. Make sure you use a B.A.B. (Big Ass Bowl) because you'll need a lot of room to maneuver. You'll probably need a slightly longer kneading time, too.

The dough should feel soft, supple, and pliable. If the dough looks too wet, add 1 or 2 tablespoons of flour. Too dry? Add a tablespoon or two of warm water.

Step 2: Let It Rise

Thoroughly grease a pizza pan with oil, sides and all. Form that bad boy into a ball and pop it into the oiled pizza pan (i.e., the pan you're going to cook it in). Flip the dough ball once to coat it in oil. Cover the whole she-bang with plastic wrap and throw a clean kitchen towel over it. Let it hang out in a warm spot for about an hour. On a cold day, you may want to heat your oven until it's just warm, and then cut the heat off. Nestle your little dough baby in that cozy oven while it doubles in size. If you use that method, don't cover it with towels because towels + oven = flames.

Make your eggplant chips (Step 3) and start cooking your sauce (Step 5) while the dough is rising.

Step 3: Make the Eggplant Chips

Preheat the oven to 375°F.

In a large bowl or plastic bag, drizzle the eggplant rounds with olive oil and mix with your hands until completely coated. I cook these on a giant catering-sized metal baking tray, but at home, two glass casserole dishes would work for cooking the eggplants. Lay the slices in the dishes in a single layer and sprinkle liberally with garlic salt. Top with grated parmesan.

Bake for 30 to 40 minutes, until the eggplant is tender and golden brown. Set aside to cool.

Step 4: Let the Dough Rise Some More

After your dough has risen for about an hour, unveil that little puffball of glutenous perfection. The dough should be puffy and approximately double its original size. Set the plastic wrap aside; you'll need it again. Press the dough down to fill the pan and mold it up the sides. Fix any holes. Re-cover the pan with the plastic wrap and towel and let it rise for another 15 minutes.

Assuming you've taken your eggplant chips out, whack your oven up to 425°F to get it nice and hot for baking your pizza.

Step 5: Make the Sauce

Melt the butter in a medium saucepan. Add the zhu-zhed/diced onion. Toss in your salt, oregano, and red pepper flakes. Cook for about five minutes over medium heat until the onion is soft. Add the nduja and break it up with the back of your spoon, letting it coat everything with porky, spicy goodness for about 3 to 4 minutes. Nduja doesn't need to be cooked before eating, so you don't need to worry about browning it. Add the garlic, tomatoes, and sugar. Simmer on very low heat for 30 minutes or so, until thickened. Taste for seasoning, and adjust as necessary. Let it cool slightly.

Step 6: Build Your Creation

Take the plastic wrap and the towel off your pan and behold your gorgeous dough. If the shape has gone funky during the second rise, press it back into submission.

Layer the mozzarella directly on top of the crust. If you use sliced mozzarella, lay the slices out with a slight overlap, as if you're making a fruit tart. Layer on the eggplant chips and basil leaves.

Pour the sauce on top of the mozzarella. Make sure the sauce covers your toppings. This is a must. The fresh basil will scorch if it's not covered in a protective layer of sauce. Then, sprinkle the grated parmesan across the top.

Super Important Note: Deep-dish pizza goes cheese, then toppings, THEN sauce. There are important, scientific reasons for this. And also, I told you so.

We are using low-moisture mozzarella here. Don't use fresh mozzarella unless you want Delilah to personally come to your house and tell you how soggy and disgusting your crust is. Ditto with any other toppings you add. Don't add anything too wet, or you will regret it.

Step 7: Bake

Pop your pan in the preheated 425°F oven and bake it for about 30 to 35 minutes. The crust around the edges should be a lovely golden brown.

Let the pizza cool for a few minutes on a wire rack. Slice, serve, and chow down.

DECONSTRUCTED PRETZEL CRUST DEEP-DISH WITH BRATWURST AND PICKLED VEGGIE DIPPERS AKA MAXIMUM BRATTAGE

Feeds: 4–6 people (appetizer portions)
Prep time: 1 hour (including rising the dough)
Bake time: 15 minutes

It's me, Sonya. Recipe invention is usually a breeze for Delilah, but I swear she struggled over this one like she was giving birth to a narwhal. It all worked out in the end, and the bratwurst pizza morphed into these pretzel bites, which are currently our most popular appetizer. The actual name on the menu is Deconstructed Pretzel Crust Deep-Dish with Bratwurst and Pickled Veggie Dippers, but among ourselves, we call it Maximum Brattage, paying homage to Jordan's infamous smoothie.

The Recipe

Pretzel Bites

- 1 teaspoon (about half a sachet, if you're using sachets) instant or active dry yeast
- ¾ cup warm water (about 110°F, which is like very warm bathwater)
- ½ teaspoon salt
- ½ tablespoon light brown sugar, packed
- 1½ teaspoons unsalted butter, melted and slightly cooled
- 2½ cups flour
- Oil, for greasing
- 5 cups water

Did you notice that this water is separate from the warm water? Keep it that way, okay?

- ¼ cup baking soda
- 1 beaten egg
- Coarse sea salt

Step 1: Make the Dough

Sprinkle the yeast into the warm water and let it sit for about 5 minutes. Pour it into your stand mixer. Add the salt, brown sugar, and melted butter to your stand mixer and combine with a whisk or whisk attachment. If you've been using the whisk attachment, remove it and attach your dough hook. Add the flour, one cup at a time, mixing after each addition. Pause and scrape down the sides of the mixer. Use your dough hook to knead the mixture for about 5 minutes.

Quick tip: If you don't have a stand mixer, you can do all of this by hand. Make sure you use a B.A.B. (Big Ass Bowl), because you need a lot of room to maneuver.

You'll know the dough is perfect when it is stretchy, but not sticky. If the dough looks too wet, add flour, one tablespoon at a time. Too dry? Add a tablespoon of warm water.

Step 2: Let It Rise

Use oil to grease a large bowl. Form that bad boy into a ball and pop it into the oiled bowl. Cover the whole shebang with a clean kitchen towel. Heck, go crazy and cover it with two towels. Let it hang out in a warm spot for about 15 minutes. On a cold day, you may want to heat your oven until it's just barely warm and then cut the heat off. Nestle your little dough baby in that cozy oven while it doubles in size, about 15 minutes. If you use that method, don't cover it with towels because towels + oven = flames.

Step 3: Prepare for Other Things

Now is a good time to start pre-heating your oven to 425°F. Line a very large baking sheet (or two smaller ones) with parchment paper. Set aside.

Bring 5 cups of water to a boil in a large pot or saucepan.

Step 4: Knives Out!

Cut your dough into four equalish pieces. Using the Play-Doh skills you honed in preschool, roll each piece into a snake, about an inch in diameter. Slice the snake into 1½-inch nuggets. The size of the pretzel bites should be about two bites' worth.

Step 5: Bubble, Bubble

Did you start boiling your 5 cups of water in Step 3 so it would be ready now? Great. Gold stars for you. Add the baking soda and enjoy the gentle Alka-Seltzer fizz for a brief moment. Now, drop about ten of the pretzel bites in at a time, and allow them to boil for 10–15 seconds. Fish them out with a slotted spoon and place them onto the baking sheet you prepped in Step 3.

Step 6: Bake Those Bad Boys

Using a pastry brush, dab each bite with a sheen of beaten egg. Then sprinkle the whole shebang with coarse sea salt. Pop the baking tray into the oven and bake for about 15 minutes, until your bites are a lovely golden brown pretzel color.

These don't keep well, so be sure to eat them or freeze them right away. Speaking of which, don't tell Delilah I said this, but if you don't have time to mess around making pretzel bites from scratch, you could buy frozen soft pretzel bites, like the ones from SuperPretzel. They're pretty good.

Beer Cheddar Cheese Sauce

- 2 tablespoons butter
- 2 tablespoons flour
- ¾ teaspoon Pampered Chef Salt & Vinegar Seasoning

You can order this online, even without being invited to your work friend's cousin's sister's Pampered Chef party. If you can't get your hands on it, substitute garlic salt.

- ½ cup milk
- ½ cups beer. (We use New Glarus Fat Squirrel Nut Brown Ale.)
- 1–2 teaspoons spicy brown mustard
- ¾ cup sharp cheddar cheese, shredded
- ½ cup gruyere or swiss cheese, shredded

Melt the butter in a pan, and sprinkle in the flour and salt & vinegar seasoning. Cook over medium heat for about 2 minutes.

Slowly stir in the milk, beer, and mustard, whisking constantly. Cook until thickened and bubbly.

Reduce the heat to low, add the cheeses, and stir until you have a smooth, velvety cheese sauce.

Dippers

Serve the pretzel bites with the cheese sauce, bite-sized slices of cooked bratwurst, and pickled onions (or other pickled veggies).

DANIEL'S NECTAR OF THE TROPICS PASSIONFRUIT MULE

I grew up in San Juan, where the air before a thunderstorm can be like breathing through a hot, dirty washcloth. Then I served in Kuwait, with heat and dust that every day make you think your eyes might shrivel up like little raisins inside your dried-out skull.

When some guy at my bar says Geneva Bay is so hot that they must have a tropical cocktail to cool down, I humor them, even though that guy is talking out of his *culo*. I know what hot is, and Wisconsin is not hot. This is one of the skills you must master to become a bartender—how to smile your beautiful smile and pretend you don't think someone is talking out of his *culo*.

Makes 2 cocktails.

Ingredients

- 6 tablespoons passion fruit pulp, divided—about 4–6 passion fruits, depending on size
- Toasted coconut, for garnish
- 2 teaspoons fresh lime juice, plus extra lime juice or pineapple juice to wet the rims of the glasses, divided
- 4 ounces pineapple vodka, divided. (I use Ciroc or Skyy. If you don't have pineapple vodka, you can use plain vodka and add a splash of pineapple juice.)
- 8 ounces ginger beer, the spiciest you can find, divided
- Ice

This is what you do:

1. To extract the pulp of the passion fruit, cut the fruit in half with a sharp knife. Then, using a large spoon, scoop out the flesh and seeds.
2. Finely chop the toasted coconut, or process it in a food processer, and sprinkle it onto a plate. It needs to be in very small pieces. Wet the rims of two mule glasses (or other short, wide glasses) with lime or pineapple juice and twist the glasses into the toasted coconut until the rims are coated. If you have trouble getting the coconut to stick, try adding a little honey to the lime juice.
3. Divide the passion fruit pulp among the glasses and pour 1 teaspoon of lime juice into each glass and muddle gently, careful not to disturb the coconut.
4. Fill the glasses with cubed ice.
5. Add 2 ounces of vodka to each glass then top with the ginger beer.
6. Gently stir and serve immediately.

Notes

If you can't find fresh passion fruits you can use passion fruit puree, or if you are very desperate and cannot find a good supplier of tropical fruits, you can use canned passion fruit juice.

BIZ'S GARDEN-FRESH TOMATO SANDWICH

I don't know why I have to even write this down. A chimpanzee with half a brain could make this. But Sonya asked me, so fine.

Time: 3 minutes
Feeds: 1 person

Ingredients
1 medium-ripe garden-fresh tomato
2 leaves basil, torn or cut into a chiffonade
1–2 tablespoons good quality mayonnaise
2 slices sourdough bread
Salt, to taste

Instructions
If you can't figure out how to make a damn tomato sandwich by yourself, then I really don't know what to tell you.